Beginning

the

game

Other books by Brenda Webster:

Fiction:

Sins of the Mothers

Paradise Farm

Memoir:

The Last Good Freudian

Translation:

Lettera alla Madre, by Edith Bruck

Critical Studies:

Yeats: A Psychoanalytic Study

Blake's Prophetic Psychology

Edited:

Hungry for Light: The Journal of Ethel Schwabacher

The Beheading Game

BRENDA WEBSTER

For, Richard and Ann Marie
with much affection
Brenda

San Antonio, Texas
2006

The Beheading Game © 2006 by Brenda Webster

First Edition

ISBN: 0-916727-24-6 (hardback)
Converted ISBN: 978-0-916727-24-6

Wings Press
627 E. Guenther
San Antonio, Texas 78210
Phone/fax: (210) 271-7805

On-line catalogue and ordering:
www.wingspress.com

Library of Congress Cataloging-in-Publication Data

Webster, Brenda S.
The beheading game / Brenda Webster.-- 1st ed.
  p. cm.
ISBN 0-916727-24-6 (alk. paper)
1. Gay men–Fiction. 2. Theatrical producers and directors–
Fiction. 3. Fathers and sons–Fiction. 4. Critically ill–Fiction.
5. Lymphomas–Patients–Fiction. 6. New York (N.Y.)–Fiction.
7. Rome (Italy)–Fiction. I. Title.
  PS3573.E255B43 2006
  813'.54--dc22
                              2005034344

For Carol Cosman
better than best friend

CONTENTS

B
e
the
e
Game
d
i
n
g

CHAPTER ONE

WINTER WEATHER

this king lay at camelot at christmastide;
many good knights and gay his guests were there . . .

           – *Sir Gawain and The Green Knight*

It snowed all night and high wind-blown drifts had trans-
formed the park into the pristine landscape of an Alaskan
wilderness. Standing at the frosty windowpane, Ren realized
at a glance that he could forget about getting a cab: there was
no traffic moving through Central Park. Still, his chest softened at the sight of the untainted snow settling over the city,
the temporary return to nature. It would be a welcome dis-
traction, he thought, looking down at Jack curled in bed, his
neck and one white shoulder exposed. Under ordinary circumstances Ren would have bent and kissed his throat, made
some campy joke about vampires and Victorian heroines, but
today he only drew up the covers with a quick embarrassed
gesture. You didn't think about sex when someone was as sick
as Jack was – or rather you did think about it, too much, all
the time, but you didn't do it much. Jack's appetite for it –
though he kept hoping it would come back – was all but gone.
Sometimes he couldn't even take Ren's weight.

    Ren walked over to the window, longing for a cigarette.
But that was another vice he'd given up for Jack. Chain smoking and chain fucking – both unhealthy. He shook his head. It
was hard to believe what an earnest little brute he'd fallen for.
But everything about this passion of his was unusual. He

smiled at the figure on the bed, glad he'd let Jack persuade him to spend the night uptown instead of in Ren's Village pad.

It meant he'd had a long subway ride uptown after rehearsal at the Village theater, but now they'd have a shorter trip to the hospital. Ren had run through the first act of his production of *Sir Gawain and The Green Knight*. The results had confirmed the wisdom of his decision to join the Back Alley Players. They were not only smart and funny, they were getting quite a bit of buzz in the press. Being with them had made Ren happier than he'd been in years. As an actor on Broadway and off, he'd been everything from walk-on to leading man. But he'd been increasingly frustrated by difficult directors and lines that had no meaning for him. What he wanted, he'd realized, was to move to the other side of the footlights and shape a play himself. Now, with the Back Alley Players, he was finally getting a chance. It all rested in his hands.

Adapting a medieval romance for his debut as a director was risky. But completely convinced the drama was there, he'd quite easily persuaded the others. Ren had always loved the story of Gawain's encounter with the Green Knight because of its mysterious plot. From childhood he'd been fascinated by the terrifying green-skinned giant who had come to King Arthur's court, challenging someone to behead him, with the bizarre proviso that he would return the blow in a year and a day. Ren had shivered with pleasurable fear when the stranger picked up the head Gawain severed, and named their meeting place with bloody lips.

The next part of the story was equally mysterious. A year later, searching for the Green Knight, Gawain comes to a castle whose genial Host leaves him alone with his beautiful, seductive wife. Gawain refuses her advances, but takes her girdle – a sash really – because he believes it will save his life. Then, and this was the part that Ren found most surprising, it turns out that the frightening Green Knight and the Host are the same person – the Green Knight is a shape-changing magi-

4

cian! Because Gawain has resisted evil, the Green Knight spares his life but nicks him on the neck with his ax to punish him for taking the girdle.

As a child, Ren didn't understand Gawain's sexual temptation. All he knew was that Gawain had been in danger of doing something really bad, resisted, and received only a token punishment. To Ren's great relief, Gawain won the Green Knight's forgiveness. Eventually, Ren concluded that it had all been a test of Gawain's worthiness by a powerful older man who, in some versions of the story, was revealed to be Gawain's father.

Jack turned over on his back, mumbling something in his sleep. Ren bent to hear it and caught sight of himself in the wall mirror, all six-feet-four of him twisted down like a giant pretzel, his face worried as a Jewish mother's. "Darling," he whispered to his reflection, "it's lucky you're going to be a brilliant director because you look a fright. And I can't imagine how someone like you who doesn't give a damn for anyone else – don't grimace, you know I'm right – can find his insides turned to butter every time this child – past twenty but still deliciously fresh – looks up at you." As if to prove the point, Jack opened his gray-green eyes and Ren felt his heart pound. Jack blinked. Smiled. There was a slight smudge of dark, like a thumb print, under each eye.

"Time already?" he asked.

The dark bruise-like shadows hurt Ren to look at. "Playtime," he answered, overly cheerful. "We're going to have an unexpected holiday in the Alps. After I make sure you're not going back to sleep again, I'm going to check out your skis." He opened the window a few inches and scooped at the snow outside on the sill.

"Hey, watch out for my fish," Jack called. There was a big aquarium on a stand near the window.

Ren put the snow in his other hand and dropped a pinch of fish food into the tank, watching as the three sunfish came up to the surface working their mouths; then he lobbed a compact snowball at Jack's chest.

Jack whooped and threw back what was left, making a snow shower that subsided on the floor. Then he got up and pushed at the window to be sure the fish weren't getting a draft. God, the kid was insane about them. Ren remembered how skeptical he'd been when Jack brought them back from one of his field trips up the Hudson to check on the spawning grounds and to tag fish that Fisheries wanted to follow. The sunfish were right in the middle of the food chain, Jack had explained to him, and if their numbers decreased or if their flesh was found to contain higher than usual PCBs, this would be a danger signal for other river populations they were working to safeguard. Ren had been sure the sunfish wouldn't survive, but they not only survived, they flourished. Ren had even gotten to like them. They were colorful little buggers, with their orange-spotted gills and yellow bellies. Unusually bright for a freshwater fish.

"They're fine. I cleaned the tank yesterday." Ren grabbed an elegant striped robe from a chair and threw it to him. "Put something on. You're shivering."

Just then the phone rang. Ren could tell from Jack's deferential tone that it was his father, Malcolm. "No, I don't need any help, I'm fine. My friend Ren's here. We're going to ski through the park to Mount Sinai."

"You're what?" Ren could hear the explosion from where he was standing.

"Parents should all be shot," he said when Jack put down the phone. "Especially middle-class parents. Parenting is the disease of our century."

"What would you say if he ignored me? That he was neglectful and self-interested? So he wanted his chauffeur to pick me up? So what? The poor guy sounded so disappointed when I said no." Jack rubbed a hand over his head and Ren hung

fire for a minute, subdued by the sight of his pink scalp showing through the gold fuzz. Then he rallied.

"If you had something less savory, I wonder if he'd be so
blasted helpful. You said yourself it was a relief to have cancer, not . . ." Ren stopped suddenly, flushed to the eyes. It was
ugly to throw Jack's words back at him that way, uglier to
want to strip him of his comfort. He'd been so childishly
happy to have family friends calling and asking for him. Glad
not to be hidden away like a leper.

"It's still a relief," Jack said quietly, but his face turned
white.

"Go on," Ren prompted, "and, and . . ."

Jack shook his head.

"Why can't you tell me I'm being an insensitive shit? It's
obvious, isn't it?"

"I'm conserving energy. Give me a break." Jack sighed,
a low soft sound somewhere between exasperation and toler-
ance, and headed towards the bathroom.

Ren followed him. "I thought a little fight would relieve
the tension. Nu? It didn't?" he asked, affecting his Jewish-
mother voice.

Jack turned around. He wasn't amused. "I know you get
off on fighting, but I don't. And especially not today. I'm going
to shower." He shut the bathroom door.

Ren put his face against the wood. "Can't you even slam
the door?" he said more to himself than to Jack. "Why do you
have to be such a saint?"

You're a big help, darling, his mirror image taunted him.
Weren't you coming along as an objective observer? Because
poor Jack would be too fuddled to take notes? Ren heard Jack
in the bathroom. Yes. He certainly was a big help. He'd given
Jack the runs. A great start to a two-tranquilizer day. But he
couldn't help it. Whenever Jack mentioned his father, bile
started to flow, giving him a bad case of heartburn. He heard
the shower go on and it was all he could do not to go in and
cover Jack with kisses.

It was awful that loving someone didn't automatically make you love their relatives. But Jack's father was such an arrogant prick, with that smug little smile of his. Always right, no matter what the argument. It was hard, hard to understand how Jack managed to love him. But what was inconceivable was that to spare his father's feelings, Jack wouldn't tell the old man he was gay.

"He's already pissed that I'm cleaning up the environment instead of practicing medicine," Jack had said when Ren pressed him. "Poor Pop couldn't believe that I'd use a perfectly good biology major just to study fish. I can't do this to him too. He'd be humiliated at his club. You know how conservative those guys are. At least now he can show his friends my photo and boast about how popular I am with women."

"What are you saying? That you're an ornament on his watch fob? A pretty little trinket? Oh, shit." Ren had known then that Jack would tell his father zilch. It was hopeless.

Ren countered the misery this memory gave him by imagining a huge success for his play. Maybe Jack would be proud enough of him then to tell his father about their relationship. Ren pictured Malcolm sitting in the audience overcome with admiration, swept away by Ren's vision. From the beginning, Ren had had a visceral sense of how the play should make the audience feel. He wanted the whole thing vivid as a dream. A dream of pleasure from the outset at Camelot, with kissing games, music and over-rich food – then a brilliantly lit nightmare when the Green Knight bursts in with his axe and issues his macabre challenge.

It was easy for Ren to imagine how much more effective the opening scenes would be when the actors were moving freely and there were costumes and lights – he wanted the sparkling jewel-like effect of stained glass. But already, even though the actors were still dressed in jeans and T-shirts, penciling notes in their scripts, they exuded youthful energy and *joie de vivre*. True, there were some problems; Gawain's voice in particular seemed too soft. But Ren wasn't going to panic and think he'd miscast her, or doubt his decision to use a woman in the part. As an actor, he'd had enough experience with temperamental directors to be patient now. Even the best actors could shut down if you criticized them too soon. And he wanted them wide open and digging deep.

Just then, Jack came up behind him and flicked him with his towel. "Admit it. You're jealous because I asked Dad to meet us at the hospital."

"Mmm," Ren said, smelling the damp skin, wet hair, a faint odor of aftershave.

"I asked him because he's savvy. He's good at statistics. Neither you nor I would know a statistic from a laundry list." He hugged Ren lightly from behind. "Just remember, you're my number one."

Ren felt his cock begin to rise, then flushed with chagrin and lust. So he was jealous, of course he was jealous, a hysterical aging queen. He kept wanting to make Jack see that his father was the kind of man he'd hate if he'd met him outside his family – a supporter of all the values that were making America a wasteland of plenty. Ren spent insomniac hours imagining car crashes and heart attacks for the old man, though he knew perfectly well that a tragic death would enshrine him in Jack's heart forever.

"Sorry," he said, leaning back against Jack's chest. "I don't know why you put up with me." He let himself drink in the warmth, savor the stillness for a minute, then he made himself go and look in the hall closet for the skis. He pulled them out, holding them in both arms.

Jack followed him. "I love you, that's why. No one has ever taken care of me the way you do. And you have a great imagination. But sometimes you can be a real pain in the ass."

He tried to take his skis out of Ren's arms but Ren pushed him away.

"Sorry if I'm getting on your nerves, darling. But at least let me be useful. Go ring for the elevator." Ren was indeed sorry, but he couldn't resist striking a languishing Camille pose for the electronic eye as they went down in the rosewood-paneled elevator. He imagined Daddy was watching. He wanted him to see how things were between them. To know that one thing he didn't own was his son's body.

Outside, the sun was glorious on the snow as they made their way along a channel that had been cleared in the middle of the sidewalk. When they got to the park entrance at Ninetieth Street and Fifth Avenue, it was all pure glitter and dazzle, blinding whiteness. Ren knelt and clamped on Jack's skis, then did his own. They followed the path that ran beside the park's snow-covered outer wall, uptown. At Ninety-fourth Street they veered slightly inward to cross the transverse bridge that arched over the street. When they reached Ninety-ninth Street, they could take one of several connecting paths that led out of the park and come out on Fifth Avenue near Mount Sinai.

It really was like a holiday. Better even than Sundays when the park was closed to cars. People smiled when they passed each other. Waved colorful mittened hands: skiers, kids with sleds, a lone snowshoer in a plaid woodsman's shirt, lovers walking hand-in-hand through the drifts. Even the line of watching skyscrapers seemed less aggressively massive than usual, their starkness softened by soft snow mantles. Some of them were beautiful with the light on their rosy brick facades.

Ren checked Jack for signs of fatigue, but aside from the smudges under his eyes, he looked radiant, his cheeks glowing from the cold air and the exercise. After awhile he admitted to being a little short of breath and Ren put an arm around him.

They moved then together, their poles like the legs of a single giant insect.

It was good moving like that, fluid, light, as if they didn't have a care in the world, with the slight crunch of the thin crust in his ears and the clean smell of snow. Ren didn't want it to end. He slowed as they neared the East Meadow and moved his free arm languorously up and down. "We could make angels. The snow is perfect for it."

Jack looked at him. "Hey," he said, "you don't have to come in with me, you know. Just get me to the door and then you can play all you want. You could let my Dad do this one."

"No way."

"I know you hate hospitals."

Ren clapped his hand over his mouth. "Hate them. Why Lord 'a mercy, Miss Scarlet! No, I love them . . . all those nurses in their cute little S and M uniforms, those gleaming needles and knives. It's better than the back room at the Fur Tunnel."

Jack laughed. "If you love it so much, why'd you faint last time when they couldn't find my vein?"

"I was just resting. And what if I did faint? Some of us are more sensitive than others." In fact, watching those poisons drip into Jack's arm every three weeks for six months had made him sick. Again he wondered how in God's name he could be here. He loved perfect, well bodies, was terrified of disease, of dying. At 45 he hated every sign of aging in himself. His stiff joints when he climbed up on the stage to show some tricky movement sequence. The way he woke up three times a night to pee, his prostate swelling like a rotten fruit. Jack was different. He tolerated deformations of every kind with the bemused interest of a Buddhist priest. Just now he was exclaiming in delight over some alpine moss that had the perverse idea of blooming in a city park in winter.

By the time they emerged from the park, Ren had worked himself up into a panic. There was no way he could wait passively for Jack's disease to gather force. The idea made him crazy. All this business about coming along to help gather facts about the new procedure was bullshit. Sure he'd help, he'd listen and pretend to weigh the pros and cons, but even if the treatment ended up being worse than the disease itself, he knew he wanted Jack to try it. He'd already started to pressure him subtly – by a slight change in intonation, slight questioning of his raised eyebrow. If Jack hung back, he'd bring up the fish. Isn't what gets you about them their determination? That no matter how much they've been spilled and dumped on, despite their PCB levels, they keep trying to survive? Unfortunately, he could imagine Jack answering that they weren't the ones asking for the chemicals. They didn't have the choice of their "treatment." He did.

CHAPTER TWO

Challenges

alcolm Firste was waiting for them in the lobby of Mount Sinai. Jack embraced him and Ren could see that instead of relaxing into it, the man stiffened and his facial muscles clenched in a parody of a Brit's stiff upper lip. Ren was just beginning to feel sorry for him – all that anguish locked up inside – when Malcolm noticed the skis and gestured disapprovingly at the snow which was beginning to drip off the ends onto the floor.

"I'll ask the woman at reception if she'll keep them for us," Ren said, maneuvering them over to the desk. The woman was obviously amused and when the skis were safely stowed in her closet, Ren turned back to Malcolm, but the man refused to meet his eyes and stared pointedly past his ear. Jack was busy registering and didn't notice, but even if he had, he would have accused Ren of overreacting.

"Transplant floor is down the hall to the end, and then upstairs to three," the receptionist announced. "Jean, the head nurse, is expecting you." Ren noticed how casually she spoke, as though a bone marrow transplant were an ordinary event instead of an experimental and extremely risky procedure.

As they started down the hall, Ren longed to curve his arm around Jack's shoulders or touch his hand. Instead, Ren

13

thought he should walk like a Suit. Keep his face blank as a Japanese clinching a deal. When Jack winked at him, Ren didn't trust himself to smile. He always made an effort to look Wasp hetero when he was with Jack's father: no gold chains of course, not even the tiniest trace of eye-liner and slacks not too tight in the ass. He was wearing the only roomy pair of slacks he had, with a button-down shirt and a sweater his mother had sent him last Christmas. You wouldn't even know he had a butt, much less an attractive one. But his mannerisms were too ingrained by now to turn off easily. He was afraid the pitch of his voice gave him away. Could imagine Jack's father asking why his son had brought this faggot along.

When they got to the nurses' station, the head nurse, Jean, took one look at them – sniffed the tension – and started to chatter as she propelled them along a corridor.

"Doctor Stevens says you've passed the physical exams, congratulations by the way, and your insurance has given a green light – so basically, you're all set."

"Did he tell you I was having a hard time deciding to do it?"

"It's natural to have doubts," she said. "Everybody's nervous. But I'm glad you decided at least to have a sneak preview and see what our facilities are like – the transplant rooms have all been re-done." She stopped in front of a blond wood door that could have been the entrance to a honeymoon suite.

Jack gave her one of his beautiful smiles. "I'm sure by the time you finish, it'll seem like a luxury vacation – nothing to do for a month but lie around, be waited on hand and foot."

"I don't know if I'd go that far," she said, smiling back as she opened the door and led them into a little antechamber. "The patient in here," she gestured towards the glass porthole on an inner door opposite the entrance, "has done extremely well. Right now she's out getting some exercise. She's going home next week. This is the wash-up area. It's where friends scrub up and change when they come to visit. All the isolation rooms have it."

The space gave clear signs of use. There was a sink and blue gowns and masks and bottles of something and big plastic jars set out neatly on shelves.

"What if someone's coming down with something?" Malcolm asked, sliding his eyes lizard-like over Ren. "Isn't there some sort of screening process?"

"Visitors have to register at the nursing station," she said. "And we recommend keeping the number down to a few trusted friends."

"We probably won't want anyone outside the immediate family," Malcolm said, glancing at Ren again, "at least until the transplant takes."

"Dad," Jack said, "I wish you wouldn't sound so positive . . . I'm still not sure."

"You should never have gone for a second opinion, it's just gotten you confused. The man was hopelessly out of date. Why have another course of chemotherapy when the first one only put you in remission for a few months? Absurd idea." Malcolm gripped Jack's arm and steered him towards the door of the absent patient's room.

Jack started to explain that the doctor had recommended trying a different chemical cocktail but Malcolm shushed him. They peered through the porthole window at the inner room and Ren looked over their heads. Surreptitiously, he touched Jack's hip, gave him a pat.

Brightly colored cards covered the wall opposite the bed. "It looks like a birthday party," Malcolm said.

There wasn't much to say after that. It was a room in which someone was struggling to live. The cards and photographs of curly-headed children were supposed to remind her of the other world out there, remind her not to give up.

Ren found himself thinking of a dungeon with a straw pallet and a concrete floor strewn with torture instruments. It seemed a more accurate representation of what Jack would have to go through than tastefully arranged glossies. But maybe he was just disassociating. He had been succumbing lately to medieval daydreams.

They went back to the transplant nurse's office and she sat them down on an overstuffed sofa under some pretty prints.

"Would you like me to tell you how things go if you decide to do this?" she asked Jack. "Walk you through it?"

Jack nodded and his father promptly whipped out a Palm Pilot.

"Well, before you're admitted to the hospital we have to harvest your stem cells so that after chemotherapy has cleared the cancer from your body, we can reinfuse them. I guess you know they're the cells all the other cells in your body grow from." She handed him a plastic card with colorful icons depicting the stem cells and branching lines showing the mature cells they developed into. "We're hoping they'll grow you squeaky-clean bone marrow, cancer-free, as good as new. The harvest itself is a painless outpatient procedure."

"And while you're harvesting, can I –" Jack hesitated, "still change my mind?"

"I suppose so, though I haven't seen it happen. You'd be surprised at how much you'd suddenly want the transplant if it turned out you couldn't have it – if your cells were damaged by your previous chemotherapy for instance – but chances are that everything will go just fine."

"If it all goes smoothly, how soon can he be admitted?" Malcolm asked.

Jean studied the calendar. "We'll have a room free January seventh." Ren began to dislike the nurse's assured tone; somehow she made it sound as if it was already decided. "So, Jack," she went on cheerfully, "your stem cells are harvested and safely stored in our refrigerator. This is when the procedure proper starts. First thing we'd do after we've got you settled, is put in a catheter." She patted herself below the collar bone.

"Does it hurt very much?" Ren asked, ignoring the scornful look Jack's father was giving him.

"It has to go through the bone there, so it takes a lot of force." Jean looked thoughtful for a moment. "But don't worry – your doctor, Dr. Stevens, is great at it. And once it's in, we'll be able to start hydration."

Ren thought of the quip he'd read recently where an astronaut says to the woman strapping him into his seat, "It's nice to know if you ever get fired, you could get a job at Helga's House of Pain." This woman wasn't an amazon or a babe, but she had just enough resemblance to Nurse Ratched to be frightening.

"Then, for the next week you'll get high-dose chemotherapy to destroy your cancer cells. So that part should be familiar to you. I know you're a veteran as far as chemo goes."

Jack's father sat with his finger poised over his Pilot and asked her about the dosage, as though the figures would give him a grip on the cells proliferating in his son's marrow. When he heard how high and how much, he smiled, reassured.

Jack, on the other hand, turned pale. "Those doses are much bigger than the ones I had last time. Aren't the after-effects pretty severe?"

She handed him a booklet. "This details possible complications," she said not unkindly. "You can look it over at home."

"Will he feel very sick?" Ren asked, putting his hands out against the sofa cushions as if to steady himself. One of his only memories of his own father was a sailing trip. Ren – who must have been about six – had been sick the whole time, upchucking until his insides felt raw. A few days afterwards, his father had mysteriously vanished – walked out of their apartment on an errand and never returned. Though his parents weren't very close, they never fought and his mother wasn't aware of another woman – she searched everywhere. Ren believed that his father left because of him. Some stupidity, some tantrum. He had never had a chance to say he was sorry. He rushed home every day to see if he'd gotten a postcard from some faraway place. When he saw a stranger looking at him, his heart would jolt, imagining it was his father returning in disguise.

He longed to be tested like Gawain, to show himself worthy of love. He didn't even mind the idea of being punished if afterwards his father would forgive him. But his father never gave him a second chance and Ren was left with a dread of nausea, associated with a mysterious absence and the sea.

"You can feel nauseous the whole time, but the last days of the chemo and then until the transplant takes are probably the worst."

Jack's father's face grew heavy, Ren saw, heavy as a mean-faced pug about to bite. "There must be lots of things to counteract it," he said, his jaw ticking. It was clear he was afraid Ren would lower Jack's morale. Ren wondered if Malcolm knew that he was the one who urged Jack to get a second opinion.

"Compazine, for starters," Jean said. "But we have quite an arsenal. We'll make you as comfortable as we can. Though there'll be some days when nothing is going to help." She clicked her tongue. "To go on with our little story here. We let you rest up a couple of days, then we put the stem cells directly into your catheter. That's what we call the 'rescue'," she beamed. "After about eight days your white blood cell count should start rising and in 30 days you should be home."

"How many people are alive after five years?" Jack asked. "I mean you've done relatively few of these transplants." Ren recognized the doubts of the second doctor. Bad as the prognosis was with chemo, he didn't believe a transplant offered anything better, and the suffering, he'd told Jack, was incalculable.

His father jumped in, nervous that the process was going to be derailed. "I've been checking out the different centers . . . sounds like about a seventy percent success rate. That about right?"

"Every case is unique," she said evasively.

"They can't give us real statistics," Jack said morosely when the nurse left them alone. "For all I know half of their patients croak."

"Don't even think such a thing," his father said. "You've got to think positive. I know if it was me, I'd do anything, pay anything."

"I'm not you, Dad."

"And here they're letting you into their study on purifying the stem cells before the transplant. It's not everyone they let in."

"I haven't heard of anyone they've turned down lately. The hospital got a big endowment for bone marrow transplants, everyone knows that. Maybe they just have to fill their quota."

Jack's father got red in the face. He knew how his son felt about big business – and medicine certainly qualified. But he seemed determined to control himself.

"You know that's not true, son," he said with exaggerated assurance. "They think this is your best chance, maybe your only chance. Your bone marrow will be clean. You heard the nurse say it. As good as new."

"They told me the chemo I just finished would fix me up too. Now they're saying, 'Sorry, but we think your disease will be back within a year.' A year is a long time. I could go to the tropics and look at the relatives of the sunfish I study here, see how they've adapted . . . and see the coral reefs – there's no richer habitat."

"You're strong," Ren heard himself saying. "You got through the chemo well. One year? You're going to have fifty."

"You think I should do it, then?"

"If you think it's your best shot, of course I do . . . but," he added in a whisper, "*piano, piano*, go slow, don't let him bulldoze you into something you're not ready to do."

After a week of reading rehearsals and preliminary blocking and a late-night argument with the costume director over the merits of various speaking devices for the Green Knight, Ren was enjoying a few hours of peace with Jack.

Now, in Jack's apartment, they lay in the dark cave of the covers, snuggling spoon-fashion after making love. Ren had been so touched that Jack wanted to, he'd kissed him all over his body – slow languorous kisses, each toe, each finger. In the cave it was dark with a faint red glow from the corner lamp, like a prehistoric fire.

"God knows what this business will do to my sex life," Jack muttered afterwards. "It may be a year before I can get it up again." He was lying back with his arms under his head looking up at a slice of lamplight that had slipped between the badly closed levelors.

"I'll wait for you, honey," Ren answered in his Scarlet O'Hara voice, thick and Southern and sweet. But he knew it was no laughing matter. He'd never gone without sex for more than two weeks. And then he had been sick himself.

"I'll be sterile as a mule."

"What's the difference? Given that you're already as stubborn as one."

"Will you be serious?"

"I can't." He fingered Jack's cock, squeezing the head, making it stand again. "Besides, since when are you interested in children? I'd rather have a dog, myself." He licked Jack's navel, running his tongue down the hairline. Better not to think. Just feel this enormous pleasure coursing through his body. He took him into his mouth.

Jack pulled him gently away. "I can't come again," he said.

"Doesn't matter." When they met last year Jack could come four times in a night. So what. Age, sickness, they got everyone by the balls sooner or later. "Doesn't matter," he repeated. "It's still good isn't it?"

Jack sighed. "Yeah. It's good."

Afterwards, he played a little game. Imagining his saliva had the magic power to protect Jack, he licked his body clean. His idea was that if he missed the slightest patch of skin still tanned from the Sag Harbor summer, it would turn purple-black. He concentrated all his energy on not missing an inch. Test me, he said to some unseen power. Whatever you ask me to do, I'm game.

"If you do this, you've got to tell your father it's okay for me to be with you in the hospital," he said abruptly.

"Are you starting that again? Of course he'll let you. There's no need to discuss it." He pushed Ren's head down against his shoulder as if he were a fretful child.

Ren popped his head up again, leaned on one elbow. "What if you're semiconscious?"

"And you're languishing outside the locked door like Peter Pan outside his mother's window? Oh please, Ren," he said. "I need help getting ready for this."

Ren could feel him trembling. "Oh, baby, I'm sorry. Are you scared?"

"Scared shitless. I read through that booklet the nurse gave me. That chemo regimen doesn't just kill the cancer, it'll kill every dividing cell in my body: the blood cells, the cells inside my mouth, my nailbeds. And if it doesn't kill me outright, it could destroy my liver, damage my heart, give me an inflammation of the lungs. I could be an old man, Ren." Jack put his face in his hands. "Shit."

Ren stroked his shoulder. He wanted to say, don't do it, but both doctors had told Jack that next time his cancer would be harder to put into remission, and after that it would only be a matter of time. If you believed Dr. Stevens, this treatment was Jack's only hope for a cure, or at least a much longer remission. And how could Ren tell any better than Jack what was the right choice?

While he was desperately thinking of what to say, Jack suddenly sat up and in a matter-of-fact voice asked him, "Which PJ's should I take to the hospital?"

It took Ren a minute to realize that Jack had just made the decision. Incredible, just like that. After weeks of agonizing. It took another minute for him to switch gears. "Your green, of course," he said finally – his birthday gift to Jack.

"Then too, I'll probably be throwing up like mad the first few days of chemo. Maybe I should wear their beastly hospital gowns." Jack got out of bed and started rummaging through the drawers looking over what he had. "Sweat pants would be good too, don't you think?"

"Cool." Ren felt like crying. I'd give my right arm for you, he thought, and immediately saw a little scene like the one in Monty Python where the docs come to take the guy's liver and cut it out while he is still alive. He looked around almost expecting to see the doctors with their knives ready to chop, but there was only Jack collecting some books on tape. Just the methodical, fussy way he was doing it, like the prematurely old man he was afraid of becoming, jangled Ren's nerves.

"Hey, you don't need to do that now," Ren said, wanting Jack to stop. "It's not like you're going to start having labor pains in the middle of the night and need your bags packed – we've got over ten days left. Come into the kitchen with me and I'll fix you a bedtime snack."

Jack had gutted the kitchen when he moved in, ripped out the dark wood cabinets and put in light ones. Two luminous spheres cast a bright, even glow over the work counters and a heat lamp set in the lone window radiated upbeat messages at a couple of ragged-leafed plants.

"Old Slim-Shanks seems to be rallying," Ren said, nodding toward a spindly plant Jack had moved in from the other room. "It looks as if it's waving its little arms. Hello, little fellow." Ren chucked the plant's imaginary chin, then poured milk into a bowl of muesli and mixed in golden raisins.

Jack glanced over at his plant suspiciously. He knew perfectly well that Ren thought the plant was grotesque. "You don't need to distract me. I'm OK. It doesn't hurt to do a little reality thinking."

"Well, sor-ry, Mr. Party Pooper." Ren handed him the bowl. "Maybe it's not ready to dance in my show, but I really do think it looks healthier."

Jack winced. "I forgot to ask how the publicity shoot went."

"Oh, that. We had to put it off." Ren always tried to sound lighthearted when he spoke about the show because Jack had enough to worry about. "Our costumer couldn't finish the Green Knight's head in time. It was more complicated than she expected. But it's okay. Even if we can't take the shots to the printer until after Christmas, he has a fast turnaround and we should be able to get the flyers out in time."

In fact, Patrick, Back Alley's producer, had been really pissed. He hated to cut things too close because, as he said, "if something can go wrong at the last moment, it will."

"I wanted to go to one of your rehearsals," Jack said, "but I've been so tired. I don't think I could stay up past nine even for you."

"Don't worry about it, you're there." He tapped his forehead. "You always are. Hey, don't look so glum. You're my inspiration; you have to be cheerful." He put out his hands.

"You're my muse, you're my Magna Carta," he crooned, shuffling his feet.

"You chase the blues, you push my starter."

"You goon, I'm trying to eat," Jack said, but he was smiling as Ren put his arm strongly around his back, drew him up and started to waltz. "Good evening, my lady," Ren said, bowing his head as he whirled past the juicer. "How about a squeeze?" He could feel Jack's heart beating against his chest. "My lord, your codpiece is simply divine," he simpered to the shining steel mixing bowl. "What heroic proportions! And what colors." Finally, they collapsed laughing in each other's arms and Ren fed Jack his cereal, kissing him between each bite.

CHAPTER THREE

Christmas Disrupted

Where is now your arrogance and your awesome deeds,
your valor and victories and your vaunting words?
now are the revel and renown of the round table
overwhelmed by the words of one man's speech.

— *Sir Gawain and The Green Knight*

A week before **Christmas**, and only four weeks before opening night, the buzzer rang in Ren's apartment on West Twelfth Street and Ren ran down four flights of stairs to collect a huge package from the mailman. He immediately recognized his mother's slanted handwriting and Upper East Side address and wondered what in the world she could have sent him. For years they had exchanged only token gifts at Christmas, usually books. The box – as he took it in both hands – felt as insubstantial as a collection of butterfly wings. Still, it was big and awkward to carry. And he waddled like a duck going up the narrow stairs, hugging it to his belly.

He kicked open the door and carried the box into the middle of his studio. Then he put it down on the rug while he searched around in the mess at the sink until he found his one dull carving knife and slit the top open. Pink confetti oozed out of the wound. Ren rummaged in the box for a moment and pulled out a wadded sphere, which he slowly unwrapped.

It was a gold egg traced with delicate lines of blue, a Christmas decoration he had treasured as a boy. Its presence here surrounded by dirty laundry and unpaid bills shocked him. What was his mother thinking of, sending him this? Then he remembered that the last time he'd talked to her, a couple of weeks ago, she had mentioned she might go away somewhere warm for the holidays. He had been so preoccupied with Jack's illness and his own show that he hadn't realized that she was giving up Christmas for good. Handing it over to him. Staring at a straggly tree all by your lonesome couldn't be much fun.

He had his usual pang of guilt. Poor Mom, left without even one chubby-fisted urchin to paw over packages Christmas morning. He had a sudden image of a small boy in slacks and a pullover lying on his stomach in front of a Christmas tree. The boy seemed terribly far away. Shaking his head to rid it of the image, Ren peered into the center of the gold egg and saw his eyes and mouth reflected, his full lips – black-buck lips, one of his lovers had called them – and the feminine eyes, dark and long-lashed.

He put down the egg with a sigh. Rummaging further in the big box, he started to find the tiny figures his mother had hung on the tree – he guessed that's what they were before he unwrapped them. He had been mad about King Arthur and his mother had built him knights out of pipe-cleaners with foil armor. Now he could see how crude they were, with their roughly painted cloth faces. But back then he had almost wet himself with eagerness to get the next one and hear his story: Arthur and Merlin and Yvaine and Gawain and Sir Bors.

Yet even as a boy, it was the idea of the beautiful male bodies under the armor that attracted him more than the fighting. Before he hit puberty, he'd already imagined himself, his own body soft and yielding, kneeling slave-like between a man's armored thighs. He'd tagged around after the school athletes, watching them under the showers. When he was in eighth grade, one locker-room hero had responded to him and they had furtive sex in the boy's bedroom. For the other boy it had been just a substitute for the real thing, while Ren had the most passionate dreams of romance, of running away together. The boy's father had sensed something was going on and broken off their idyll.

He'd done it quite subtly, by poking fun. Ren remembered the day they'd been swimming at the Y. The father had noted the way Ren's long arms flailed when he did the crawl. Awkward and effeminate at the same time.

"Here he comes," the father had said, his voice moving up the scale in a passable imitation of Ren. "Wow, what style. Just like a water nymph." And his friend had suddenly been ashamed of him. Ren could see it in his eyes. Ren had held his breath and submerged to hide his tears.

He'd spent that summer at the movies. When the curtain went up and the lights went down he'd soothe himself with the words and colors, putting himself in whatever role he chose – the more he despaired, the more powerful the role.

One night his mother took him to a play in a little theater in Greenwich Village. A wildly unsuccessful painter, Thelma relieved her frustration by working at an art gallery on Fifty-seventh Street and imagining herself a superior appreciator of the arts. Afterwards they chatted backstage with a friendly set designer. Ren was fascinated with the way the man had created the illusion of a forest.

"It's all done with gauze and lights," the man had explained to him, "nothing expensive. You could do it yourself."

Ren had gone back on other nights and the designer, clearly amused by his interest, showed him some of his tricks. That was the beginning of his career in the theater; first backstage designing sets, then bit parts, and finally, after a lucky break when he was understudy in *Living Dangerously* and the lead came down sick on opening night, a string of stellar off-Broadway roles.

Ren sighed and set the figures in a circle on the rug – the old Round Table. In his mother's mind, the knights on the tree gave Christmas a fairytale air, making it okay for a Jewish family. She thought of the knights as the good guys, rough and ready like the cowboy heroes in the Westerns she loved.

Ren wondered what she'd think of his production of *Gawain*. Maybe he'd ask her to a rehearsal. She liked the fact that her son was an artist – a theater artist, she called it – though he had the feeling she didn't get half of what he did as an actor and director. Once when he had played in a camp version of *Antony and Cleopatra*, she hadn't even guessed that Cleo was a man. Ren bet she wouldn't notice that *his* leading man was a woman. This was ironic in a way, because it was his sympathy and tenderness for women that led him to cross-cast his play. The original Gawain poem, for all its beauty, was misogynistic. Gawain's bond with the Green Knight came at the expense of women, who were seen in the end as witches or temptresses. As a gay man, Ren knew that the patriarchal system that underlay the poem would have excluded him too. He couldn't stop himself from loving the story, but he desperately wanted to expand its boundaries. His mother wouldn't understand, but he was doing it for them both.

Now, he left the knights in their Round Table circle, then, searching carefully, found the globes. They were still as bright and gleaming as they had been, and as he took them, he got the idea of making a Christmas for Jack the way his mother used to for him, with all the trimmings from his childhood.

He hadn't discussed Christmas with Jack but he assumed they'd be together, especially now with the transplant hanging over them. Ren went down to the corner market and got the biggest tree he could find, carrying it on his shoulders up the stairs and filling his whole studio with the smell of pine. As he set it up, he imagined scenarios. Maybe he shouldn't mention anything until Christmas Eve, pretend he hadn't even thought of a tree then casually invite Jack up for dinner. The uncertainty of that made him nervous. Better to invite him now. The surprise could be in the tree. Maybe he'd blindfold him, lead him in and let him smell the pine, or do a little show for him, pretend they had been magically transported to some distant time and place, talk him into an Alaskan forest – Jack was always wanting to go to Alaska – then whip off the blindfold and there would be his tree, with Ren's knights nestled in its branches.

That night, after a contentious and back-breaking rehearsal, Ren slept at Jack's place. They were lazing around in bed the next morning, getting a slow start when Jack laughed out loud.

"What's funny?" Ren asked, nuzzling his side.

"Nothing."

"Tell me." He tickled him.

"No . . . it was something Dad said on his book tour . . . you wouldn't think it was funny." Jack looked suddenly unhappy.

Ren's stomach clenched. It was bad enough that Malcolm was a powerful chief executive, but now he'd written a best-selling memoir. Ren tried to think of a quick joke to lighten the atmosphere, something to do with Malcolm's new book. Someone less involved might have found a lot to laugh at in his attempt to portray his rise to CEO of Seaboard Power as a sort of Horatio Alger story. His setting out his shoe-shine kit on a corner of Park Avenue when he was a kid because his own father had wanted him to learn what people had to do to earn a dollar. I mean please, give us a break. The worst part of it was the smarmy way Jack's father wrote – his advice to think positive, to listen to tapes from *Jonathan Livingston Seagull* every morning, his uplifting business-speak. "Remember, everything can be a 'win win' situation!" was a suggestion Ren found particularly repulsive. Everything? Really? How about dying? Or losing your mind?

"Book tour going well?" he asked with studied casualness.

Jack visibly tensed. "Oh, yeah . . . holiday sales are up. Dad's tired though, glad he'll be home for Christmas. . . .

I told you I was going over there, didn't I?" he asked, not meeting Ren's eyes.

"When? Not for Christmas?"

"Some photojournalist is coming to do a story on him and his family." He gave a little laugh. "That's me, I'm afraid. And my sister, of course – though Henny wasn't exactly enthusiastic. Dad thought it would be easier if we both came Christmas Eve and spent the night. I'm sure I told you," he added, seeing Ren's face.

"You didn't," he whispered, his voice suddenly lost.

"Remember, I told you it was the only clear time he had before – oh damn, I'm forgetting my shot." Jack jumped up and went into the kitchen. Ren could hear him opening the fridge. He returned with a syringe and a vial of clear liquid and stuck the needle in through the rubber top. Then he picked up a fold of his belly between two fingers and deftly jabbed the needle in. "Don't you remember? We were coming back from the Mexican restaurant after brunch. You had the combination plate."

"Uhhh," Ren murmured uncommittedly. What more could he say when Jack was sticking himself with that needle?

"Look, I'm sorry Ren," Jack put the needle down. "I guess I should have told him I had other plans . . . but when the moment came, I couldn't. I saw him looking at me and I just . . ."

"Don't fret sweetie, I don't usually go for that 'tis-the-season-to-be-jolly stuff anyway. It was a moment of atavistic yearning, a pull from the primeval swamp of my early life. It's totally totally unimportant. Forget it."

Jack looked as if he'd like nothing more. "You haven't done anything special, prepared anything?"

"What would I have done?" Ren asked, fighting down an urge to hug him, "made a figgy pudding? Oh heavens." He determined to get rid of the tree before Jack saw it. "Christmas is a bore really, an unappetizing mixture of sentiment and sales."

Jack's face relaxed, his eyes lightened. "That's what I thought you thought," he said, and threw the empty syringe and vial into the garbage. Ren retrieved the *Times* from outside the front door and they sat peacefully reading until lunchtime, when Ren found bugs in the pasta that he'd intended to cook.

"God, Jack, I don't know why you keep these old boxes around," he shrieked histrionically, taking a box of yellow cornmeal off the closet shelf. "They've infected everything." Small brown bugs leaped from the box onto the counter. "You should know better."

"They're kind of cute," Jack said. "I should know what they are."

"Cute? Make a collection then . . . keep them next to your plants. Here . . . " He shook the bug-ridden contents under Jack's nose then handed him the box.

Jack dropped it in the trash. "You don't need to have such a hissy fit."

"I'm not having a hissy fit. I'm just being efficient. I'm sure your father has a rule for getting rid of nasty undesirables. Nasty bugs, nasty attitudes, nasty . . ."

"Ren, stop! This is really off the wall. You know if there's one thing that could break us up, it's this crazy obsession you have with my father." Ren knew it was true. Even the tender tone in which Jack said "father" offended him. He hated it.

"Can't you see what he's up to? Did he ever have holidays with you when you were a kid? When your mom was still alive?"

"No."

"Then why the hell is he doing the Christmas thing now? To publicize his damn book."

"Well, what's so wrong with that? He's killing two birds with one stone. He wants to see me and he wants to get some publicity. Why shouldn't he?"

"He's using you, that's why. If he could he'd make you into an ad for Ivory soap – ninety-nine and forty-four one-hundredths percent pure. He would!"

Jack put his arm around him. "I thought you loved me because I was clean-cut."

"I loved you for your ass."

"Well then . . . " Jack threw up his arms. "Nothing more to say."

"There's a lot more, but I won't say it." Ren considered saying "I wanted you to come for Christmas dinner. I got a tree." He imagined how Jack would take him in his arms and say "Oh baby, I'm sorry." But the words stuck in his throat. He was still too mad. He knew he was hurting himself worse than Jack – depriving himself of a pleasure. But he just couldn't. He turned and went back to clearing the closet. He swished up some soapy water and washed down the closet shelves with maniacal precision, humming a Fascist march tune. Damn Jack for making him so miserable.

That night Ren made up with him – as of course he knew he would – but he didn't tell him about the tree. He lay awake half the night watching the moon shift its position in the rectangle of the window.

It had been so much easier not to love someone. Whenever he wasn't working, he'd prowl the streets, or go to one of the clubs. He thought about the last time he'd been at the Fur Tunnel and picked up the Puerto Rican with the soft lilting voice. When he'd brought him home he'd been surprised at how powerful he was in bed. His long brown prick hard as steel hammering into him. The hot mouth. And then afterwards the exchange of confidences, smoking in the stained bed. A mini-life in an hour. His shrink would have said there was no emotion in it, but he would have been wrong. It was intense, easy, and there wasn't this awful pain of always wanting more than you could get from one man.

CHAPTER FOUR

old plots, new plots

in his one hand he had a holly bob
that is goodliest in green when groves are bare
and an ax in his other, a huge and immense
a wicked piece of work in words to expound

— Sir Gawain and The Green Knight

The theater was in a basement on Third Street just off
First Avenue, in an old building that the city was always
threatening to condemn. The auditorium, though dark,
was spacious enough to accommodate a decent-sized prosceni-
um stage with a small apron and faded maroon velvet curtain.
The seats, taken from an old movie palace, were worn but
serviceable and set in slightly sloping tiers. They held about
three hundred people.

When Ren arrived the next evening for rehearsal, he
found his trinity of leads, Joe, Grace and Ellen, sitting on the
edge of the stage arguing about whether the boys who were acting the court ladies had camped it up too much last time.

Ren pulled off his gloves and blew on his numb hands. It
felt almost as cold inside the theater as out. The brick back
wall was covered by a fifteen-foot-high, bronze-colored hanging. In front of it was a raised dais for the court feast. The rest
of the stage was bare except for a partially finished wooden
hearth with a painted fire on the left, its lintel surrounded by
festive boughs. Well, this was going to be his Xmas – paint and
paste at Camelot, instead of tea and sympathy with Jack.

Joe, the big, soft-bodied man who was playing the Green Knight, was flapping a false arm to and fro. Ren was pleased to see that Joe's fake head, finally finished, was resting on the stage beside him. Ren had insisted on getting Joe's full costume early, and looking at the giant head, he was sure he was right. The thing was beautifully ugly, surreal. Its weight alone should affect the way Joe played.

"Hey Joe," Ren smiled at him. "How're you doing? I see you've got your head." Ren had chosen Joe for the part because of his exotic looks and enormous size – he was the son of a Samoan knife thrower and he had the heft of a Sumo wrestler.

"I don't know," Joe said. He had the top of his over-the-head green costume open so he could talk freely. "I thought it would be cute if I had a bit of black stocking showing under my tunic."

"Cute but not what we want here," Ren said calmly. He saw Ellen flash Joe a look of annoyance. It had been apparent from her first readings as Sir Gawain that she thought Joe something of a prima donna, and disliked his jokes and constant chatter. Ren hoped there wasn't going to be serious trouble. He clapped his hands,

"Places, everyone. Act one, scene two, from the top. Let's go." Ellen got up and stretched vigorously, her small breasts curving against her muslin rehearsal tunic. The interns, all male, some in mock-up gowns, the rest in tunics, were coming out of the wings and taking their places on the dais. Ellen, who Ren could see had been practicing her masculine walk, stalked over to the center of the board that was serving as a banquet table, and sat, legs apart, pretending to drink from an imaginary glass. She was clearly eager to get started. Ren waited until the others were seated.

Pacing the narrow aisle in front of the stage and looking up at the interns, Ren began: "Here we are again in Arthur's court, in the midst of Christmas revels. You've been flirting, dancing, stealing kisses. Your pleasure is at its height. But

first," Ren said, "we need to be a little warmer. Would someone plug in the heater? Thanks." Ren himself wasn't noticing
the cold anymore but some of the interns still looked stiff and
uncomfortable.

"I know the heat situation isn't good. But let's try to forget it." He swept his arm around, energizing the space. "Close
your eyes for a moment and imagine you're in the great hall in
front of a blazing fire. Each of you has images for what you
desire most. Imagine this is it . . . or as near to it as you can
get. You are warm, fed, content, you've never been so content
and suddenly this creature, this bawling Green Knight,
appears and starts taunting you. I want a violent change of
mood, from pure elation to pure panic. Okay. Let's start from
the Green Knight's entrance."

The Green Knight strode into the court. Already tall, Joe
towered over the others with his false trunk and enormous
head. As he strode in, the dance music changed to something
eerie, and the light, managed for now by the student tech,
flickered.

Ren had overseen the design of the magnificent papier-
mâché head. It was a wonderfully vibrant green with a thick
green beard and scintillating red eyes. The effect was unnerv-
ing. Even a jaded audience would get a jolt from Joe's powerful presence. Then all of a sudden, Joe made a swish gesture;
the mood broke.

Ren was furious. He got to his feet and stopped the scene.
He knew that Joe would resent it if he told him that he was
supposed to play the Green Knight straight. Ren decided to
direct Joe indirectly by addressing the other players. He
forced his voice to sound laconic, cool. "We need stronger
reactions here," he told them. "Look at him," he pointed at
Joe just off center stage. "He's come in as if he owns the place.
He's huge, his green skin is creepy, he makes the hair on your
neck stand up, he stalks around taking your measure in a
scornful way, asking who dares cut off his head. You need to
gasp, jump to your feet, show more terror, put your hands to

your swords. Remember. You've never seen anything like this."

Ren's stratagem worked. Joe understood that his sashaying was out of place here. He took his hand off his hip, assumed a wide macho stance and lightly caressed his ax, testing the blade with the tip of his finger as if it were razor sharp. "Good moment, Joe," Ren said. "Be sure to keep that next time. Ellen, I want you to stand and take two steps towards him when he gets near you. You're as frightened as the others but from the beginning, you want to protect your king. Okay, take it from Joe's entry."

If Joe was irked at not being able to play for laughs, it only made his taunts more venomous as he walked along the line of knights jutting his big head into their faces and making quick feints with his axe as though it were an animal whose force he could hardly contain. "My God," he roared, "are you all beardless children here, have you no leader? No one willing to play my game of a blow for a blow?" When he neared Ellen he chucked her maliciously under the chin. Startled, she moved back a pace.

Joe kept up his taunts. "It's not as if I'm asking you to fight," he said. "None of you is man enough for that. I'm offering you an easy chance to be a hero. Here's my ax." He held it out. The thing was huge and double-headed, painted bright silver with a green ribbon wound around it. "Take it, cut off my head. . . . All I'm asking is the right to strike a return blow a year from now. Oh, come, now. Don't tell me you're afraid of a dead man, you the bravest knights in the world. Doesn't someone want to do it? Come on, you know you do. Cut it off. I promise I won't resist, I'll kneel down for you and make it easy."

He danced around Ellen on his toes, holding the ax by its handle, shoving it towards her, goading her until – Ren wasn't sure just how it happened – the protruding end of the ax head hit her breast.

"God damn it." Ellen turned white, then red. "What are

you doing, get away from me, you hit my breast!" Her voice was shrill, almost hysterical. "I'm not taking this. . . . " Then she burst into furious tears and ran offstage.

Ren called a break and went after her. He found her in the closet-like space that served as a costume room, huddled on the only chair, next to a rack of half-finished costumes.

"I can't play with him," she said, choking back tears. "Find someone else. From the start he's been upstaging me and now . . . where does he come off hitting me like that?" She clenched her fists and leaned forward.

Well, she was intense, all right. That's what he'd liked about her in the tryout. And even now, blotched with crying, her looks were perfect. With her short black curls and classical chiseled features, she was ideal for his new model of the heroic. Ren clucked sympathetically, letting her get it all out, giving her time to recover her poise.

He knew better than to put his arm around her shoulder or to defend Joe and say it was an accident. When her anger had diminished a little, he simply told her how much he valued her. He'd talk to Joe, it wouldn't happen again.

"You say that. But it shouldn't have happened in the first place. I took the part because I thought it would be liberating to play a man, and the first thing that happens is this guy jabs his ax into me."

"What happened with Joe was bad," he said more matter-of-factly. "I'm not denying it, but you're a professional. Why not see if you can use your anger, put it into the part. This green bastard insults you, threatens your king. What happens then? Tell me."

"I want to kill him," Ellen said. Her voice had been too soft before. Now it was low and vibrant. Ren left her to collect herself while he went to talk to Joe. A half-hour later she was back on stage and they took up where they had left off.

This time the scene went without a hitch, Ellen's voice was clear as a bell and when Joe offered Ellen his ax, she leapt forward to receive it with as much ferocity as Ren could have wished. And Joe managed to add a touch of bitchiness, telling Ellen to hold her tool steady, without losing his power. Then he knelt and threw his green hair dramatically forward to bare his trunk-like neck. There was a pregnant silence before Ellen, teeth clenched and using her whole body, brought the ax down on that ugly neck.

For now there was a cardboard sleeve that retracted as the ax came down. Ren made a note that they should add a sound effect here, the crunch of breaking bone. But even without that it was startling to see the giant head fall to the ground, the silk streamers of red blood spilling out as it rolled across the stage, its mouth gaping.

Ellen gave it a tentative kick. With one heavy lurch the Green Knight got to his feet, strode over to his head and picked it up by the hair. The bloody lips – their speaking device operated from backstage – challenged Gawain to meet him in a year and a day at the Green Chapel for a return blow. Ren saw a quick succession of expressions – horror, amazement, pride, fear – pass over Ellen's face. Good girl.

Ren played with ways of turning up the power still more. What if he projected slides of a lizard's tail regenerating – resurrecting – in slow motion, puffing out in enlarged close-ups while the Knight retrieved his head? He made a note on the small note pad he carried with him along with his script.

While he was focused on the small intense space of the stage, the play was his whole world. His painful emotions were sucked into the play, which seemed to fatten and gain in power. But when the Green Knight stalked off the stage and Ren closed the stage door behind him and started home, he felt his own worries staring at him from the dark, watching him from behind, waiting to leap.

Christmas came and went in a flurry of snow and hurt feelings. Jack managed to send Ren an e-mail but it only made Ren feel worse since it was on Malcolm's computer and had his name emblazoned on the top, Malcolm Firste. At that moment, he could have gladly axed the man. To make up, Jack brought champagne on New Year's Eve and told Ren he could take him to his harvesting sessions without *le père*. Ren felt his eyes tear up. They held hands in front of the TV like an old married couple. For a moment, as they were counting down to midnight, Ren missed being somewhere noisy and glamorous; then gratitude flooded him for what he had. The noise and glitz would mean nothing without Jack. He relinquished it without a second thought and hugged Jack closer. The shorn head rested against Ren's shoulder and, snugly wrapped in an old quilt, they watched the ball drop in Times Square.

On January second, five days before Jack's scheduled entry into the hospital for the transplant, they took the bus up to Mount Sinai together. The snow had been pushed to the sides of the streets, where it formed huge crags and peaks slowly turning black or streaked at the base with yellow markings of dogs staking out their turf. Above them, tinselly green and red Christmas decorations were strung across streets, plastic trees and reindeer, pathetic reminders not only of primitive forests with their steamy-hided, antlered creatures, but of the Christmas they hadn't spent together. Ren had ended by inviting a downstairs neighbor, Marge, a feisty older lady who it turned out loved tales of chivalry almost as much as his mother.

Jack had been giving himself Nupogen shots to boost his stem cell production for a full week before the harvest and it made his bones ache. He climbed stiffly onto the bus, looking, with all his clothes, like an overweight Santa. He had long-johns under his clothes, and an extra sweater – the nurse had told him to keep very warm so his veins would be plump and relaxed – plus a fur hat and mittens. Ren guided him down the aisle past an overweight businessman with a briefcase and a middle-aged woman reading the *National Enquirer* – and shoehorned him into a newly available seat. The woman, noticing she'd been aced out, gave Jack a dirty look. Ren could see Jack blush. In a minute he was going to play good little boy and get up.

"Got to keep your eye on the game, lady," Ren whispered to the woman. "Reading smutty stories has its price."

She glared and edged towards the exit.

"What did you do to her?" Jack asked.

"Just suggested that if she was creaming in her pants wishing she were Monica Lewinsky, she was going to miss out on the seats. She thinks I'm a poivert," Ren added happily in a Brooklyn accent.

"Well? That wasn't very smart."

Ren stood touching Jack's knee with his knee, pressing it when the bus lurched. "Yeah, I know. Don't want to give us girls a bad name." He could feel Jack draw away from him and straighten his shoulders. He didn't know why he had to push things, why he couldn't just let Jack be his Ivy League self, the self he'd fallen for.

"Why do you always have to do this?"

Now was the time to apologize but the wrong words spouted from his mouth. "I'm always silly when I'm happy."

"That doesn't mean you have to act weird. God knows what that woman will tell her friends."

"You didn't have to listen to years of some pompous shrink telling you what a sicko creep you were. I don't care what anybody thinks anymore." Not true, of course – ridiculous macho posturing. Ren could feel scorn coming at him from behind just by the way his shoulders started to tingle.

Jack's eyes became a warmer shade of green. "I shouldn't beat up on you. Stop me next time. You could rap me on the knuckles with a rolled up newspaper – once for being pompous, two for being tight-assed. Behavioral re-conditioning. What do you think? "

Ren slid into the seat that had just opened up next to Jack. "It's not bad idea. I like your concrete approach to therapy."

"Why'd you'd go to a shrink in the first place?" Jack asked. His voice lowered discretely to avoid people's attention. "Were you trying to shift gears?"

"Me? Never. My mom was worried – though actually I think she rather enjoyed my being queer. It kept us close." As he said it, he realized it was a new thought. "She used to take me in bed with her and tell me stories. The shrink blamed her for messing me up – you know the way shrinks always do – and it cooled things off between us. 'She treated you like little Lord Fauntleroy and Einstein in one package,' he said. 'No wonder you're too self-involved to really love anyone.'"

"Wow! I like the tentative nature of his interpretation. He sounds like a really humble guy." Jack gave Ren a sympathetic pressure with his knee. "I bet the first thing my father would do if I told him I was gay would be to pack me off to someone like that."

Ren didn't want to think about Jack's father, or the shrink, for that matter. Get out of my head, boys, he said, picturing them trying to crawl inside a rotund tube of his gray matter. There are no vacancies. He wanted to be happy just being with Jack and taking care of him. He put his hand on the back of the seat behind Jack's shoulder. Not touching, but close enough to feel the heat, he looked out the bus window. "Hey, nothing can be that small," he pointed to a tiny dog, his body only inches above the ground. "Why don't we go to a pet shop after your harvesting today, and get a dog. I could keep him at my place and we could have soulful conversations while you're in the hospital."

Jack seemed suddenly uncomfortably conscious of Ren's hand touching the back of his neck.

"Ren, I don't think you quite grasp . . . after the transplant I'm going to have to be in a sterile environment. I ought to be thinking of a cleaning lady, not a dog." Jack stopped and shook his head like a horse trying to get rid of his bridle.

Ren removed his hand. He knew Jack didn't like displays of affection in public but God, people rest their hands on the back of seats for all sorts of reasons. "Maybe I ought to stay away too," he said sulkily. "I mean God knows what filth I come in contact with at the theater."

Jack groaned. "I don't think there are many germs that are strong enough to co-exist with you, doll. But actually, I kinda hoped you'd come and clean for me. You could skate around my place with rags on your feet the way they do in Italy, singing arias from *Pagliacci*." The bus lurched to a stop and Jack struggled to his feet, knocking his mittened fist softly against Ren's chest as he did.

"What? Where?" Ren had the sudden fear that Jack was running out on him.

Jack turned him towards the door. "Hel-lo. Reality check. This is where we get off. Come on." He held Ren's arm above the elbow and they pushed their way out into the glare of sun on snow. The hospital towers rose across the street like the turrets of some impregnable fortress.

After Jack signed in at the front desk, they went straight back to one of the treatment rooms – the same one in which he'd had his chemo – where they set Jack up on a bed facing the tiny TV that hung from the ceiling.

The nurse was a big blond man named Tommy. You could sense his muscles bulking up under his green hospital shirt, the kind of man queens used to swoon over before gays started going macho. Ren thought he was eyeing Jack with unusual sympathy. Jack looked up at him under his long lashes and dutifully opened and closed his fist.

"I hope they told you this would take a long time," the nurse said while he palpated Jack's veins. They were small and tight despite all the warm fluids he'd been drinking and the warm blanket Ren had piled on his feet.

The needle looked like something you'd use for a horse. Ren knew that if he couldn't get it in, they'd have to shove an even bigger one through Jack's breastbone. He felt himself getting faint and made himself breathe. When Tommy finally managed to insert the needle, Ren wasn't able to turn away in time and he saw it going into the blue vein on the soft inner arm that he had so often held against his mouth. He winced and saw Jack's smile. Yeah, he knew he was a sissy. The nurse, all professional now, pretended not to notice. He secured the needle with blue tape. As far as Ren could see, there was a sort of circle game. Blood was being drawn out of Jack's right arm and passing through a hovering machine, then shunted back into Jack's body through the left arm.

"The grim reaper," Ren said and reached out to pat the machine. "How does it know what to harvest? Mightn't it take out some innocent little white cells by mistake?" It occurred to him that he wouldn't have made that joke if it had been AIDS they were in for. Too many ideas of sin and punishment still floating around.

"You should be careful with your metaphors," Tommy said, unexpectedly serious. "The way a patient visualizes his treatment can influence the outcome, so it's important to get the images right. We're not killing anything, we're simply collecting cells, the way a farmer collects seed. These stem cells are going to jump start his whole system when we put them back in again."

"Sorry," Ren said. "It was stupid of me. I'm sure the stem cells are something special." He tried to picture them swelling inside Jack's marrow until it was full to bursting, then in an orgasmic whoosh spilling into the peripheral blood.

"But to answer your question about how the machine harvests the right cells, cells have different weights. The stem cells fall about here" – he indicated a middle level in the belly of the machine – "the more mature reds and whites here and here." The machine had the stolid look of a water cooler.

Jack shifted uneasily on the bed, trying to keep from jerking on the lines in his veins. "What if there aren't enough stem cells?" he asked the nurse. "I heard that sometimes production is diminished by chemo . . . and I've just had six months of it."

"Dr. Stevens wouldn't have suggested this if he didn't think you could make it," he said, kindly. "You look very well, considering what you've been through." Ren thought he saw Jack blush. "No point in worrying about it now. You have to come in at least once more anyway." Tommy checked that the tape was holding. "I'll be at the station if you need me," he said moving off. "Name's Tommy," he added over his shoulder.

Ren reached out and touched Jack's leg under the blanket, re-establishing possession. "That guy got on my nerves," he said. He could see Jack's blood moving along the thin tube – a deep dark red. Despite the scientific trappings, the slow snaking of the blood struck him as mysterious, even sacred.

"Really, I thought he was nice."

"I don't care for those bulky types myself."

"You should talk."

Ren stretched out an arm and examined it. "I don't know what you mean. My muscles are long and elegant . . . I could be a ballerina."

"Yeah, if they made point shoes the size of loaf pans."

"You're behind the times, honey, they do."

Dr. Stevens, the oncologist, poked his head in. He had a dapper black goatee and black eyes like agates. "You seem to be having a good time. How's it going? Got you hooked up alright?" Jack nodded. He was still wearing his fur hat – convinced that it helped to keep his body heat up and his veins open – and despite the grin elicited by the idea of Ren on point, he looked like a little boy home sick. All he needed was a set of toy soldiers on the blanket. "I was wondering what you'd decided about the purging to get rid of any cancerous cells included in the harvest," Dr. Stevens asked. "Do you want to go ahead with it? It means an extra harvest session."

"Do I really need it? I mean, I thought the chemo put me in remission."

"It did. But there are probably some of those little devils wandering around in your blood. We found just one cell when we did a marrow biopsy. But I'm afraid they grow rather rapidly."

"I admit it doesn't make much sense to put back cancerous cells. Are there any reasons why I shouldn't try it?"

While they were talking, Ren tried to remember what he'd heard about this latest addition to the transplant protocol. They had some sort of centrifuge that whirled the cells and pulled out the cancerous ones. Or was it a magnetic field? He'd been lousy at science.

"None I can think of," Dr. Stevens was saying. "Though it might make it harder to get enough viable cells. It reduces them by about a third, sometimes half . . . we might fall short."

"And then?"

"Then we could try to harvest directly from the marrow. I personally like the blood better. It's cleaner. Gives better results. But none of this may be necessary. I'll check back in the afternoon and see how the counts are doing."

The morning went quickly enough. Around noon Jack was hungry and Ren brought him a sandwich and an orange from the snack room. "I should have brought my red checked tablecloth," he said as he peeled the orange and divided it into slices. "*Voilà*, Paris on the Hudson." He popped a slice into Jack's mouth.

"Want me to read to you?"

"What have you brought?"

He rustled in the Takashimaya bag Jack had given him as a present. Very elegant and minimal, a bit clonish, not at all him, but he carried it because he knew it made Jack happy. The poor kid was too young to understand that consumerism was even more dangerous when it was understated.

"Well, If you want something light, I have Agatha Christie, *Death on the Nile*, and" – he hefted a large, color-

45

fully illustrated volume – "Lord Norwich's *A Short History of Byzantium*, or we could watch a video – I brought *Priscilla Queen of the Desert.*"

"I like the idea of turning the lights out," Jack said without missing a beat.

Ren patted Jack's leg, then excused himself and went to the bathroom, where after opening a window to dissipate the smell, he locked himself in a cubicle and smoked a joint. It was a weird thing to do in a hospital – someone might come in – but he'd done weirder things in toilets and he needed it. The sterility of the place was getting to him. All the chrome and gleaming surfaces, the lights that illuminated every corner. It made him feel as if he were trapped inside the body of a giant space ship like the sperm-men in *Everything You Always Wanted To Know About Sex*. He drew in the sweet smoke and let some of the tension out.

When Ren came back, Jack sniffed once and gave him a look, but he didn't say anything. The video hadn't been rewound and started near the end with a shot of a tour bus with a flurry of purple chiffon on top. The camera moved in and long purple streamers whipped by the wind parted slightly to reveal a young drag queen, arms outstretched, belting out an Italian aria.

"Ohhh, that gown is to die for," Ren moaned.

"What's in it isn't bad either."

"I thought you liked more of a GI look."

"Why do you keep saying this stuff? I like bulky, I like GIs. Just because the nurse has a nice body you don't need to panic, so do a million other people. It's you I want. Oh, this is ridiculous. I can't believe I'm having this argument with you now." He glanced down at his taped arm. "Isn't it enough that they have me splayed out like this? Do you have to torment me too?"

"I was just wondering whether you're getting tired of me," Ren said meekly.

"I will if you don't shut up."

"Hate to bother you when you're in the middle of a movie, boys," Tommy said, raising his eyebrows. A surreal blue face, red lips splayed wide, filled the small TV screen. "But I need to check some things." Ren glowered at him and stopped the video but Jack smiled.

"I'm glad you're here, actually. I need to pee."

"I'll get you a bottle. I'll be right back."

"Being rude to him isn't a big help to me, Ren," Jack whispered when Tommy went out.

"I didn't do anything."

"You did too. You glowered."

"Something bit me."

"Sure."

Tommy came in with a glass urinal. Ren wanted to take it from him but Jack was frowning at him so he just watched while Tommy unzipped Jack's pants and held it for him. The yellow liquid foamed up. God, he must really have had to go. Another nurse called Tommy away for a minor emergency in the next cubicle and Ren got to zip Jack up. While he was doing it, Jack accidentally knocked the urinal over – he had put it on the little swinging table – and the warm urine sloshed all over his flannel trousers.

"Damn, these are a mess . . . and I have nothing to change to. It'll look like I went in my pants."

"*Calma-ti, calma-ti,*" Ren crooned. "I'll wash out the stain in the head, then I'll dry it under the hand dryer, don't worry. You'll be fresh as a dream." He levered Jack out of his pants, careful not to derange the lines, then rushed off to the toilet. He stopped long enough to smoke the rest of the joint, then rinsed out the stain and held the pant leg up to the dryer. It went on with a roar and he not only had the virtuous satisfaction of standing in an uncomfortable position doing something tedious for Jack but of being rewarded with a grateful smile when he came back. It struck him not for the first time that the most meaningful battles weren't in hand-to-hand combat, they were in coping with piss and shit.

CHAPTER FIVE

diverse blows

now liege lord of my life, my leave I take;
the terms of this task too well you know –
to count the cost over concerns me nothing.
but I am bound forth betimes to bear a stroke
from the grim man in green, as god may direct.

— *Sir Gawain and The Green Knight*

By the next day's harvesting session, Ren had gotten over his fear of the procedure. If he'd been able to forget about his show, it would have been almost cozy. But of course he couldn't – the best he could manage was to turn off his cell phone for several hours while he curled up on the foot of Jack's bed and read to him. Except for the insertion of the needle in the beginning and his anxiety that the vein might collapse, Jack didn't seem to be in pain. Ren tried to turn the sterility of the place into an asset: he told himself that being together in that small windowless room was like being in a space capsule going to the moon. They didn't even have a porthole where they could look down at the earth under its curtain of blue haze, and see with a shock how far they'd come.

They gave Jack a day of rest before the final harvest. Dr. Stevens came in at the beginning of the third session and told them that this day's harvest should do it. The Nupogen shots had boosted cell production well beyond the required amount. They'd gotten over the first hurdle. This had been much less grueling than Ren had expected, and he began to hope that the terrors of the ordeal to come had been exaggerated.

In the congratulatory atmosphere produced by Dr. Stevens' announcement, Ren remembered the interrupted video. He dug it out of his bag and inserted it in the VCR slot. Then he climbed up on the high bed by Jack's feet and held them in his hand, pressing the toes while they watched the "girls" performing at a bar surrounded by rednecks. "Nasty looking group of brutes," Ren muttered.

"Shush," Jack said.

The apheresis machine hummed lightly as it skimmed off the precious cells while the young drag queen Felicia was chased by a group of men, thrown roughly on the ground and her legs flung open.

Ren leaned forward. "Jesus, they're going to cut her."

Jack was trying to peer round Ren's shoulder. "Ren, shush."

Ren drew back, startled. "Oh sorry, babe, sorry." Ren was terrible at movies, he knew. He always talked in a stage whisper, and at the scary parts he clutched Jack's arm so hard it left marks. "I won't say another word." He looked meekly up at the screen where a sobbing Felicia was being rescued by a man in a beard whom the girls had befriended on the road. "Hey," Ren blurted out, "want to bet Red-Beard marries one of them? That's how I'd end it." Then he squeezed Jack's toes hard. "Last comment, I swear."

Jack closed his eyes and reached for Ren's hand. "I'm awfully sleepy all of a sudden . . . would you mind terribly if I took a little nap?"

For answer, Ren switched off the video and moved to the chair at the foot of the bed. In less than a minute Jack was lightly snoring. Ren hadn't realized how tired this was making him. Maybe taking the stem cells out made you anemic. Anyway, it must be a jolt to Jack's system having his blood moved around like that. Ren had fainted the last time he went to give blood. And that was an operation of just a few minutes.

Jack was hooked up for hours. Poor baby. It was so typical of Jack – cheerfully watching Ren's movie when he probably wanted nothing so much as to be left alone to sleep – always playing the good host even when he was the one who was supposed to be entertained. He could have dozed hours earlier.

Ren got up and looked down at Jack's face. The heartbreaking eyelashes, the beautiful square jaw. Was he grinding his teeth? He ran his hand lightly over Jack's cheek, willing him to relax and sleep peacefully, then he curled up in the chair, put a blanket over his legs, rewound the video and replayed the chase scene from the beginning without sound.

When Felicia first showed up in the circle of men, she was wearing a miniskirt and the heavy makeup of a whore. They leered at her, clearly attracted, then furious when they realized they couldn't get it.

Ren winced as they chased her. Why didn't they just make love to her? They wanted to. He wondered how much violence would be done away with if men could admit they loved each other. Instead of trading blows, they could take turns being twinkies. That's what he and Jack did, took turns being on the bottom. Though they still quarreled over style. But this wasn't like taking a knife to someone.

"What about women?" Jack asked, when he woke up and Ren told him his idea for world peace. "Your utopians would die out like the Shakers."

Ren was about to answer when Tommy, the bulked up nurse, came in to check Jack's leads. "I'm going off in a while. I wanted to say goodbye and wish you luck with the transplant." He rested his hand on Jack's shoulder and Ren resisted the urge to snarl.

"Thanks," Jack said, opening his green eyes wide.

"Remember the Greeks," Tommy said to Ren (he'd obviously overheard their conversation). "They made love and war. Men will always have the urge to beat each other."

Ren studied him trying to figure out if he was gay or straight. "Maybe so," he said annoyed. Tommy gave another pat to Jack's shoulder then started to massage his neck. Ren got to his feet. "Hey, is that medically necessary?"

"Ren," Jack said warningly.

"Do you mind removing your hand."

"I don't understand what's bothering you. His neck is very stiff. I need to loosen it."

Ren lurched forward with a gesture of protest and without really meaning to bumped Tommy's arm.

"Watch it! Don't touch me when I'm working on him." Tommy, off-balance, stumbled. The needle pulled out and blood spurted from the wound.

"Oh my God," Ren sputtered, aghast. "I'm sorry . . . I didn't mean . . . " He didn't get a chance to finish. Just then Jack's father appeared in the doorway – hat still on, nose red from the cold. "What in God's name is going on here?"

"This man attacked me," Tommy said. "Damn! I have to reinsert the needle." He held a piece of cotton hard against the vein, which was still leaking blood, while he tried to find a fresh vein to put the needle in.

"Let me hold the cotton for you," Jack's father said. "I did First Aid in the war." Tommy shook his head. He'd already gotten the needle in. "You alright, son?"

"Fine Dad. He's got it back already. It's cool."

"It's anything but cool," his father spluttered. "My God, what kind of a person would start a fight in a hospital room. It's inconceivable to me." He turned toward Ren. "You could have disrupted the whole process."

"That's right," Tommy said. "As it is, I'll have to check with the doctor."

"It was an accident," Ren pleaded, near tears. "I came too close, I know, but I didn't mean to bump him, I tripped."

Malcolm didn't even pretend to listen. "I knew you'd be trouble the moment I laid eyes on you. Would you mind getting out of here before I call security and have you thrown out?"

Ren couldn't very well say, "That faggot was feeling up your son, why don't you throw *him* out, book him for sexual harassment." His face felt hot as fire. Then he saw Tommy smirk, knew he'd been right about him all along and instinctively made a fist.

Jack's father's eyes bulged. He looked out the door at the nursing station, afraid to leave his son alone with this madman but clearly wanting to summon a guard.

"Go Ren," Jack said in a low urgent whisper, "please." He looked thoroughly miserable. "You'll only make it worse. Let me handle it. I'll call you tonight."

Ren pictured the security guards running up and had an urge to let them come so he could clunk their heads together the way they do in Kung Fu movies. But he saw from Jack's eyes that he was really angry now – almost siding with the enemy.

"The last thing in the world I want is to hurt Jack," Ren said to Malcolm as he headed towards the door, "but it'll obviously be better for him now if I go."

It was snowing when he got outside. Panhandlers lurked in doorways, their pleas and handicaps scrawled on brown cardboard signs. He dropped a quarter in one of the cups.

"Thanks, pal," the man said. "God bless." He was a tall man with a patch over one eye and darkish skin. "The demons of spice are after me," he whispered confidentially. "Won't give me no rest."

Jack called later. He had managed to calm his father and the apheresis had survived the disruption, but he was shaken and angry. Ren asked if he could come up but Jack wouldn't let him – he said he was afraid his father might show up unannounced – but Ren cried and finally Jack had pity on him and took a taxi down to his West Village flat.

"I shouldn't reward you for acting crazy-jealous," he said after he let himself in, "but you seemed so desperate . . ." His voice was colder than Ren had ever heard it.

"I'm sorry, I'm really sorry." Ren embraced him – Jack standing rigid – trying not to cry again. "I don't know what came over me. I smoked some pot before we went to the hospital; maybe it made me clumsy. I was mad but I didn't really mean to bump him."

"Your stupid jealousy is what came over you. And pot doesn't help. I thought you were going to stop it." Jack pulled away, lifted a jacket off a chair – Ren had obviously been sewing on a button – and sat down.

"I am going to stop. I know, it was stupid of me. I promise." Ren hovered over him, terrified that he'd go back to the arguments they'd been having about commitment before Jack got sick. "Do you still love me?"

"Of course I do." Jack impatiently pushed away a mockup of the Green Knight's head that was staring, mouth agape, from the table. "But you've got to control this stuff." He avoided Ren's eyes. "You came within a hair's breadth of being locked up. You could have been raped ten times before I could get down to the precinct." He put his head in his hands.

"They would have put me with the whores," Ren said. "I wouldn't have been raped." It was true enough, but it sounded facetious.

"Ren!"

"Sorry. I'll do anything you say. I'll wear shackles . . . put rings in my balls so it'll hurt if I move too fast."

"Do you have to turn everything into a joke?"

"Ex-cuse me." To hide his chagrin, Ren picked up his jacket and hung it in the closet.

"Sorry," Jack said, "but this isn't a play – this is my life. Now I have my father worrying about my unstable older friend. I don't think he suspects anything. It's too far from his mind. But he's begun asking me questions, like where did I meet you."

Ren had an instant picture of Jack, sober and single, at the opening night party, where everyone else was making out in dark corners. He'd loved Ren as Prospero in Back Alley's

production of *The Tempest* and had come backstage afterwards to talk. That's how it started. On Ren's part it had been
a *coup de foudre*.

"Why can't you tell him?" he asked, remembering how
dazzled Jack had seemed. "If you showed him you were
proud of our relationship, don't you think he'd see me differently?"

"You don't know how many times I've started to tell him
the truth. I wanted to . . . but I just freeze up. Still, one of
these days I'm going to do it." He paused, bit his lip. "I know
I'm letting you down, but can't you see how hard you make it
for me when you act like this? It sets us back, that's all I'm trying to say. It makes him so much more suspicious. He really
grilled me."

"I can imagine." When Ren was in high school, his mother used to cross-examine him about his dates and he had to
feign interest. It had been such a relief to tell her when he
graduated.

"He wanted to know if you took drugs." Jack hung his
shorn head. He looked terribly tired.

"I'm an idiot. How could I let you in for this?"

"I'm going to be very sick," Jack said simply. "Maybe all
this is your way of telling me that you want to cool things off."

Ren was next to him in an instant. "I would have moved
in with you months ago, if it hadn't been for your father."

"But now?"

"Even more. I want to take care of you. It's him . . ."

Jack flared up again. "He didn't make you pick a fight
with my nurse, for God's sake."

"If I lived with you I wouldn't feel so scared."

"Maybe. Maybe not. You might get more scared.
Sometimes it seems to me that the closer we get, the more we
fight. Anyway, I am letting my father take me to the hospital
for my check-in on Monday."

Ren felt as if Jack was waving a red flag to see if he'd take
the charge: anger churned up in his stomach. But given the

trouble he'd already caused, all he could do now was pretend to be a rational human being.

"Fine," he said. "If that's what you want, fine."

"He insisted. Don't look so glum. You're not missing anything exciting – I'll probably spend the whole day with a dietician talking about what I won't be able to eat."

Good old Jack, introducing a perfectly bland topic. Well, he'd go along. Win points for good behavior. "I read somewhere that you can get an aversion to your favorite foods after high-dose chemo" – but please no aversion to me, Jack baby, he thought, not to me.

Jack smiled at him, obviously relieved that he hadn't gone into a tantrum, then suddenly looked at his watch: eight p.m. "Hey, aren't you going to rehearsal tonight?"

"Oh God, yes," Ren said. "But I wish I could stay with you. I need to hold you. Shit."

"You've never missed a rehearsal or even been late for one for as long as I've known you. Get going. I'll even come with you, if you like."

"No, you get some sleep. I've been selfish enough. Got to hurry, though." Ren grabbed his jacket and ran into the bathroom to pee. Over the mirror was a quote from Artaud about getting out of the body into the mystical realm of art. Good trick if you could do it.

From outside came the metallic clash of garbage cans hitting the asphalt. Some stoned kids drove by several nights a week and tipped them over. Ren checked his face, combed his hair and ran his razor dry over his five o'clock shadow. Then he went out and pressed his cheek against Jack's. "I'm sorry again," he whispered. Jack gave a grunt, whether of exasperation or forgiveness he couldn't tell, and nudged him towards the door.

"Just be quiet coming in," he said. "I'll probably be asleep."

Ren smiled. He had been afraid for a moment there that Jack wasn't going to stay the night. He went downstairs two stairs at a time to counter his urge to go back. When he opened the outer door, the night air blasted his mind clear. As he walked quickly through the garbage littering the sidewalk, he lectured himself. Jack loved him and he needed care, not jealous rantings. He soaked up nurture like one of his straggly plants. Ren wished he could whisk him away to Italy, as they'd planned last spring. Their bags had been packed. Jack had bought himself new shirts and a fancy raincoat and then he'd gotten what seemed like pneumonia and had been rushed to the hospital. It was hard to believe this had been just a year ago. Then there was the endless testing and waiting.

It had taken them both off-guard to be attacked from a completely unexpected direction. AIDS had been the obvious thought, the shadow under which they were living. But to be carried off by cancer before you hit thirty?

He looked at his watch and started jogging slowly, trying not to slip on the icy patches.

When Ren got to the theater, Jerry, one of the interns, was checking out the film clips that showed the seasons passing until it was time for Gawain's return blow – a scene of spring lambs gamboling in front of a moated castle was projected on the back wall. Ren felt as if he'd walked out of hell into a fairy tale. His stomach was still churning from the stress of the day.

"Let's begin with the farewell," Ren said. It was a brief scene that, luckily for him, needed only the lightest adjustments.

The projected images turned wintry: the castle stood deep in snow, heavy mounds along the tops of fir boughs. Ellen, as Gawain, came onstage to say preliminary farewells to his friends and his mother. The character of Gawain's mother, Lady Helen, was Ren's own invention and he had given the part to Grace, a willowy blond with striking green eyes who also played the Green Knight's wife in the crucial final act. She was made up to look like an older but still beautiful woman.

Her flatteringly tight rehearsal gown emphasized her breasts without being in any way indecent, and she was wearing a peaked hat and light veil.

When the curtain opens she is seen sitting at a little table holding a silver hand mirror and admiring her face from different angles. She is so engrossed she doesn't hear Gawain come up behind her. When she sees him in her mirror, she rises to embrace him.

"Grace, why don't you push the mirror away from you, turn it facedown. It should be obvious that you are ashamed at being caught in an act of vanity. It's not how you see yourself."

Grace began again. "I wish you hadn't to do this thing," she tells Gawain, "that you'd left it to King Arthur. I've prayed for you. Prayed to the Virgin to keep you safe." She turns toward a little shrine set in the wall. A large shield with the Virgin's face clearly painted stands on edge below it.

"I am her knight, Mother," Gawain says simply.

"And mine." Grace strokes Gawain's arm and looks up at him adoringly.

Ren had worked out a series of increasingly intense gestures, from the touch of hand to their final kiss, that showed their erotic fascination with each other. He wanted everything they did, every movement, to counter their talk of chastity and containment. He was thankful that the chemistry between the two actresses was so strong. They reacted to each other naturally. Now he noted with satisfaction how vulnerable and boyish Gawain looked as he leaned toward Lady Helen to brush a wisp of hair out of her face . . . how Lady Helen seemed unaware of the way her hands were behaving as they roamed his body.

"Good work," he said to them when they finished. "That was a pleasure to watch." Grace moved off left and stood next to Joe just inside the wings where they could see the stage.

An intern preparing for the next scene brought an elaborately decorated stool to center stage and Ren motioned for

Ellen to sit down.

"Okay, Ellen, a year has gone by since you gave the Green Knight his blow and now the time has come for you to face him on his own turf. What do you feel?"

"I've been trying to shut it out." Her clean jaw jutted forward, on the defense. "I'm young after all, not sick or wounded, it doesn't seem real that I'm going to die. But even my mother seems to think I'm finished. And now that they're getting my armor ready, I feel like that sacrificial goat the Jews used to push off a cliff loaded with their sins. I mean, why me?"

"A knight has to arm up and take risks," Joe called to her, flashing her a grin, "it's part of the job description." Ellen scowled at him. Ren wished Joe could rein himself in; he must know by now that she bristled every time he made a comment. And it made it harder for Ren to get the effect he wanted. She was tensing up.

"Ellen," he said in a soothing voice, "I need you to show vulnerability at the beginning. You might hunch your shoulders forward a little, touch your bare throat. You're sitting here, exposed. Let the arming slowly transform you."

Ren turned to one of the squires who were going to buckle on Gawain's armor. "When the scene starts I want the gear piled in front of her under a light. This whole arming scene should go fairly slowly – not so slowly that the audience gets bored, but slowly enough to show the importance of the transformation."

The armor was spray-painted leather. Ren had picked it up at a flea market for a song. It had just been finished – Lisa was doing things in order of priority – and this was the first time they had used it in rehearsal. Ren was thrilled at the way it looked, gold paint gleaming. Ellen had complained the cardboard mock-ups were unconvincing, they made her feel like a child dressing up, and it had been hard for her to work with them.

Two squires knelt in front of Ellen putting on her shoes, then they moved up to the calves, then the knees, turning her into a golden idol. "A little slower," Ren suggested. "And Ellen, let us see it affecting you even more. This is burdensome, confining . . . but it's also an honor and gives you enormous status. That's the hook that makes the enterprise so irresistible. I want both qualities."

It was astonishing how well she was responding to her carapace now that it had real substance. Her shoulders straightened to hold the mail coat, her hand went down naturally to the sword at her side. She really seemed to feel stronger. And the blue-gold light emphasized her purity and hardness. When she reached for her shield, there was a swell of church music from backstage. Ren couldn't help himself; he was moved. The shield with the Virgin's face was a goddamned fetish. Ren disapproved of the whole chastity/righteousness deal, but every muscle in his body was tensing along with Ellen's, telling him to go for it. It would be a glorious death.

Gawain moved to the chapel to pray and, right on cue, the music swelled again. When Ren was a kid, he'd thought of converting to Catholicism just so he could pray to Mary. Nothing beat the Catholics for stimulating gestures and emotional punch. Ren had had an orgasm in church once listening to Bach's B-minor mass. Joe had suggested that Ellen play Gawain as a martyr for camp art, have him ogling the altar boys. But that would be too easy to dismiss as silliness. And Ren wanted this to be taken seriously.

Because unlike Judaism – his own faith – Catholicism was so beautiful, it was hard to see where it went wrong. Not just the purity business and the inquisitional prying into people's sex lives, but the violence – the Crusades, the holy wars. Doing this play was Ren's attempt to come to terms with opposing impulses – to celebrate the beauty but resist the message at the same time. It was proving harder than he'd thought.

CHAPTER SIX

Rescuing damsels

was gawain in good works, as gold unalloyed . . .

— Sir Gawain and The Green Knight

Jack managed to call Ren from the hospital late in the morning of January seventh – his father had gone to the bathroom – to tell him that the worst part of his first day was over: the catheter was inserted in his chest. Ren had run into someone he knew once when he went with Jack for chemo and she told him that they didn't use anesthesia. She'd said it was a horrible aching pain like a bone breaking.

When Jack hung up, Ren sat hunched over his coffee picturing Jack under a white sheet waiting for the needle – big as a knitting needle – to hit. He could see him lying there perfectly still, being too polite to mention his fear. And then, as soon as it was done, calling to reassure Ren. Jack was such a sweetheart. Ren didn't deserve him.

While he was sitting there feeling worse than useless, the phone rang and he leapt at it, hoping it was Jack again, but it was only his mother. "I'm feeling so blue today, honey," she said. "Someone wanted to buy one of my watercolors. You know, the beach one with the honey-colored sand . . . he really seemed to like it. He said it reminded him of his place in Miami but at the last minute he changed his mind. I was so positive this time," she told Ren. "But I should have paid attention to my horoscope. It was right there in black and white. Not a good time for business." It was what always happened.

"Sorry Mom, next time, chin up." He'd always encouraged her to be optimistic but maybe that had been the wrong strategy. Maybe if she'd worried more, his father wouldn't have walked out and left her, a former Jewish princess, without any visible means of support.

"How's the gallery going?" he asked to distract her. He could imagine her fidgeting with the phone cord. She wore Ann Taylor skirts, all beige and fawn with just a touch of the exotic – a heavy silver necklace from the old city in Jerusalem – to certify that she was not merely bourgeois but an artist too.

"How should it be going? It goes. It puts food on the table. It means nothing to me. I never thought I'd end up this way."

The words triggered an image of her from so far back, he couldn't even remember his size or shape. He had come into the living room of their Madison Avenue apartment – it must have been before his father left – and she was sitting by the window painting, her hair flecked with gold from the light. She'd been so beautiful to him then. Later, when they'd had to move to a dingy flat on Third Avenue and she was working so hard to support them, he'd felt fiercely protective, lying on his bed, fists clenched and swearing that when he grew up he'd restore her to her rightful place. But as he got older, her disappointments only depressed him; in fact, he came to feel them as an intolerable burden, something he had failed to set right. It led him, especially in his tormented adolescence, to mock her.

His fears for Jack opened up that earlier time again and for a moment he felt sorry for her – even though he knew that once he gave her an opening, the litany was hard to stop. This time he bent his head and accepted it. After every pause he said, "Ohh Mom," or, "that's rough," as she gathered momentum.

"Even Van Gogh wasn't appreciated in his lifetime, Mom," he said after half an hour. She took herself with the deadly seriousness of an older generation. He heard her give a satisfied sigh, and at the same time, caught a glimpse of himself in the mirror across from the phone – long hair, jutting nose, shapeless khakis. Yeah, his mother resembled Van Gogh the way he resembled Marilyn Monroe.

"I've got to go now, Mom," he said. The light outside his none-too-clean window was so dim that even at noon, it seemed as if morning hadn't happened.

After he hung up, he thought that he'd have to make an effort if he wanted to lighten things up today. Maybe later – when he could face going out in the cold – he'd go and pick up the wigs they needed for *Gawain*. Afterwards, he could get himself something snazzy to wear to the next Wigstock festival. Treat himself to that crazily gorgeous blue one. Meanwhile, he puttered around, eventually plunking himself down to look at his notes for the Temptation scenes. The image of Jack getting the catheter inserted wouldn't leave him alone. It got tangled in his mind with the sound of splintering bone when Gawain lops off the Green Knight's head.

Ren's mind flicked to the end of the play, where the Green Knight nicks Gawain's neck with his axe. Ren loved the way the Green Knight made peace with Gawain after hurting him just a little to punish him for not being truthful. Ren had always thought his own father would have liked him better if he'd been more obedient, more the son he wanted. But seeing Jack with Malcolm made him less inclined to indulge the fantasy of being a good boy. Certainly he wasn't going to give up his love – not for anyone. Ren felt a chill up his spine. Jack's getting any sort of blow at all made no sense unless . . . he was taking Ren's punishment.

But maybe power wasn't the most important part of being a father. Wasn't he in the best sense an older benevolent father to Jack, didn't he love him more than he could love any son?

He had a fleeting physical memory of someone tossing him in the air and him shrieking with pleasure. He had lost his father from one day to the next. His father had vanished so completely Ren couldn't remember a word he'd said to him. He had only these occasional ghostly sensations that – to feel less alone – he called "father." Until he'd met Jack, he'd been frozen, unable to risk loving. Unable even to feel more than a transient fear when a friend died. And an embarrassment to be still alive at his age, with so many of the younger men gone. It would have been fairer in a way if he'd gotten sick. He'd wasted far too much of his life.

The doorbell rang and when he opened the door, Sarah, his upstairs neighbor, was standing impatiently outside, shifting from one foot to the other, her blond curls in disarray and the usual cigarette dangling from her mouth.

"I've got a big problem," she said and waited, hand on her hip.

"What's up?" He wasn't exactly in the mood for helping a damsel in distress, but he liked Sarah – and it would keep him from brooding. He thought a bit guiltily of the late-night talks they used to have before he got so engrossed in Jack. How he used to go up to her apartment for a companionable beer.

"My cat, you know, Horace?" She blew a strand of hair out of her face.

"Of course." Every time he went up there, he got covered with thick black fur – the animal was a regular shedding machine. "What's the matter?" Horace was always climbing out on the fire escape and yowling in the middle of the night. Ren would hear Sarah's anxious "Here, kitty kitty," followed by curses if she was drunk.

"I've got to stick a needle in him and I can't get him to stand still. Sorry to bother you but . . ." She shrugged – a charmingly helpless gesture he couldn't resist.

"Sure, let's go," he said. He watched her cute blue-jeaned behind negotiate the dirty stairs. It had a sad sort of wiggle, as though it were saying, "Here I am, but I know you don't care."

They could hear the cat's yowl reverberating down the stairwell, a mournful drawn-out cry for help. When Sarah opened the door, the cat made a dash for freedom but Sarah caught him, scooped him up and murmured soothingly. She led Ren down the hall past Indian wall hangings and promo pictures for her latest book – Sarah in a black dress with a necklace of animal teeth, blond curls combed back.

In the bathroom, she thrust Horace into his arms and told him to hold on while she attached a bottle of clear fluid to the shower head. The bottle was connected to a small syringe like an IV drip. It reminded him uncomfortably of the hospital.

"Good grief. What are you doing to him, chemotherapy?"

"Dialysis," she muttered. "Put him in the bathtub."

He knelt awkwardly and the cat twisted and gave him a long ugly scratch on his right hand. "Oww. You devil," he hissed. "I need steel gloves to handle you." He'd have to cover the scratch with make-up, but he held on while she inserted a needle into Horace's back. Being a knight errant was dangerous work.

"Shit," she said, as the cat bucked. "It must have gone into the muscle. That's why he's jumping so much. I'll have to try again. Keep a strong grip." She pulled the needle out and threaded it in just under the skin. "Come on baby," she crooned, her voice catching. "It's almost over now, hold on." The cat's squalls subsided into an occasional mew like a hiccup and Sarah gave Ren a wry look. There was smudged mascara on her lashes. Her voice quivered and Ren noticed for the first time how soft her mouth was and the way one front tooth stuck out a little, making a faint indentation in her lip.

"Sarah, doll . . . it's really none of my business. But why don't you take Horace to the vet?" He was still holding the cat, its tail flicking angrily against his arm.

"Money with a capital M. Not that I'm against lining doctors' pockets per se, especially my cute vet's, but a weekly cash bleed? Uh uh. I've been doing this for eighteen months. Go figure. It's beginning to get to me." She coughed, covering what sounded like a sob. "I may be crazy, but this cat is the sole survivor of a major wreck. Refugee from the good ship Love. When we split, I was afraid John was going to feed him rat poison just to spite me. You wouldn't believe the custody battle we had over this guy." She took the cat and rubbed its ears lightly with one hand. Lost in her memories.

Ren stood looking at her, not knowing what to say. She usually seemed so tough. Like a sort of female Humphrey Bogart, with her slangy, street kid way of speaking. He was surprised to see her so vulnerable. He wondered whether if something happened to Jack, he'd nurse his spindly plants, putting drops in their water. Propping them up. Maybe even joining one of the pure air, pure water groups, even though he was bored to death by those people. "Love can be brutal," he said finally.

"Water under the bridge," she said, rubbing her nose with the back of her hand. "What about you? How's Jack?"

Ren shook his head. "He's in the hospital right now. For a stem cell transplant."

She whistled through her teeth. "I was wondering why I didn't hear bedsprings. Is it likely to work?"

Boy, she got right down to it, didn't she. Ren's stomach lurched. "Sure. I mean, what do I know? The doctors hope so, but I've read that things can go wrong. Liver. Heart. I'm scared to death."

"I suppose you won't love him without his looks," she said bitterly. "Ten pounds in the wrong places lost me a husband."

Ren had a shocked awareness that she didn't know how much he'd changed. She had seen him alleycatting around, not being too good about visiting his friends with AIDS, while she spent long hours reading to three of her friends in the hospital.

"You need a new scale," he said. "You don't look a day over twenty."

She pulled scornfully at her waist, grasped some flesh between thumb and fingers. "Fat," she said. "I used to be really cute."

"You still are, Sarah," he said. "You're at the age the French call the age of mystery. They've always been more savvy than we are."

"The mystery is that I'm still alive," she muttered. She made herself a stiff drink, kicked off her shoes and tucked her feet under her – clearly preparing for a bummed-out day.

"Hey, why don't you come to the store with me," he asked her, "to pick up some wigs for my play. We just had a costume review under strong lights and a couple of our hairpieces didn't make the cut. Our costumer has enough to do with fixing squeaky boots and too-tight crotches, so I volunteered. Come." He put his hand behind his head and struck a pose designed to make her smile. "You need a purifying aesthetic experience after all this" – he waved his hand airily – "messy reality."

"I've got my own aesthetics to attend to," she said. "I should be writing."

"It would cheer me up."

"Well . . ."

Cheering people up was as hard for her to resist as it was for him. She put her shoes back on and gave him one of her funny crooked smiles. Her new novel was going badly anyway, she told him. She'd planned the whole book around the metaphor of the endangered golden eagle and it wasn't taking off. It had the energy of a dead fish. No wings, just flippity flap. Dead. And the book cover for her new paperback – it had just come out with Penguin – was impossible. It was blue and they put her name in pale blue letters. You couldn't even see it.

"I see it perfectly," he said. To hear Sarah complain, you'd never know she had good mainstream publishers, enough money to get by, and a lot of respect. Her short story collection, *Breakdown*, was practically a classic in literary circles. But besides being a perfectionist, she was an expert at self-torture. The paperback sat on her coffee table and he picked it up and looked at it attentively, rubbing his hand over the glossy surface. "Perfectly," he repeated. "Sarah True."

"Well, of course – you've got it two inches from your eyes," she said, but her look cleared.

A low blanket of clouds covered the afternoon sky. Ren didn't feel like walking in the depressing greenish light that managed to filter through the dirty cotton, so he decided to splurge on a cab. Twelfth Street, with its secret lofts and chipped outer facades, could look quaint in sun or bright snow but right now it was sending off purely negative vibrations.

"You're good with women," she said as they sat in the cab loosening their scarves, "at least with me. Have you ever considered living with one?"

"Not since I was a teenager. Though I suppose if I'd been born twenty years earlier, I would have married. I can get it up."

"But?"

"It wouldn't have been fair." He didn't want to risk hurting her feelings by telling her that what he had now with Jack was in a whole different realm.

The taxi let them off on Eighth Street right in front of the shop and they descended like royalty, walked a few steps through the dirty snow – cars honking around them like disconsolate beasts – and descended the steps into a small brightly lit cave. Every time Ren came here, it made him happy. It was so deep, in its subterranean basement, deep and magical.

Rick, the proprietor, had his hair done in a new way, shaved on the sides, with the back caught up in a bright red ponytail. He was working his spells on an enormous blue wig.

"How's it going, maestro?" Ren asked him. The wig blossomed in front of him like a flower.

"Great. Haven't seen you around in awhile."

"I need to pick up some wigs for my new production, and I brought a friend to show her your fabulous collection."

"Rick is our transformative goddess for the Wigstock Festival," he explained to Sarah, after he had chosen a lovely dark wig for Guinivere and a dramatic red one for Grace. "You know that they have one every year?"

"I was actually set to go last year," she said. "I thought it would be nice by the water – I like Battery Park – but Horace was up on the roof . . . well, I couldn't get him down." She gave her helpless shrug.

"It's never too early to get some ideas for next summer," Ren said, guiding her over to the shelves of Rick's past glories. Rick went for blond in a big way. Sarah eyed the intricate braids and teases.

"I used to play dress-up for my ex – a different costume every night."

"I did it once for Jack," Ren said. "He was sweet about it but it's not really his thing," he sighed, "so all of it went to the back of my closet. I guess I'm lucky he liked to see me act. Came to all my shows, though I think he liked the straight ones best. You should see my box sometime. I have some silk kimonos that might look good on you. And a fabulous gown, a copy of the one I wore when I played Hamlet in drag. And the black vinyl costume I wore as Theseus with cut outs you know where."

"I bet you made a great Hamlet," Sarah said.

"I did, I was sensational."

"When I was a kid, my mother put old dresses and wraps into a special box for me. It was one of the few good things I remember. But if Jack doesn't . . . I mean, don't you ever just dress up and go out on the town?"

"Seldom. It's one of the many sacrifices I've made for love."

"You have the most expressive face, but you don't look like a martyr." She was edging over to the for-sale wigs and he followed her.

"More like a satyr?" She tried on a long-haired silver one.

"Like someone who wants to get back onstage."

"Ahh, well." Ren sidled up behind her and put his hands on her shoulders, looking at her image in the mirror. His head next to hers.

"Gorgeous," he said.

She giggled and took it off. "Doesn't fit my present life style, I'm afraid. You try it!" She reached over and put it on his head slightly askew.

"Not me," he said. "Besides, what I really want is the blue."

"Get it then, for shit's sake." She'd lapsed into her tough-girl voice. "No point in wasting good money on a taxi, then going home bare-headed." She made it sound slightly obscene.

"Well, I tell you it's tempting. I could dress up like the American flag. I have the red and white parts already. May I?" he asked Rick, who hadn't quite finished teasing. The wig was glorious and he could already picture the make-up to go with it – a sort of surreal blue-white. Maybe silver eyelashes. He looked at himself in the mirror. Big hungry eyes, full mouth. A bit too much nose. If he ever made money again, maybe he should have a nose job. "I've got to have this," he told Sarah. "I can already see the headlines, 'Fag Queen Represents the True America. Get With It. Be Androgynous for the Millennium.'"

He strutted to and fro in front of the mirror. He felt suddenly strong enough for anything. Jack's father might have kept him away today, the first day of Jack's hospitalization – because he was weakened by that caper with nurse Tommy – but Ren determined not to let him do it ever again. These might be the last months of Jack's life, for God's sake. The doctors said five percent didn't make it through the transplant – they flatly refused to say how many succumbed after it. Ren stopped and hitched up his khaki pants, stared at his pale face under the ferocious blue. "Yes," he said, "yes yes yes." He could already feel the bullets bouncing off his bracelets.

When he woke up the next morning, he still felt strong. In his dream, he'd been wearing his blue wig and riding on a

white horse, galloping through the New York streets bare-
chested – a medieval version of the Cockettes with their motorcycles – and every so often he'd dismount to help someone.
He'd rescued a baby perched mysteriously on a window ledge;
another time, prevented a beating. Just before he woke up,
he'd put a homeless woman in front of him on his horse and as
they ambled along, keeping each other warm, she offered him
sips of a revivifying aromatic drink she had concocted from
herbs which she carried around her neck in a velvet bag.

In the old stories, Gawain had had his share of rescuing
damsels. Though in the ones Ren had read, he couldn't
remember the damsel ever having a real conversation with her
rescuer. A demure "May God reward you" could have been
delivered just as well by an answering machine as by a woman.
Ren preferred his dream's suppler version of the old chivalric
model. It kept the good parts: the horse with fantastic muscled
flanks and the pleasure of rescue. But the glittery armor
served as decoration, not defense – and the woman in his
dream offered as much to the dream hero as he did to her.

The dream affected Ren like a cold shower after a warm
bath, leaving him exhilarated and relaxed. He stretched and
rubbed the sleep out of his eyes and then it hit him – this was
the first day of Jack's conditioning regimen – the medical
euphemism for high-dose chemotherapy. He glanced at the
clock, ten o'clock. Then raced into the bathroom and ran his
brush vigorously over his teeth. If he was going to get through
his difficult, sometimes hellish rehearsals – his schedule was
getting more strenuous as they neared opening night – and still
be with Jack at least part of every day, he'd have to discipline
himself to wake up earlier. He made a desultory stab at his
back molars, which, he had been warned, gathered plaque.

Thank God Jack had been able to argue his father out of
issuing a restraining order forbidding Ren to go within a block
of the hospital. "I just kept insisting that it was an accident,"

he'd told Ren, "that the nurse had blown it up out of all pro-
portion. I could see he didn't believe me, but he took it. For
now, at least, you're off the hook."

Jack's voice registered an unspoken reproach that Ren
was making things hard for him with his father, but still, Jack
hadn't given in to Malcolm's pressure, he had hung tough. Ren
was proud of him and determined that he wouldn't regret his
loyalty.

Ren spat a mouthful of fluoride foam into the small
round bowl of the sink and wondered if he should make a
chart of the month Jack was going to spend in the hospital. It
would make him feel more in control if he pictured it as a siege
that they were fighting together. He had been through chemo
with him before but this was different; the chemicals were ten
times as powerful. It would be as if Jack was being battered by
sledgehammers or run over by a truck. Jack had told him the
"conditioning" wouldn't just kill the cancer, it would kill every
dividing cell in his body: blood cells, hair follicles, nail beds,
everything. And after this wholesale slaughter, Jack might not
make it back.

Ren concentrated on what coming back would entail.
During Jack's treatment last year, Ren had considered the
poisons with horror. This time he had to put himself on their
side, because whatever he felt about the treatment was going to
be picked up by Jack. He and Jack were like those Siamese
twins who shared a vital organ: sometimes when they made
love, Ren couldn't tell their heartbeats apart. So somehow he
had to see the poison as positive.

Once at his doctor's office in the Village he'd read an article in a dog-eared Zen magazine about a cancer patient who
thought of his chemo as the Host: a dose of the Father. Since
Ren didn't believe in God, he'd have to invent his own magic.
He decided that every morning when he got up and every
evening before he went to bed, he would visualize the chemicals
getting rid of the cancer cells. He thought he'd imagine them as
versions of his dream – blue-wigged knights on white horses.

But they wouldn't be killing. That didn't feel right. They'd be bringing Jack, quite simply, his love. You are a sentimental old cow, his inner voice mocked. What are you imagining, you pathetic creature? A holy grail filled with your gysm?

When Ren got to Mount Sinai it was near noon. After he took off his coat and scarf and rubbed his hands together to warm them – it was bitter cold outside – he found himself looking for Malcolm. He half expected Malcolm to leap out at him from some corner. But the halls were blandly filled with the usual white-coated interns. He took the elevator up to the transplant floor and asked the nurse for Jack's room number. It was such a relief not to have to face that beastly Tommy again – Jack had discovered that he was working on another floor. This nurse had honey-blond hair and the hint of a dimple on her chin. She looked much too young to be in charge of critically ill patients – little more than a child. Without thinking he ran his hand through his own thinning hair. It's me, he thought, I'm getting old.

"Are you expected?" she asked, with grown-up seriousness. He nodded and hastened down the hall, her "Don't stay too long," echoing after him. Now that he was so near to Jack, all Ren's muscles suddenly ached to hold him.

He threw open the door to the scrub area in front of Jack's room, rushed to the porthole and looked through the glass. Jack was lying on the bed, eyes half closed. Standing next to him, was a tall young woman with long blond hair. Ren's neck and chest flushed as if he were coming down with the flu. For a second, he was in a panic. What if Jack had a secret lover? What if the stress of being gay was too much for him and he'd decided to get married? Then the woman half turned around and he saw it was Jack's younger sister, Henny. It took him a minute to calm his breathing. Then he went over to the sink and washed his hands thoroughly with Phisohex and put on a blue gown.

Ren had only seen Henny a few times. He knew she was finishing her senior year at Columbia and lived with a roommate in a small apartment on West Ninety-sixth Street. Once, on Jack's birthday, she'd taken him to lunch and Jack had insisted that Ren come along. He couldn't tell if she understood about him and Jack. If she knew, she hadn't let on, treating him respectfully, decently, like any other friend of her brother's. Another time when they'd gone to the zoo, she'd been livelier. She'd fed the elephants peanuts and giggled when the soft trunk nuzzled her palm.

"It's so delicate," she'd said, "almost as if he's kissing me."

Ren liked her. He asked Jack why they didn't see more of her. "Because Henny and Dad are on the outs," he said, "and she always wants me to take her side. I love her but it's an awful drag." Ren knew he shouldn't say anything. He just let Jack talk about how his father and Henny fought. How she looked quiet but she was as strong-willed as his father – they had the same lantern jaw.

"Why can't she just go along with him?" Jack asked another time after a particularly difficult family dinner. "Why does she have to provoke him?"

Because he's an ass, Ren was on the verge of saying, a righteous ass. Why should the poor kid go along with him? But anything to do with Jack's father was a taboo subject. It was hard – a little like being a Muslim married to an Orthodox Jew. Once he had listened to an awful radio shrink named Dr. Laura. Some poor guy had been complaining that his wife's mother followed them every time they moved. The doctor asked if it was part of the wife's culture to have tag-along mothers.

"Yes," he says.

"And you knew about it when you married?" she shot back.

"Oh, yes, but you don't understand, her mother . . ."

The doc cut him off. "It's marriage. If you knew, you have nothing to complain about. Adjust."

Well, Ren had known ever since the beginning that Jack

loved his father and was proud of him. When Ren had tactless-
ly made some comment about how hard it must be having his
father's power plant as a neighbor to the fishery where he
worked, Jack had responded defensively. Most power plants
had responded to regulation. And when there'd been an oil spill
some years back, his father's plant had donated money and
supplies for the clean-up. He showed Ren a photo from some
magazine of baby fish darting around looking perky and a
headline in big letters: Seaboard Power Cleans Up. Yeah, right.

But even if this hadn't been just PR, which Ren deduced
it was from Malcolm's later comments about simple-minded
environmentalists, what did a dollop of clean-up money
amount to in the whole scheme of things? Jack knew perfectly
well that his father's water cooling system sucked up larvae
and baby fish and returned them dead or damaged beyond
repair. He had talked about that happening in other plants on
the river, but if Ren had asked about his dad's, Jack would
have gone ballistic. Ren wondered if his exaggerated reactions
came from the fact that deep down he had the same thought.
Just hated to recognize it.

Now, Ren sighed and pushed the door open. Henny
turned around and he could see at a glance that she had been
crying. "I can come back later," he said.

"No need," Jack motioned him forward. "We're done.
Hey, it's good to see you. The room is brighter already." Jack
looked tired but otherwise all right.

Ren started to sit down beside him on the bed but then he
remembered it wasn't allowed. He reached out a hand to pat
Jack's shoulder, then drew it back in alarm.

"We're not really done," Henny said, barely able to contain her tears. "Dad's being a bastard. "

Ren looked at her, surprised. The word "bastard" didn't
fit with her pale hair and soft voice.

"Oh, come on, Henny. Don't exaggerate." Jack said.
"Ren has trouble with him, too." he added, and then bit his
lower lip.

"Do you?" she asked, wiping at her eyes with a Kleenex taken hastily from her oversized bag. "Really." She looked at him with a flicker of interest. She had Jack's beautiful face, the strong classic profile.

"Your dad has such a . . ." Ren hesitated, "a presence. All that silver hair." He tried to keep it light but a glance at Jack told him he wasn't succeeding. Henny half smiled.

"You forgot his perfectly upright carriage," she threw back her shoulders in imitation, then her face clouded again. "Oh shit, I'm so tired of it. Everyone's always on his side. It's like complaining about Billy Graham to the people at a prayer fest."

"Henny," Jack put in, "lots of parents have expectations for their children. Don't make such a big deal of it."

She ignored him and looked at Ren. "Excuse me for bringing you into this little family tiff, but I thought . . ." she looked quickly from one to the other of them.

"You're right. It's fine," Ren said.

"Well, what do you think? A dad who's furious when his daughter wants to get a master's in education?" she asked. "Wouldn't a normal father be pleased? But no, he said it had no "class" – that was his word – "class." Can you believe it? He wants me to do a degree in history or political science – as if teaching kids has no value at all."

She looked suddenly so young. Like a forlorn little girl, lower lip trembling. "Is he threatening to cut off your funds?" Ren asked.

Jack raised himself on one elbow in bed. His striped gown rumpled. "Of course not. He'd never do that."

"Oh, never never. What do you know?"

"I did what I wanted, didn't I? I didn't wait to see if he approved. He didn't, as a matter of fact."

"Yeah," she said, looking puzzled. "How'd you do it?"

"He probably agreed pleasantly to everything your father said about the Green Party," Ren said when Jack didn't answer. "Your brother has a way of pulling his head in and then when you think he's given up, he goes for it. Haven't you noticed? Don't worry. You'll find your own method. The hardest thing is toughening up so it doesn't hurt so much."

"Jack's more like Dad than he thinks," she said. "That's why he knows how to deal. Isn't that right Jack?"

Jack shrugged.

"Do you think he ought to rest awhile?" Ren asked Henny softly. "He seems tired." He'd always wondered what it would be like to have a sister. A creature very like you, but female. With the same family situations and memories to chew over. It struck him that when he first thought of having a woman play Gawain, he'd imagined her as Gawain's sister. Gawain could have been killed in battle and she'd disguised herself and taken over his quest. He couldn't have imagined what trouble his idea might have led to with Ellen, talented up the kazoo but always on the verge of exploding. He just figured that an outsider, his hero(ine), would be able to see things that her brother didn't.

He smiled at Henny. One day maybe he'd invite her to have tea with him and talk some more. Get some fresh angles on Jack's family life.

But Jack had obviously had more than enough of this. He was looking pale and strained.

Ren picked up some of Jack's get-well cards from the night table, fanned them out and fluttered them towards Henny. "Doctor say too much talk no good for treatment," he said in a fluting Asian accent. "Beneficent action much better."

The girl seemed suddenly aware of where she was. Or, more significantly, where she wasn't. She wasn't embattled in her father's posh living room. She looked at Jack on the bed in his striped prisoner gown, surrounded by the stark white walls, guarded by an aquarium window, then thrust her balled up Kleenex back in her purse and ran a hand through her blond mane. "I think I've done enough damage for today," she said. "God, I don't know what I was thinking of." She went over and bent close to Jack. "Sorry I lost it," she whispered. "Love you." Then something more Ren couldn't quite hear.

"Don't be so hard on yourself," Jack said. Ren felt glad Jack wasn't being hard on poor Henny. From the splayed out cards, he drew out one that caught his eye, noted it was from Jack's colleagues at Fisheries and taped it up on the bulletin board provided by the hospital for the purpose. It was sappy, the easy sentimentalism that he usually made fun of, but somehow he found himself warmed by it: a brilliant child's sun, scalloped waves full of fish and the motto, "It's your river, take care of her and she'll take care of you."

CHAPTER SEVEN

a different journey begins

among the mountains in the morning, merrily he rides
into a deep forest, exceedingly wild

– Sir Gawain and The Green Knight

All Ren needed was a call from his mother on a morning
when they'd had an excruciating tech run-through the
night before, all stops and starts and missed cues, and he
was trying to squeeze in a half-hour of extra sleep before he
checked up on Jack's apartment and went over to the hospital.
Jack was two days into his chemo conditioning regime and,
though he seemed to be taking it well so far, Ren was anxious
to see how he was doing. But Thelma wanted to tell Ren about
a man she'd met on her vacation in Miami – Morris, an old fur-
rier, a New Yorker.

"He has a son who toured with the Jewish theater," she
said, her voice sounding brighter than it had in years. "I was
telling him about your big success when you did Hamlet in a
cocktail dress and got those good reviews. You actually were
making some good money for awhile there." She paused delicately. "I never understood what happened."

Ren grunted, remembering the way he'd spent whatever
windfall he'd gotten on treats for an ever-changing parade of
impecunious lovers. Even if an affair lasted only a week, he'd
do something romantic with his lover like take a turn around
Central Park in a buggy. If it was longer, a cashmere sweater
or caviar at the Ritz. But the good times hadn't lasted: there

was his sensational flop as Heathcliff in a musical version of "Wuthering Heights."

"What happened? I turned forty and lost my ingenue appeal," he said, half-joking.

"Morris said there are so many gay parts on TV these days. Why don't you try that, instead of starving yourself directing off-Broadway? Or ads. There's lots of money in ads and people get used to your face."

"What did you tell him?"

"I told him I'd be wasting my breath," Thelma said with a mixture of frustration and pride. "I told him you were an artist. You didn't do that sort of thing."

He almost laughed remembering the times – most recently when he'd joined the Back Alley Players – that she had urged him to find some way to combine integrity *and* money-making.

"You're learning," he told her. "By the time I'm eighty we'll understand each other perfectly."

The conversation ended on an amicable note with his mother expressing concern about Jack and Ren reminding her that opening night was only ten days off. She said she'd bring Morris.

Ren took the subway uptown to Jack's place, bringing a bag of amusing books and tapes and his new wig for later. He had felt so up the other day shopping with Sarah, he wanted to communicate some of it to Jack, brighten up the sterility of the hospital. If a nurse walked in, he'd just start clowning.

Now, despite the winter sun streaming through the windows, the apartment seemed gloomily vacant, like a stage set without the chief actor. Jack's colored ink drawings of fish in various stages of development stared from the walls, reminding Ren that it had been months since he'd seen Jack drawing, not to speak of working. His field notebooks crammed with data about his fish were stacked neatly on his table – data he would have been analyzing right now in the lab, if he hadn't been so sick.

Reality was either too grim or too dull, Ren thought as he checked the mail — opening, with Jack's permission, any envelopes that had people's names in the corner to see if anything needed urgent attention. There was a huge oversized envelope from a friend of Jack's in Fisheries with a note about a joint project and a segmented photo of the river that he thought Jack might enjoy. It had been taken from the air at low tide, when the underwater plants were exposed, and the floating eel grass and water chestnut made a lovely pattern of light and shade along the borders. Ren couldn't imagine how you could tell what they were, but he thought it might cheer Jack to see his river flowing along so tranquilly.

It reminded him of the time Jack had insisted on taking him along on a field trip. Thank God it was calm. He'd held the rail while the duck-like mergansers floated by. He'd watched as Jack and the other technician dropped their wired electrodes in the water and gathered up the stunned fish in nets to tag them and take scale samples. The tags looked like the plastic ones you get on clothes, except they were coded with the date and place so Fisheries could keep track of them. He'd always been a city person himself, but Jack had been so excited it was exciting to watch him. He was practically orgasmic about the way you could tell a fish's age from its scales, just the way you could tell a tree's by its rings.

Ren added some water to the tank and fed the fish. One of them seemed to be swimming less vigorously than the others and he watched it for a few minutes. He had a nervous dread that if any of them succumbed during the course of Jack's treatment, Jack would weaken. Die wasn't a word that he'd allow himself to think. Not die, weaken.

He mixed up some of the special plant food Jack was experimenting with and watered his plants, giving special attention to the spindly one in the kitchen. "Look, we're all damaged goods," he murmured to the plant. "Don't think you're special. You've got sun on you now, make use of it, get a bit of green in your veins." He snorted, looked around embarrassed. Who was the idiot who'd invented this idea that plants respond to love? That all you have to do is talk to them daily and show your concern? It was hard enough for people.

After he watered, he went back and looked at the fish again. One was definitely ailing; his scales had a faint white fuzz. Ren scooped it out and put it in a bowl with a little of the vegetation. If it got better, he'd put it back but if not, he wouldn't mention it to Jack. He tried to remember what Jack had told him about the chemicals that had been dumped in the river by power companies way back in the fifties and sixties. He knew they'd done a lot of damage. And Jack had said the stuff, PCB, was still there in hot spots along the river bottom. Maybe when the sunfish was hatching he'd gotten a dose of something. Right now he looked like a Hiroshima survivor. Ren thought of a picture he had seen of survivors and shuddered.

Later at the hospital, when Ren saw that Jack was awake, he gowned up, washed his hands, slipped on the rubber gloves from the supply shelf in the scrub-room and went in with his bag of books and tapes. On the subway, crammed between an old lady and a Suit with a spreading belly, he'd been cheering himself up by imagining how he would read to Jack for hours, the way he had during his chemo a year ago. That treatment had been spread out over six months. This was much harsher, but shorter too. In eleven days – just a day after opening night – Jack would receive his cell transplant (the "rescue") and, if all went well, his blood cells would start to regenerate. But there was constant risk. In the next few days Jack's immune system would be completely destroyed and the slightest infection could flare up and kill him. Ren carefully washed and re-washed his hands with antibacterial soap, then put on his gown and rubber gloves and went into the room.

"How're you doing? I brought you some goodies. *Flesh and Blood*, sound appetizing?" Jack didn't smile, some clear liquid was dripping through his IV. "There's a note from your friend, Chuck, and a gorgeous photo." Ren opened up the photo so the river rippled over Jack's chest, put the book next to him on the bed, then started making a neat line of books on the windowsill. A hard bright light was flooding in. Down below, he could see people hurrying along hunching their shoulders against the cold.

Jack glanced down at the photo for a minute but didn't pick it up, didn't even read the note. He ignored the book completely, just lay there in his green silk pajamas with his hands out flat on the white sheet and looked at him with a slightly bewildered expression. "Ren, I don't know . . . I'm not sure I can concentrate." He reminded Ren of the plant they'd seen in Central Park, gamely sprouting in the snow. He had an urge to pick him up and carry him off, IV pole and all, to Fregene or Capri. Instead, he sat down in the iron-frame arm-chair.

"With me reading, how could you help it?" he asked, cupping his chin and leaning towards the bed. "Didn't you know? I rivet audiences around the world." He picked up an information manual from among the pile of things on the bed-side table – brochures, syringes, yesterday's mail – and opened it at random. "To prevent infection you must clean your gums very carefully," he said in a low caressing voice, "rubbing them with soft sponges" – here he pantomimed a circular rubbing motion with a blissful expression on his face. "Well?"

Jack laughed. "Very juicy. They should have you reading texts to school kids. You'd really turn them on."

"You think so?" Jack's eyes had momentarily brightened when he laughed but now they had a glassy look. "You okay?"

"Just tired. A little woopsy. My white cells took a nose dive this morning, the reds too."

"But isn't that what's supposed to happen? " Ren heard his voice stupidly cheerful. "And last time you had chemo you did so much better than you thought. You didn't even barf."

"This is different. It sounds so good – fresh marrow, bones all new and clean – but what they're actually doing is bringing me as close to a mortician's slab as they can without actually killing me."

Ren moved his chair closer. "Hey, how about a safe hand hold." He held out his hand sheathed in a rubber glove and Jack took it, squeezed it hard.

"Just promise me you'll keep coming," Jack said. "That you'll sit right there and keep on making your silly jokes. I don't care what you say. I know this sounds stupid but I'm afraid I'll be lying here, not able to talk or maybe even to nod and you'll give up on me. But unless I'm dead, I know I'll sense you're there. So keep talking to me, okay?"

Ren shivered and looked at Jack more closely. He was paler and maybe a little puffy, but nothing really drastic. "Of course, I'll be here, Miz Scarlet, honey. I'll always be here for you. And I'll talk so much you'll wish you hadn't of aksed me." He shook Jack's hand gently, then got up and emptied the tapes he'd brought out of his sack, setting them up in neat piles next to the books.

Jack gave him a funny look. "I don't think you're taking it in," he said finally, "but this is already pretty bad. I feel like I'm going to take off. . . . No, no, don't freak!" Ren had turned from the tapes and looked as if he were going to fling himself on the bed. Jack patted the air, pushing down Ren's alarm. "I just mean . . . well, if I split for awhile, it may be hard to come back. I have the feeling I'll need you to keep me in place. Like the weight on the end of a balloon." He looked up into a corner of the ceiling as if planning a getaway.

Ren had had drug experiences where he seemed to be floating above his body. "I think I get it . . . and don't worry – if you need a heavy, you've got one. I'm going to bulk up on ice cream starting tonight."

An hour later, Henny showed up. Ren noticed with mild curiosity that she was wearing jodhpurs, dark brown, and a tight sweater. "They're clean, no horse hair on them," she said defensively when she saw him looking.

"I was just admiring. I didn't know you rode."

"It's amazing she finds time to do anything else," Jack put in, raising himself on his elbows to look at her. She went over and gave him a kiss, on the shoulder of his gown. "I brought you some photos," she said, holding out a collage mounted on heavy green paper. "Of good times."

She sat down on the straight-backed chair next to the bed and Ren pulled up the armchair next to her. "Here's us in our tree house," she told Ren. "Us, playing touch tag. That's my horse, Trigger," she laughed. Henny had short hair then and looked like Jack's twin. Ren felt a twinge of excitement. He imagined her dressed in yellow-gold armor like her hair, a cross between Joan of Arc and Greta Garbo. He couldn't decide if she should have her helmet on or off. He liked the idea of the soft silky mass against armor. But a helmet would accentuate the high cheekbones and the softness of her lips. She could do a lot more with her hair, Ren thought. Create more drama. The way the woman did in the adjoining photo, whose red gold hair rippled and caught the light unevenly in folds of bright and shadow.

"Your mother?" Ren asked. The woman stood next to a mysteriously wooded lake in a white linen dress, her arms curved protectively around Jack and Henny. Henny nodded. "She was lovely. Such a warm expression. With just a touch of mischief. And all those freckles."

He noticed Henny's face soften. So she liked her mother, then. Jack rarely spoke of her – she had died when he was an adolescent – and when he did, he seemed to blame her for the divorce. Ren was sure there was more to it. Once Jack had said rather casually that her being so soft and yielding led his father to hurt her. "Her 'yes yes yes dear' drove him up the wall." Well, she didn't look soft in the photo, though she was clearly in need of psychic rescue: she'd been miscast.

Even though Ren didn't know her, Jack's remark had provoked one of their first fights. "Blame the victim. Is that what you're saying? I can't believe you. I mean you just can't say things like that. It's like blaming the Jews for provoking the Nazis to torture them. Come on, man." Jack had gotten flustered and admitted that when he was a child, he'd been terrified by their fights and wanted to protect his mother. "But then after awhile, I didn't want to anymore, I'm not sure why. I began to feel angry at her for being so weak, and crying . . ." He sputtered to a halt and wouldn't talk about it again.

Ren couldn't help noticing that Henny hadn't included any images of her father in her composite. While he helped her pin it up along the line that ran across the room, a dietician talked to Jack about the bacteria-free diet he was going to need to follow after the treatment. Ren asked Henny about school.

He could see himself. Drag Queen talks to young beauty in an avuncular fashion. Advises her about life. What the hell did he know about life? He didn't have a clue. Except he loved Jack, and with him he'd apparently gotten a family or part of one.

"I have to admit there isn't much intellectual content," she said after describing one of her lighter courses at Columbia. Admit to whom, Ren thought. Do parents have any idea of the harm they can inflict on their children? He couldn't imagine having a child. He'd always be bending over the other way, not to do any harm.

"I wouldn't give a damn about it. So bloody what," he said. "You're taking this stuff, some of it boring, some useful, so you can get to the kids and put something in their little heads. You know you'll be good at it. So you go through the hoops, the rigmarole, just the way everyone else does. Right, left, march. That's it. Simple." Henny widened her big brown eyes at him like a fawn startled in the underbrush.

"I had dinner with Dad yesterday," she said, following

her own associations. "Thought he needed some cheering," she grimaced, "but he hardly spoke a word to me. He used to do that to my mom when they quarreled. 'No speeksies,' she called it. Once he didn't talk to her for three weeks. Can you imagine!"

"I'm too impulsive to even consider it."

She smiled at him, then frowned. "Do you think it's weird for me to want him to approve of what I'm doing?"

"Not weird, but unlikely to have a good result." Ren thought of telling Henny he'd given up the idea of graduate school because it was a pompous crock of shit.

The dietician was a pert redhead who looked more as if she belonged in a beauty school than a hospital. "Nothing raw, that's the main thing to remember," she said, going over to the fridge on the back wall and pulling open the door. Ren saw with surprise that it was full. Jack clearly hadn't touched any of the things they'd brought him.

"Juice. Yogurt Popsicle. Ice cream. All good stuff. Do you feel like anything?"

"Not at the moment," Jack said politely. Too politely, Ren thought. A bit like a zombie. She shrugged her pretty shoulders and smiled. She was nice, Ren thought. Looked as if she really cared. Or maybe it was just her luminous skin and bright eyes. She exuded health from every pore. "I know you don't believe you'll ever want to eat again. You probably wish I'd throw all this out." Jack nodded wanly. "But don't worry, you'll be looking for it one of these days," she spread her smile over Henny and Ren, "so keep squirreling it away."

When the dietician had gone Ren and Henny went back to the bedside and while Jack shut his eyes and tried to doze, Ren asked about her riding. "I do both hunter jumper and dressage," she told him. And then she was off, telling him about her horse, an elegant bay with white socks. "He's a big boy," she said, proudly, "sixteen hands, with a chest that can propel him over almost anything, and a heart to match." When she'd talked about school and her father, she'd had a wispy little voice. Shy, diffident, worried. Now she was back to being a young knight. He couldn't grasp all the details – the types of bit, the special saddle pad, the leg commands given so subtly they seem invisible – but he loved her excitement and the way her cheeks flushed pink when she talked about it. He told her he'd like to see her ride. He'd never been around horses except in museums or briefly glimpsed on the bridle path when he was walking. Seeing her ride might suggest some subtle adjustments for the hunting dance in the last act.

Then suddenly Jack pushed himself upright. "I hate to disturb you two, but I need someone to help me to the head." Ren was up in a minute, leaning over him. "What's the best way to do this? I don't want to disengage anything." He looked worriedly at the IV pole with the tube snaking its way into Jack's arm.

"Just help me get my legs around. Oh shit."

Ren had pulled back the covers and with one arm around Jack's shoulder supporting him, was gently pulling Jack's legs. "What is it? What's the matter?"

"Head spinning."

"Sit still for a minute then," Henny said, coming to the other side. She moved the IV pole slightly so that it wouldn't interfere with his getting up.

"I'm going to call the nurse," Ren said, picturing Jack falling, pulling the needle out. He still couldn't stand to look at the bruised purple spot where it entered the vein.

"No need. It'll be all right. It's just the change in position. Okay," he said. Ren slowly lifted him to his feet, Henny supporting the other side. This was the first time Ren had helped this way and he was shocked to feel Jack's ribs against his hand. He must have lost ten pounds. How could he have lost so much so fast? He shuffled along the floor, barely lifting his feet, seemingly afraid that if he raised them, he'd topple.

None of this had happened during his first chemo. Sure, Jack had felt a little weak. His heart had beat too fast if he

tried to do stairs at more than a snail's pace. And Ren had had
to remind him to slow down so he wouldn't have a heart
attack. But nothing like this – and after only two days. Maybe
he should have finished the booklet the hospital gave Jack
about side effects, but he'd thought it would be time enough
when things happened. The truth was, he'd been so horrified
when he read about the long-range possibilities like heart damage or blindness or secondary cancers that he'd slammed the
booklet closed. Had he really thought this was better than
AIDS? Now, he and Henny maneuvered Jack to the door of the
bathroom and Ren motioned to her to wait in the room while
he went in with him.

"I'd rather you didn't," Jack said.

"No way I'm going to let you stand here and faint with
that thing in your arm."

Jack rummaged in his green pajamas – Ren had insisted
on exchanging the hospital gown for something pretty – and
after a minute let loose a stream into the bowl.

"Jesus, it's red."

"Gut's bleeding," Jack said. "But that's not the worst of
it." He turned to sit. "I've got piles so bad . . . I don't want to
gross you out."

"You're not."

"They're hanging out . . . hurts like hell," he grunted
painfully and Ren turned away not because he was embarrassed but just to give him a moment of privacy. He could hear
the quick intake of breath and a suppressed sob. Then he heard
him reach behind and flush. But he still didn't get up. He was
reaching behind with his left hand trying to do something.

"Need help wiping?" Ren asked, then he realized Jack
must be trying to push the mass of piles back inside. "Stand
up," he said. Jack shook his head. "Go on, do it." He felt suddenly competent and peaceful, unlike himself. Jack unbent
himself from the pot and Ren pushed with his gloved finger
until all of it went back inside, then he took off his glove and
threw it in the pail, washed his hand and put on a fresh glove

from the box on the shelf over the sink. He ignored the fact that Jack couldn't seem to look him in the eyes.

When he got Jack settled back in bed, Ren opened his bag, took out the blue wig and sat with it on his knee. His knee was shaking so the hair did an odd little jog, and Ren could feel hot tears sliding down the back of his throat. Two nights ago, he felt as though he were Wonderwoman. Today he felt more like King Lear's poor forked radish.

On the way downtown to his rehearsal he bought a sandwich, but though he unwrapped it, he couldn't make himself eat. He closed his eyes, letting himself bounce slightly to the subway's swaying, trying to shake off his tiredness. In comparison with the pain of Jack's treatment, the preparation and rehearsals for his play seemed thin, faint, even frivolous. As he struggled to focus, it struck him that Ellen should convey more of this kind of bone-weariness as she searched for the Green Knight. He pondered ways of eliciting it.

Tonight they were working on some rough spots in the last act. After they had tackled a technical problem with the lighting and were ready to begin, he climbed on stage to suggest a new adjustment to Ellen's movement in the opening scene:

"Try circling the stage slowly several times . . . show us how exhausted you are and then, I want to feel your tremendous relief when you see the palace. Remember you've been travelling for weeks," Ren said. "No people, nothing but Bruegelesque monsters. You're starved for human contact. Someone to care for your wounds. You're also scared stiff because when you find what you're looking for, you'll likely lose your head. When you see the castle, it reminds you of Arthur's court, maybe even stirs some hope." He paused. "But in reality this is different; what you're going to get is something deeper and darker."

Ren jumped down as the lights dimmed. A light designer had taken over from the intern for the final week-and-a-half of rehearsals. The student had only been able to give a rough idea of what was wanted so Ren had spent much of the tech run-through working with the new man to modify and refine the lighting plan. Ren noted with satisfaction how striking the set looked when properly lit.

The castle seemed to hover on the top of a high hill sur-rounded by dark trees. It was like a child's cut-out, glistening white with multiple battlements and turrets.

The Green Knight had magically changed his appearance in order to test Gawain further, and when Joe came on with his russet beard and hair and jovial manner, he looked for all the world like a friendly Host. Graciously, he welcomed Gawain to his castle, then disarmed him. Here Ren wanted them to mir-ror in reverse the first act's arming. He stopped the actors and suggested they slow it down.

"I want people to have time to think about what it means to change clothes. You've worn protective armor but now you're putting on a richly sensuous robe. I need to see how this changes you. The mood should be dream-like, you are in a place of startling transformations. The castle opens its doors to you. It seems warm and hospitable. You are as susceptible as a hungry child. You have no way of knowing that your Host is really the Green Knight or that he has set his wife to seduce you and that if you succumb, you will lose your head."

After being immersed in the story for months, Ren was still fascinated by the Green Knight's cleverness and power. "The Green Knight forces you into a corner," he told Ellen. "He's not only brutal, he's a genius at manipulation. It's diabolical, really." At the beginning, when Ren tried to imagine dramatic alternatives to Gawain's loyal self-control, his mind hit a wall. Now, though Ren still had no clear idea of what he was going to do, the wall was disintegrating. Through the cracks, he was beginning to glimpse soft shim-mering forms.

Armor off, Ellen softened and relaxed. They dressed her in a flowing robe embroidered with flowers. The lights paled to a gold glow, servants moved slowly, bringing food and drink on elaborate trays. The Host came in, leading his beautiful Wife, played by Grace, and they sat down with Gawain by the fire, looking for all the world like a noble family.

But something persisted in going wrong. No matter how hard they'd worked on it, Ellen tensed when Joe moved close to her.

"Let's play a game to pass the time," Joe suggested in an insidious tone, "a game of tit for tat: each night I'll exchange what I kill in the forest for whatever you win here by my hearth."

Though she held out her hand, Ellen's body arced away from him, her eyes narrow with suspicion. And Joe wasn't helping. He looked anything but sincere and friendly.

Ren stopped them. "The tension's way too high. The mood here is still supposed to be friendly. I think it might help if you weren't physically right on top of Ellen, Joe. You could get up and take a few steps away from the table, then stop and look back at them as if you've just had a great idea. Ellen, when he does that you could lean towards him. You're curious, eager to hear what he has to say. Remember, you're sitting around after dinner, replete and slightly bored. The game of exchange is proposed as an amusing diversion."

"Fine," Ellen said, "but I was just reacting to the way Joe's playing. Anyone can hear the scorn in his voice. He thinks I'm a fool to take his bait."

"The Host has the power," Joe said, flexing his huge hand. "That's how I'm playing it. I'm letting Gawain feel the iron under my velvet glove."

"What's restraining Gawain isn't your force, it's his loyalty," Ellen rejoined in her crisp Boston accent. "You've given him hospitality, he's eaten your bread." Joe gave her a dirty look. Since he'd hit her it was almost assured that if Joe had a strong opinion about how some bit of business should go, she'd have the opposite one.

"Look," Ren said, making his voice stay calm, "if we're going to find a plausible mood for this scene, both of you are going to have to make some adjustments. Let's try a quick switch. Give yourselves a chance to see your part from the other side. Ellen, take Joe's lines from where he proposes the bargain, show us what you mean. Joe, you take Gawain."

"Swear now, sweet friend, to swap our winnings," Ellen said, exquisitely polite, an arm outstretched in invitation.

"If you think it good sport," Joe responded cheerfully, "I'll gladly take part."

When they finished the exercise, Ren pointed out the adjustments he thought were good, making sure he noted Joe's ready acceptance of the bargain as well as Ellen's increased courtesy in asking and adding – since Joe clearly wasn't happy – that if he wanted to hint at his dark side, the best time to try that would be in the hunt scenes: "You could be more brutal when you handle the dead animals; you might caress them, or touch them in a way that reminds us of what you did in the first act with your ax."

Joe agreed, somewhat sullenly, to try.

Ren moved to the back of the auditorium and lowered himself into one of the worn armchair seats. It was always good to move around so you could see how the set and the actors looked from different angles. In front, up above him, he could see the array of lights on their black tracks. The lighting director had added some dappled shades to the forest lighting, and there was a shimmering pool of light in the center of the stage.

A dancer dressed as a deer moved slowly into the glade accompanied by music from the bucolic brook section of Beethoven's *Pastoral Symphony*. Since Jack's illness, music irritated Ren's nerves in a way it never had. It seemed to open in him a feeling of depression that he tried to keep down for Jack's sake. Now, the music switched right on cue to the storm section of the same piece and the doe crossed the stage in a series of startled leaps, followed by the hunters. Ren felt her vulnerability. Her painted mask had the beauty of an animal, the reddish fur and large doe eye, but a remarkably human expression. Dying, she crumpled slowly to the ground in slow spirals while the hunters clustered around her with knives, slashing at the carcass, pulling out innards, then swirling and stamping with the hooves and furry skin held triumphantly above them.

In the center of the circle, Joe was dancing with the deer's head with an intense ferocity that Ren hadn't seen before. Gradually the dance slowed and the music of the opening returned as the hunters, their blood lust sated, attached the broken bodies to poles, hoisted them to their shoulders, and moved off with Joe in front still clutching the bloody head.

The light dimmed; the black curtain that hid the castle set behind it lifted and revealed Gawain and the Host's wife standing by the big open hearth, warming themselves by the fire. Outside through an arched stone window you could see a black night sky and snow falling. Grace, her neck and throat bare and gleaming white, stood with one light jeweled finger lying across Ellen's wrist. Grace leaned seductively towards Ellen and gently kissed her on the lips. Ellen stood with lips slightly parted as if entranced.

The stillness lasted only a moment, just long enough to contrast it with the movement and noise of the preceding scene, then there was the sound of boots on the stairs, a shout and the Host burst into the room followed by his men carrying the flayed carcasses.

As they threw them down and started to count them, the Host asked Gawain, "What do you have to offer me in return?"

Then, without waiting for an answer, he snatched the

deer's severed head from the pile of parts and, holding it with one hand, advanced on Gawain swinging the head to and fro in front of his face.

Ellen exploded. "Back off Joe, you're too close. You're not giving me any space." She was in fact standing with her back to the fire with Grace on one side, a pillar on the other.

"You're supposed to be genial here, Joe," she said, "not murderous."

"Gawain just kissed my wife."

"And I was going to give the kiss back to you. How do you expect me to kiss you, if you're swinging that head in my face?"

"Wait! Wait! Ellen, Joe," Ren broke in excitedly. "You two have helped me see things about the story that I didn't see before. When we started, I saw the bonding between Gawain and the Green Knight at the end as positive, but it isn't. It's really about forced submission, not respect or friendship. And the reason Gawain can't fight back, can't even question the Green Knight's right to judge him, is because he doesn't understand who he is. I've been thinking. What if Gawain were as suspicious as Ellen wanted him to be, feels that he's in a trap. . . ? Why not let him prowl around the castle and find the Green Knight's ax? Let him find out that the man who seems like a benign father is really a manipulative shape-changing bastard . . . a Big Daddy threatening to cut off his head if he doesn't behave. If Gawain understands who he is dealing with, I see how to make a much more satisfying ending. Do something really new with the play. Could you handle some new lines so near opening night?"

Only Joe was reluctant. "The ending's been around for 400 years or so and I didn't see what's wrong with it." Joe was obviously getting off on playing a character with power. Ren imagined he didn't get many chances to exert it in his everyday life. Just the other day he'd come in with white make-up covering a nasty shiner. But Ellen was excited that Ren was going to give Gawain more initiative. She couldn't wait to see the new scenes and Ren, high on his new idea and unable to feel the cramping ache of fatigue, promised it to them by the next rehearsal.

CHAPTER EIGHT

A Tourney

Gawain was always one to pity lovers in difficulty.

— Malory, *Le Morte D'Arthur*

The next morning, having been up most of the night working on the new scene, Ren had a talk with Patrick, their producer, about a tie-in he'd engineered with a Soho Gallery that was having a show of faux medieval watercolors — strange surreal paintings of knights and horses in dream landscapes. The artist had quite a following and lots of people were picking up the play flyers.

An hour later, Ren ran into Henny in the hospital corridor. She'd come early, she said, because Malcolm was planning to visit Jack after lunch. Her look implied that she didn't want to be there at the same time. Ren didn't want to be there either and he was at the point with his scene where he'd gotten the essentials down and needed to let it settle, so he said yes when Henny asked him to come with her for a couple of hours to a horse show. It might be inspiring now that he was creating a more powerful Ellen to see Henny engaging in an energetic knightly activity, overcoming obstacles. At the very least, it would be a refreshing break.

"You'll be there *in loco fratris*," Jack had said when Ren told him. Despite his doped state, Jack was clearly pleased.

So here he was, sitting in the front row of a big outdoor arena, muffled to the teeth against the cold, waiting to see Henny ride.

A friend with a three-horse trailer had brought up Henny's horse for her, and as soon as they arrived in her little Toyota, she dragged Ren to the barn to watch her prepare. It was a dark cavernous space floored with rough wood and lined by stalls on either side. Each stall had a tiny window that let in a watery winter sunlight. The whole place smelled of horse shit and hay, and everywhere Ren looked there were glossy rumps and people with brushes working them over.

Ren had thought it would be fun to wear the appliqued jeans that he'd done himself. Someday he was sure they were going to be the rage. But right now he felt stupid. Absolutely everyone was wearing jodhpurs and slick black boots. Henny patted a reddish brown rump affectionately, then pushed it to one side and dove into a stall. A moment later, the rump lurched backwards and Henny appeared holding her horse by the halter and hitched him between two posts.

Ren stood against one of the posts, feeling a bit like Saint Sebastian about to get shot. The horse kept doing a little two-step. Mincing forward and back like the primo ballerino in the new gay dance troupe. Trouble was, his dance slippers weren't just big, they were cast iron. Ren imagined the crunch of hoof against the top of his foot. Besides sidling up to get a closer look at a mounted policeman with a cute butt, this was the closest he had ever been to a horse.

"Stormy, this is Ren," Henny crooned. "You're an angel, not stormy at all, are you?" She kissed the horse's nose. The horse's liquid brown eye peered round her at Ren with seeming alarm. There was a perfectly formed white star on his forehead.

"He's nice, but I've always preferred smaller animals myself," Ren said, keeping his distance. "Teacup poodles, for instance." The kind he'd wanted to get for him and Jack.

"Don't be so freaky," she said to the horse, "you're scaring Ren. Here, pet him." She took Ren's hand. "He likes his nose rubbed." She rummaged in her bag. "You can give him his treat – he's a regular glutton." She pressed the cool quarters of an apple into his palm. Ren definitely preferred imaginary horses to real ones, but Henny looked so happy and pretty that he was glad he had come. All her hesitation and self-doubt seemed to have vanished.

Funny how different people could be in different circumstances. He watched her rub her nose against Stormy's, telling him to be patient, that he'd get his apple in a minute. Maybe even Malcolm had another side – some private passion that would make him more likeable. Maybe when he was jogging around the reservoir before work, he stopped to feed the ducks. Or maybe he gave money to the bag lady who stationed herself at the park entrance.

He carefully opened his hand, holding the apple flat the way Henny had showed him. The horse's nose was soft but the lips opened and nibbled at his hand and he got a glimpse of enormous white molars. They could take quite a chunk out of you. Ren withdrew his hand and wiped off the slobber. The horse kept eyeing him ominously while Henny braided his mane into tiny dreadlocks. He tossed his head, turning it from side to side keeping his eye on Ren. "I think I'm bothering him," Ren said, trying to compress his six feet into the smallest possible space against the pillar.

"He's trying to see that red cloth you have sticking out of your pocket," Henny said. "What is it?"

"Just a handkerchief – really, a kerchief," he said, pulling it out. He'd had the idea of waving it at her as she rode, or letting her pin it to her saddle, something like that. The way they did in the medieval romances. He gave a little wave. The horse snorted and jumped to the side, breaking one of his leads. Ren shrieked. Henny swore, and a slender young man ran up and hung on Stormy's broken rope, talking soothingly to him.

"What scared him?" he asked Henny as the horse quieted down.

"Just a handkerchief," she said and giggled. Ren tucked the thing back in his pocket. It was oversize and he felt ridiculous. The boy was looking him over carefully. His eyes rested on the applique of a butterfly surrounded by pearls.

"Ren's my brother's friend," Henny said quickly. "Ren, Franco." She pronounced the name tenderly with a perfect trill. Her tone made Ren forget his embarrassment and stare. Her cheeks had flushed a warm, very becoming pink. Franco wiped his hand and stuck it out.

"Hi. I like your jeans."

"Thanks." Ren was intrigued. The boy spoke with a strong Spanish accent and was as stunningly handsome in a dark way as Henny was in her blondness, with a high-nosed, sensitive face and the agile body of a young bullfighter. Henny put her hand up and pretending to take out a wood-chip, touched his hair which was black and thick. "Franco's my one-man support team," she said to Ren, "better than ten trainers."

"Henny exaggerates," Franco said, but he looked pleased. "I don't do anything much. Just watch." His voice was relaxed and mellow. But when he looked at Henny his eyes were intense.

"Franco listens to me bitch and helps muck out the stall – you know he even does that," Henny said.

Franco smiled. "My father owns a breeding farm in Cochabamba. I grew up around horses." He had startlingly white teeth.

"Franco wants to see how breeders work here." She picked up the horse's foot, rested his foreleg against her knee and started to clean out the manure with a little yellow pick.

"And learn some American history," he said. "I'm – how do you say it – a history buff. Up to now it's been mostly classical."

Ren laughed. He liked the kid.

"He's going to grad school," Henny said digging hard. "As soon as he gets a little money saved up."

"I think he'd probably learn a lot more from bumming around," Ren said.

The boy looked at him with a sly smile. "She thinks an advanced degree will make her papa like me better, but the truth is, nothing is going to make him like a foreigner from Bolivia unless some movie star makes me an heir. Are you a movie star by any chance?"

"I wish. Nope, just do a little theater. Some dance. A mixed bag." Without thinking, Ren put his hands on his hips and struck a pose.

The boy looked at the applique of red pumps on Ren's right thigh and Ren could see the wheels click into place. "Oh, I see . . ."

"Papa doesn't care for me much either," Ren added.

Henny dropped the hoof she was doing and blew out her breath in a little snort of annoyance. "You better go out and get a seat," she said to Ren. As he exited the barn he saw the boy put his arm around her waist.

He'd found a place near the front and put down his cushion. His ass was so trim he needed to have something soft under it. Now he was sitting there bundled up waiting for her and thinking about what he'd seen. So that was the real trouble with papa. The business about taking a degree in education was probably minor. He was saving her for something special. This boy's family was probably land-rich and money-poor. And Malcolm wouldn't see that they were the same class as he was. He probably saw the kid as a barrio Latino. He wanted a rich Anglo preppie. The boy came by and whispered that Henny was going to ride fifth. "That's very good," he said. "It gives her a chance to warm up some more, and I can look over the competition."

"Can't we go somewhere and have a cup of coffee? I'm freezing."

"We're not in New York," Franco gestured at the pastures stretching in back of the arena, "but as it happens, Henny brought me a thermos. I'm not the only one taking care. She takes good care of me too."

"I don't doubt it." Ren was interested that the boy wanted him to know it wasn't all one way.

"Hey, they're coming. It's the opening parade." The boy
ran back down to the railing. Henny didn't look at him but
Ren thought he could see her back get a little straighter as she
rode by. After the parade, the riding started. Ren sipped his
coffee. He huddled down in his jacket and watched the first
rider, an elegant prematurely gray-haired man, prance into
the ring. He had a chiseled little nose and clamped tight lips –
like Malcolm.

Without wanting to, Ren suddenly remembered sitting
in Malcolm's living room a little over a year ago when he had
just started with Jack, his hair neatly brushed, wearing his
best slacks and a jacket, wanting the old man to like him. He
could feel the apprehensive flutter of his stomach, the abject
way he'd stood, his gold painted toenails safely hidden under
his black socks. Malcolm was sitting across from him on a
white sofa drinking a martini. It hurt for Ren to remember
how impressed he'd been by the authority the man exuded.

He was tall and square-jawed like Jack, with silver hair
and those marvelous suits. It was those custom-made suits that
sucked you in, with the wool you could die for. So you wanted
him to like you, so big deal. But Ren knew it was a big deal. It
was just like his semicrushes on teachers or older boys, all of
them hating him when they got an inkling of what he was.

And the Fifth Avenue apartment was to die for too, all
filled with antiques – even though later he found out they'd
been picked by a decorator – and all those gorgeous leather-
bound books. Ren had taken one out to look at and found the
pages weren't even cut. It was all show. The things that really
mattered in the apartment were the machines: computers,
scanners, faxes, laser printers. The other rooms were filled
with TV screens winking and flashing. Stereos everywhere.

DVD players. Cordless phones in pastel colors. The bedroom had a pull-down movie screen. The kitchen was a high-tech operation; the oven had a thermometer that could maintain the roast at a preselected temperature.

Actually, he remembered now – he was watching the next rider, a woman – that Malcolm had talked about Henny's riding. The old man had known Marshall Field's daughter at school, he'd told them, and had never forgotten seeing her ride in Madison Square Garden. Now his beautiful blond daughter was riding too. He'd gotten her a peacock-blue outfit. He wanted her to show, to win. Ren cringed now, remembering how he'd oohed and ahhed at the photo on the sideboard. How he'd thought this was all pretty charming.

But what really hurt was his little daydream, in Hollywood technicolor, about how Jack's father was going to be a father to him too. Make up to him for the one that went away. I mean, how stupid can you be? You thought when he bought a castle in Europe and filled it with art he was going to invite you to swish around on the terrace and, in front of a landscape that could have been painted by a Renaissance master, dance on the ramparts? Because even if he wasn't quite sure you were gay, he could certainly tell that you weren't making it in his world.

The more Jack's father realized this wasn't a chance acquaintance, the stiffer he got. When Ren, having drunk too much in his nervousness, made the mistake of hugging him goodbye one night, he felt the older man's body go rigid. He stopped trying to hide his disdain. Ren had been too hurt to talk to Jack about his father's scorn, so instead he concentrated on the superior tone Malcolm took when he talked about blacks or Latinos or women. Jack, of course, defended him.

"Look, you may be right about his gut instincts – but he resists them, you have to give him that."

"Yeah maybe," Ren had said. Jack could talk until he was blue in the face, but it didn't matter. One day Ren pocketed one of those pretty leather books: the poems of Rossetti.

Jack was furious. They had a big fight and Jack insisted Ren return it.

Finally it was Henny's turn. She came into the arena and held Stormy still for a minute, though he was clearly impatient to go, his nostrils flaring, slight flecks of foam on his lips. Henny had the bearing of a young princess. Like one of the androgynous beauties at Arthur's court. Robes of gold brocade flashed through his mind, embroidered gowns, white fur, making him yearn to feel them.

Henny was walking around the ring, slow and stately. Ren rubbed his gloved hands together briskly, trying to warm them, then gave up and stuck them in his pockets.

Henny paced by, her horse lifting his feet up to a surprising height. Maybe Henny trying it on with this boy would serve as a sort of dry run for him and Jack. If the old man quieted down after awhile and accepted the kid, maybe Jack wouldn't be so frightened. He wondered what kind of sex they had. The kid obviously brought out Henny's protective impulses. And maybe her feeling confident led to great sex. Who knows what turns people on. Henny usually looked so inhibited, held her arms and legs so stiffly, but trotting around the ring today she was quite different. Her horse's feet hit the ground, first one side then another, the shining haunches working like pistons, and a supple power seemed to flow upward into her body.

"Go baby," he whispered to himself as she rode by barely rising in her seat. "You're beautiful, and without all the shit." He instinctively straightened his body, imitating her. She didn't care a damn about anything but the beat, the music of the trit-trot. Now she was going into a canter so smoothly he couldn't even see the signal she gave. What was it, a press of the knees? A slight movement of the reins? He stared, really trying to see, but he couldn't. It was like magic the way the horse turned and circled now, with her hands seemingly perfectly motionless above his neck. Nice if that magic could be bottled and Henny could use it in her confrontations with Malcolm. But unhappily, you could be a brilliant rider and still fall flat when it came to dealing with your parent. Ren leaned forward intently as Henny danced sideways across the ring.

There was one rider after Henny and then the judges announced she'd won the blue. She brought it to show them in the stands, eyes sparkling.

"I was afraid Stormy wasn't quite up to this," she said. "He's young and I've only been training him for a few months. But he was great!"

"*You* were great," Franco said hugging her. "You kept him high all the way through."

"Beautiful, too," Ren said. "It was a joy to watch you. You made it look so easy." He knew she had a passion for horses, that was obvious from the start, but he hadn't realized she was such a winner.

Ren only wished Jack had been there to see her, blue ribbon clutched in her hand, flushed and pleased with her triumph.

CHAPTER NINE

humors

*In medieval medical theory there were four humors whose distribution
was responsible for the health of the individual. Hot, cool, dry, wet.
Too much of any one threw the system out of balance. The cure was
to restore balance by adding cool to hot, dry to wet. The humors were
responsible for states of mind as well as physical health. What went
on in the body was reflected in the body politic and in the world in gen-
eral under the principle of Hermes Trismegistus: as above, so below.*

– from Ren's college notes

It was the fifth day of Jack's week-long chemo and Ren was weak-kneed from the stress of dealing with emergencies on two fronts. Arriving at the hospital, he ducked into a phone booth for a last-minute phone call to check on the remote-controlled speaking device for the Green Knight's head. It had suddenly gone dead during rehearsal, and the thought of a malfunction on opening night – only a week away now – made him shudder. Thanking God that it seemed to be only a loose wire, Ren was pleasantly surprised when he found Jack, face intent, listening to his phone messages instead of throwing up.

"How you doing, babe?" Ren leaned down and stroked his shoulder. Jack had a small note pad in one hand. Ren glanced at it and saw there was only a single line straggling across the page.

Jack shut off the machine. Ren noticed that his cheeks and lips seemed badly swollen. Jack struggled to open his lips, to let the words out, but his voice was thick when it came and the words were garbled.

"What?" Ren asked, startled. It made no sense at all. Had he had a stroke?

Jack kept mumbling, "wri mbe lets," looking straight at him as though he expected him to understand.

"I'm not quite getting it, sweetie."

Jack seemed to realize from Ren's face that he wasn't coming through. He lay back with a groan.

"Never mind," Ren stroked his shoulder, "it's okay. I'm a bit slow-witted this morning, that's all. Had a bad night." Jack's shoulders began to shake with dry sobs. Ren longed to get in bed with him and hold him, but all he could do was squeeze his hand. "Hey, hey."

Jack stopped sobbing and muttered something unintelligible. Ren felt his stomach clench. He tried to imagine himself as a war nurse or a monk visiting plague victims, someone calm and unflappable. So what if Jack couldn't talk, right? If Ren calmed down, he could sense what Jack wanted, couldn't he? Isn't that what lovers did? Interpreted the minutest clues. When Jack's eyes went from green to gray, that meant he was angry. Green with a touch of warm blue meant love. But now his eyes were glazed and unreadable.

He reached toward the pad and Ren handed it to him.

"Want to try again? Maybe it'll be better this time."

Jack pursed his lips, gripped the pencil, and began to write. After a minute Ren looked down at what he'd written. A series of meaningless scrawls slanted across the page. Ren decided to let him go on, the way you would with a child who was tying his laces all wrong.

After a few minutes, Jack put down the pencil in disgust and motioned Ren to come closer. Ren bent next to his mouth. This time he made out the word, message. It was such a relief to get this little nugget of meaning that he almost cried. And such a simple thing, too. What an idiot he was not to have guessed that Jack wanted him to answer his messages.

Ren reached for the pad, which had slipped down into a little valley on the cover. "I've always wanted to be a social secretary," he said. "Wear Gucci heels and a short skirt. How do you think pink would go with my complexion?" Better than yellow, certainly, he thought as he lowered himself into the offensively yellow armchair. Why did hospitals think this puke color was cheerful? "Better start from the beginning again, huh?" he said, pressing the "play" button. He noticed his hand was trembling and took a deep breath.

The first message was from Henny wanting to say good morning. "The nurse says you're not in the mood for talking, so I thought I'd leave you this silly joke I heard at the party after the show last night. I won first, by the way."

Ren noted the "by the way." Why couldn't she tell him she'd been triumphant, glowing with pride. Hugging her boy. Hugging Ren. "Okay, are you ready? A woman takes her little boy to the beach and he's suddenly swept away by a big wave. 'Oh God,' she prays, 'just give me back my son. For the rest of my life, I'll be grateful, I'll do anything.' So God sends the boy back on the next wave, but still the woman stands on the edge, lamenting. 'What's the matter?' God asks her. 'You have your boy, he's there in your arms. Nu?' 'But God,' she wails, 'you forgot his hat.' Hope it makes you laugh. It did me. I'll be in before you go to sleep."

Ren snorted into his hand. Just what they needed, a little comic relief. "Doesn't she think you have enough Yiddishkeit with me around?" He had told her a few jokes himself the day they were at the zoo together. He'd wanted to loosen her up, get rid of some of that Protestant uptightness. Now she was reminding Jack that he'd have something to laugh about if he hung on. It was sweet. But when Ren looked down at Jack he couldn't tell if he was smiling or grimacing in pain. His face was like chalk.

Never mind the hat or the hair or even the voice, he thought. Just give me the boy. He wondered if Henny had thought of that too. Or was she making fun of her own wishes? God, let me have my boy and a blue ribbon too? Funny how people's minds worked by association. The other day he'd

heard about a lawyer trying hard not to mention to a client
that he knew her husband had jumped from the tenth floor. So
when she asked if she could afford a possible stock loss, he
said, "Well, you wouldn't throw yourself out a window over it.
Oh my God."

He thought of telling the story to Jack but decided it was
too lugubrious. He played the next message. It was from one of
his colleagues at the Fisheries office, sixty miles up the river.

Jeez, the man either had a bad head cold or permanent-
ly clogged sinus. "We're all so sorry you're sick," he said,
making all the s's sound like b's. "I haven't been so well
myself, bad case of flu."

Yadita yadita, that-a-boy! You really know how to make
a man feel better. Like, Oh, you just had your balls removed,
well let me tell you about my tummy tuck. Never again, he
promised himself, would he respond to a serious illness with an
account of his own minor pains. His neck flushed as he
remembered times he had done this. The only thing worse was
the over-the-top phony cheer. This guy managed both. Then,
his voice dropping, he told Jack that the River Keeper had
caught someone dumping waste in the river. It was the plant that
Fisheries had suspected for some time of trying to cut corners by
hiring a cheap waste purveyor. Someone who wouldn't be bothered to take the stuff to the treatment facility. It was almost
impossible to catch these guys but finally they'd lucked out. The
moon had been full and there he was upending his truck bed.
Jack's colleague was exultant. He was particularly glad they'd
got him before the spawning season, when the fish nursery not
far from the plant would be particularly vulnerable.

Jack would ordinarily have been riveted by this kind of
news but he didn't stir. His hands lay on the sheet like wax
stumps.

Ren put the pad down on the bedside table for a moment
and straightened the covers. He wondered if this stuff seemed
to Jack like something happening on Mars. "We don't have to
do this now," he said gently.

Jack seemed distressed. He shook his head and motioned toward the phone. Ren had a sudden image of a brain with its frontal lobes cut. What torture not to be able to connect, but at least Jack was trying. And he'd clearly gotten something from that nasal voice droned into his ear.

"Okay," Ren picked up the pad again. "Okay. What'll we tell 'em?"

Jack pressed his blistering lips together and muttered what seemed like a warning but also an encouragement.

"How about, 'Be careful, but keep at it?'" Ren asked, guessing. Jack nodded and shut his eyes. After waiting to see if anything else was coming, Ren made a note of the name and number on the pad. He'd been stupid to think that Jack shouldn't try to answer his messages. "You take care of the river for me," Ren added, "and I'll take care of my cancer."

He knew that Jack thought they were linked. Poison water or plants and it will eventually get back to the body. Plants and animals, humans too, were linked by a chain that went from the smallest amoebae out to the stars.

"We think we're getting smarter, but we're not," Jack had said. "We're just getting better at cutting ourselves off from the things that matter."

Ren loved Jack for saying things like that. "You don't just have a perfect Greek body," he told him, "you have a Greek mind."

Marci came in around lunchtime and started a transfusion. There were several nurses in the transplant unit but this was the one Ren liked best. Barely five feet tall, she was full of energy that gave Ren a sense that she had things under control. She had large, brown, compassionate eyes and a bosom like a shelf.

"He's having trouble talking," Ren whispered as she moved around, quietly straightening the room.

"I don't wonder," she said in a normal tone, "with all the pain medication he's been getting. He'll be in and out for awhile." Ren could feel his anxiety level plunge like mercury in a thermometer held under cold water.

"BM today?" the nurse asked Jack. He shook his head and she entered his negative on the chart at the foot of the bed. "How's the headache?" she asked, with real concern.

He made a mewing sound with a slight upward motion.

"Better? Good. Looks as though your transfusion's gone in just fine. And I've brought you lunch." She briskly detached the blood bag and hooked up the glucose. Jack watched her carefully, struggling to take it in. "We like to explain everything," she said to Ren.

"Sounds good." Ren remembered hearing that nurses talked even to coma patients, maybe especially to coma patients. Trying to call them back. "Can't he eat anything at all anymore?" he asked, eyeing the glucose, pale the color of nothing real.

"He'd just throw it up. Besides, his throat is very painful."

"Awful," Ren murmured. Jack had already told him that the chemo had made everything taste like metal, or cotton batting.

"Be a lot nastier if we didn't have this," she said, patting the bag.

"Food's pretty basic," Ren answered blandly for Jack's ears. Dead is what he would have been without it, plain dead. Might also have been dead by this time if his father hadn't paid what the insurance wouldn't cover. Ren watched the slow drip of the sugared syrup and tried to imagine what it would it be like not to be able to chew or hold something soft and deliciously slippery on one's tongue. Not to feel warmth or cool and above all not to taste. That would be the worst. The fluid looked like nothing real, and the technical coldness of the whole process gave Ren the creeps. What if technology was catching? If it turned Jack into a zombie or a robot?

Ren found himself thinking about having a corned beef sandwich in the cafeteria. He could picture it sitting in the center of its white plate on the counter. He could smell the rye and the meat and taste the pickle. The beef was salty, the bread fresh and crusty. His mouth filled with saliva, a thin line trickled out of his mouth and he wiped it away. "I guess I'll get a bite," he said shamefacedly.

When he came back he found Jack trying to clean his mouth with little sponges. His movements were uncoordinated and jerky and he clearly was exhausted by even this tiny effort.

"Let me help. I've got my safeties on," Ren held up his gloved hands. "And I know how. I read the manual."

Jack didn't make the faintest protest; he just lay back gratefully on the pillow with his mouth open and Ren took the sponge. From up close, he saw that Jack's teeth had turned a distinct shade of yellow, and there were ugly lesions on the gums. Jesus, they were festering. "Hate to see this happening to your precious mouth," he said as he ran the sponges as gently as he could along Jack's gums.

There'd been a note this morning from a mutual friend telling them that their friend Roger had died. Of course he wouldn't tell Jack. Ren had avoided visiting Roger when he was in the last stages of AIDS, his face covered with lesions. Jack had gone. He was a better person. Ren sighed and got a fresh sponge from the packet on the bedside table, sprayed on the medicine and started on the other side of Jack's mouth.

Just after he'd read the note, he'd picked up a paper to read on the subway going to the hospital and there'd been a letter to the editor from someone from the religious right about the AIDS plague as a punishment for sin. Those bastards. Hypocrites, all of them. He wished all of them would be caught with their pants down like that Republican candidate for Speaker of the House.

The phone rang just as Ren had finished and he answered. When he heard the voice he recognized Jack's father and felt his heart race. He doesn't know who you are, he told himself. You're the nurse. And anyway you have a perfect right to be here. "He's resting," Ren told him, "he's having some trouble talking."

"Well, tell him when he wakes up that I can't come in today," he said, in a voice hard as steel beneath the silk. "I've got an important conference."

"You can say hello to him yourself," Ren said quietly, "just don't expect an answer." He put the phone next to Jack's ear.

Jack held the phone close with a happy expression on his swollen face, then a minute later, closed his eyes with a look of misery, put the phone down and squinted at Ren suspiciously.

"Why didn't you come yesterday?" Jack asked, having temporarily phased back into awareness, his voice an aggrieved croak.

"But I did. I've come every day."

"You didn't."

"Ask the nurse, ask Marci when she comes back."

"You're always slipping off somewhere, promising and not . . ."

"Jack, stop it. I'm here now and I've been here every day since you checked in. Yesterday, I helped you shit. You had piles, remember? It's your father who isn't coming. Your goddamn father who isn't really there for you." All the things Ren had been suppressing came pouring out. "Why do you think you're so hungry for his approval? Because except for money, and the loan of his chauffeur, he gives you zilch. But I'm not going to let you take me for granted while you cover for that old bastard." Ren stopped short. What was he doing? This was crazy. How could he have said this? He'd thought it was all safely locked in his head. Jack looked distraught.

"Oh God, babe, I'm sorry."

Jack rubbed one crusted eye with his knuckle. "I'm sorry," he said, like a child who's been reprimanded. He obviously wasn't up to a fight or maybe miraculously he hadn't been able to process what Ren said. "Don't be mad."

"How could I be?" Ren said quickly, "It's just my usual defensiveness. I love you."

Jack lay back against the pillow and closed his eyes.

Ren sat next to him miserably, replaying the fight in his mind. How could he have said those things when Jack was in such pain? Ren bit his lips in frustration. But though he shouldn't have spoken, the bitter fact was still there: he was never going to break Jack's father's grip over him. Ren might be able to show Gawain what his opponent was really like – make him rebel and fight for his freedom. But no matter what Malcolm did or didn't do to him, Jack was going to be loyal. If he had to construct a figure he could be loyal to – he'd do it. He'd explain away bad behavior and seize on the slightest thing that would allow him to keep loving this man. When Jack's love for his father wavered for whatever reason, fear of him would take over. It was no-win.

Ren touched Jack's cheek very gently with one finger.

CHAPTER TEN

descent

Vero e che 'n su la proda mi trovai
della valle d'abisso dolorosa
che trouno accoglie d'infiniti guai.
Oscura e profonda era e nebulosa
tanto che, per ficcar lo viso a fondo
*io non vi discerna alcuna cosa.** *

— Dante, *Inferno IV*

Waiting for the infusion of Jack's purified cells at the hospital seemed unbearably slow, while opening night advanced at a reckless pace. Ren couldn't believe how many details there were still to attend to. He had gotten the revised scripts typed up and handed out to the actors. The moves flowed easily enough from the changed dialogue, but because the relationship between the Green Knight and Gawain had changed, Joe had to do some remotivating of his character in earlier scenes. Then the lighting cues had to be gone over again and a more sinister light introduced in the Green Knight scenes at the castle. Ren wanted more back-lighting to pick the Knight out ominously against a dark back-ground, and the roaring fire which had seemed cozy before in the Knight's castle had to be a more flaming dangerous red. The last-minute changes entailed all-night sessions with the lighting man and two interns who wore facsimile costumes and

---

* I found myself on the brink / of the abysmal valley of pain, / which resounds with noise of countless wailings. / It was so dark and deep and full of vapours that, / straining my sight to reach the bottom, / I could make out nothing there.

walked through the parts under the lights. In addition, the new scenes themselves still needed more interpretive work.

And though it had seemed endless, it was finally the last day of Jack's chemo. Now Jack would rest up for three days and then, if things continued to go as planned, the day after opening night he'd have his "rescue."

Ren had rushed up to the hospital after a last-minute meeting with the light designer, who hated working with such an antiquated system. During the last tech run-through the board had gone haywire and lit the forest hunt with the lights for the bedroom scene. Now, one of the colored gels had caught fire because two wires touched that should have been safely sheathed. They were lucky they hadn't had a full-out electrical fire. As if that weren't enough, the costumer had called to tell him that there was a loose board on the dais that had snagged two of the court ladies' dresses. She was repairing them as best she could, but someone should be sure to take care of the stage floor. And then there was a problem with the publicity. An important theater critic had inexplicably vanished from their database and Ren had to get one of the interns to run over an opening night invitation with tickets.

Looking through the porthole in the room door, Ren thought at first that Jack was asleep. He was lying back on his pillows, the catheter protruding from his chest, and his beautiful eyes seemed shut. But when Ren came near the bed, he saw a glimmer of green between the lids. Jack wasn't asleep at all. It was just that his eyes had some sort of gunk collecting between the lids, pulling them closed. His face was strangely puffy.

"Hi," Jack said in a small voice. He put his fingers up to his eyes and pulled them open.

"Don't expect me to be entertaining, I'm sick as hell." Ren saw with a shock that his lips were covered with oozing blisters that obviously made it painful to talk.

"Oh, baby," he murmured as Jack leaned over looking for something on the little shelf in his bedside table. Ren, realizing what he wanted, reached down and found the white basin for him, held it while clots of blood as big as a fist came out. Ren felt the gorge rise in his own throat and the sour taste of breakfast. He gritted his teeth, terrified. What was this inhuman mess? Was Jack hemorrhaging? Were his insides dissolving and coming out? In a panic he rang the call button for the nurse.

"This just came up," he said holding the basin out to Marci when she came in. He felt as if he were going to scream. She glanced at it, then went into the little bathroom and threw it out, making a note on the chart.

"Hey, we expected this," she said kindly. "It always gets worse at the end of the treatment. If you want to help him, you can wipe his lips," she handed Ren a medicated wipe, "but be careful with the blisters. They're very tender."

"Sure," Ren said. He didn't really trust himself to say more, didn't want to ask questions that would show how afraid he was or let Jack see that he thought he looked awful. He tore open the envelope and touched the wipe gently to Jack's lips, avoiding as well as he could the oozing sores. "Hurt you?"

Marci stood next to him, her starched uniform making a crinkly reassuring sound as she bent over Jack and smoothed on some Vaseline.

"I'm putting some more Compazine in your IV for the nausea," she said, "and a diuretic for the swelling." Jack mumbled something.

Jesus, even Ren couldn't keep track of the things that were going into Jack's body. Medicines to combat nausea, dizziness, funguses, medicines for sleep, for pain, for herpes. When Jack had had his earlier chemo, Ren had worked up an expertise on the drugs. Their names, their doses. He had been trying to fool himself into thinking this was going to be manageable, too. But it wasn't. Preparing for it – with all the tapes and books and pretty pictures – had been as ridiculous as preparing for a trip to hell. Bringing a fan for the hot weather, a thermos with iced coffee, extra-strong insect repellent.

As soon as Marci left, Jack had another spell of vomiting. This time it was painful dry heaves that went on and on. He lay with his head over the side of the bed, too weak to hold his head up. Ren held the basin with one hand and patted Jack's back with the other. The truth was, there were some things you couldn't prepare for. Lying in a snake-filled swamp in a war zone, surrounded by friendly fire, was probably another.

This chemo was sort of a combination. It was friendly and it burnt you from the inside out. Unimaginable hell. Ren made lists of even worse hells in his head as he held Jack's shoulders and tried not to listen to the rasping, tearing sounds: Alzheimer's, Auschwitz.

He let go of Jack's shoulders for a minute and wiped his forehead. They even had seminars on the stages of dying now. He tried to remember what they were. Denial was one of them. Anger. Acceptance. Yes, I'm in denial, you were supposed to say to yourself. Please don't crack my defenses now. Let me think I'm going to beat this.

"Jack, let me push the pain button and give you a hit." he said. They had the painkillers – Ren wasn't sure what they were today – hooked up so you could give yourself a dose just by pushing a button next to the pillow. He thought Jack nodded but he didn't care. He had to do something. He pressed it, and imagined Jack submerged by a blessed numbness.

As though you could possibly know how you'd feel when pain and sickness had weakened you. He'd known black-leather clones who lost it completely, while some queen who went into a tizzy over a rip in her gown went out like a hero. But Jack wasn't going to die. That was it. Period. End of report. He didn't need a seminar.

The next day, when his body was supposedly resting up from the ordeal of the chemo, Jack had a raging fever of over 104. Ren felt it burning through his latex gloves when he touched him. His own skin beneath the gloves was clammy cold. Jack was painfully thirsty. Ren kept offering, holding a small plastic cup of water to his lips, but he just took it into his mouth, swished it around and spat it out; he couldn't seem to swallow.

"I don't see how he can keep on like this," Ren said to Marci when she came in. He was desperate for reassurance.

"He's young, he's strong. He will," she told him. "You have to remember how high the doses were. He's burnt from stem to stern," she added, inexplicably calm. "He's at the height of his reaction. After this, the chemicals drain and we can give him the good stuff."

She was speaking kindly, almost as though Ren were a child, but suddenly it seemed as though she were only a robot going through the motions. If she knew Jack was dying, would she be saying the same things, following the drill? The walls of the room pressed in on Ren like waves of ice carrying their flotsam of cards and greetings. Jack's head against the pillow looked like a bleached skull, like something you'd find on a windswept beach.

Ren forced himself to ignore the greenish light coming off the walls and sat down in the chair near the bed where he could hold Jack's hand. He pictured Jack sliding away from him down an endless tunnel of ice. To hold him there in the bed, he started to sing a lullaby.

"*Guten abend, gut' nacht, mit rosen bedacht . . . .*" His mother had sung him that when he had had measles as a child. He'd been delirious and thought trains were rushing over his bed. He hoped it comforted Jack the way it had him, pushing away the sound of the oncoming wheels. It seemed as good as anything. Gentle streams of sound.

While Ren was remembering the scratchy feel of his mother's blue wool dress as she leaned over him, Jack signalled for the basin and began another ferocious bout of vomiting. God, the stuff was black as pitch this time. Devils couldn't have made anything more foul.

"It's okay," Ren murmured, though he could tell by the look in Jack's blurred eyes that he wasn't present anymore. Wasn't understanding, was suffering the way an animal suffers, without consciousness. Probably wouldn't even remember this.

Ren rang the bell and when Marci came in they looked at the contents of the basin. Like Delphic priestesses, Ren thought, reading the entrails of some poor sacrificed beast.

"You can toss it," she said, scribbling her prophecies on the chart.

He carried the basin to the bathroom as if he were an acolyte and tried to think positive thoughts as he watched the contents go into the bowl. The cancer is being brought up, he whispered in a priestess voice. All the blackness, all the poison is coming up. But it looked deadly as an oil slick clinging to the side of the bowl. The kind that clings to feathers and fur, that can't come off without pulling the skin. He'd seen a painting once of a saint being flayed. He'd been fascinated by the aliveness in the man's face while his body was a bloody mass. Jack was being flayed too, but from the inside. He was just one long tube of brutally inflamed tissue.

Ren rinsed out the basin slowly, glanced at himself in the mirror. They should cover the mirror, he thought. He was glad Jack couldn't see how he looked. He'd been so proud of his hair, his glowingly healthy skin. Was it Augustine who said we were all just bags of putrid guts? Or some other church father? Needing us to hate our bodies so we wouldn't sin. He wondered how Jack's body could possibly recover from this scourging. Inside his inflamed intestines, microscopic creatures were growing, like maggots in a corpse.

A large black woman came into the fish-tank room carrying one of those bags of mysterious liquid. Ren didn't remember seeing her before. She was wearing gold earrings and her lipstick was bright red. She seemed to have a positive effect on the walls, as if they were a little less cold.

"Okay, honey," she was saying to Jack, "we're giving you a little more Dilaudid." She replaced one of the plastic bags on his IV stand with a fresh one. "You're a lucky young man. I don't want to come in tomorrow and see you drooping, understand?"

The idea of Jack being lucky was so absurd that Ren giggled and the nurse looked over at him questioningly. You're going gaga, honey, he told himself sharply. Laughing, crying, seeing oracles in the toilet. You better pull yourself together. He felt his face draw itself together into an acceptable mask of reasonable manhood.

"Now that was the good news, this is the bad news," the red lips were saying. "I have to give you your antifungal and it can make you a little uncomfortable." Oh, uncomfortable again. Ren imagined the devils apologizing before they shoved a damned soul into boiling pitch. Sorry, it's going to be a bit uncomfortable, but these are my orders.

It took only a few minutes of the new anti-fungal drip to send Jack into painful spasms, making him shake all over as if he were having an epileptic fit.

Ren pressed his hand but he didn't feel any answering pressure. Jack's eyes were clamped shut, his face contorted.

"Hold on, baby," Ren said. He'd had enough of this cheerfully hellish place. When the nurse left the room Ren took off his shoes and climbed onto the bed alongside Jack. He knew he was taking a chance. If someone came in he was going to get into trouble, but so what, he'd swear never to do it again, tell them Jack was shaking so hard he just couldn't sit there and watch it. He lay outside the covers and tried to hold him still with his body, whispering into his ear telling him about how the room seemed to be changing. I love you and I'm scared, he whispered. Scared shitless. I think I'm losing it. He knew Jack wouldn't blame him. Wouldn't say, who do you think you are, Virginia Woolf? Ophelia? Jack would never say things like that. He didn't tease him except when he was angry. He didn't mind that Ren was emotional, that things played on his nerves. Ren could feel their hearts beating together, comforting him. After awhile the spasms calmed and even the walls looked less sinister.

When he got home after that night's rehearsal, Ren threw himself down on his bed fully dressed, and shut his eyes even though he knew it was hopeless. He was in that keyed up state – too tired to sleep. He twisted and turned, his mind filled with grim images, half expecting a call from the hospital. A vigorous knock on his door made him jump. "Who is it?" he called – the bright face of his clock told him it was almost one.

"It's me," came a faint voice, "Sarah." He staggered up and opened the door. "Want to go dancing?" she asked with that crazy crooked grin of hers. He could smell the alcohol stink on her breath. "You look . . . did I wake you?"

"No, just having a major bout of insomnia."

"Jack doing all right?"

"Yeah, I think so. At least he's holding on."

"Hey, he's alive, we're all alive, even Horace the cat . . . that's something to celebrate isn't it? I have some dope. Let's party, go to a disco and dance 'til dawn."

"The discos I go to are all gay. Besides I'm unbelievably tired."

"You can't sleep and I want to dance, we make a great pair. Don't tell me you can't get me in. You know everyone. Everyone," she squinted at him. "I want to go to one of those clubs where all those macho guys show off their pecs and lats to each other." He closed his eyes experimentally. Maybe with the dope and the dancing he could at least get a few early morning hours of sleep in before he went back to the hospital.

"Does it have to be the heavies? How about going to see the Latin Queens do the tango. There's some really elegant dancing – and I do know someone there."

"I don't want Fred Astaire tonight. I want to see all that gorgeous manpower going to waste. It'll be pure torture but that's what I like. Didn't you know I was a masochist? I can sniff the air and remember the last time I got laid. Think about how deprived I am."

"You're a perverse child, that's what you are, but I'm so wasted already it doesn't much matter. If it will please you." He tried to remember what Sarah had told him about her one true love – the one who had left her the cat. Apparently the guy made a point of visiting her from time to time just to keep her from forgetting him. He'd take her out for a walk or a movie and she'd be hopelessly hooked again. She pretended to be looking for a man. But she wasn't, not really. She was still carrying an invisible torch.

Sarah struck a macho pose in her men's jacket and snug boy's jeans, then crammed her curls under a cap.

"How do you think I'd be as a man?" she asked him while she lit a joint and then passed one to him.

"Cute," he said. "But I like you better as a woman."

"I've been so desperate lately, I've thought of going AC DC," she said, suddenly serious. "No, really. Women are more interesting than men – straight men at least – and there are so many more of them. I mean, why not?"

Ren shrugged. "It's not usually a matter of choice. If the chemistry's not there. Or is it?"

"I like women, I love them. I think they're beautiful. More beautiful than men, but no," she laughed, "it isn't. I guess that messes up my prospects, huh?"

They splurged on a taxi and got to the disco around 1:30, when things were just getting started. He knew one of the door-keepers here, too. Sarah was right about that, though when the man let them in and stamped their hands with a purple cherry, he raised his eyebrows inquiringly. The dope made the strobe lights vibrate in waves of yellow and blue and the men danced through that electric current like dreaming gods. He took Sarah by the hand and led her to the edge of the floor, where they could watch for a minute before going in. The speakers blared. Sarah pulled him onto the dance floor. The music would normally have seemed too loud but now it seemed incredibly rich and sent him into a semitrance. He leaned against her, watching the blue and gold wash over the tank tops and the gleaming muscled flesh. The room was hot and smelled of sex. Ren would never get taken for one of these boys, even if he put on Nikes and tattooed his biceps. They had a male confidence – or was it bravado? – that he hadn't known recently. Still, it was glorious in a way, if he didn't let himself get threatened by it. A man danced by him with the neck of a bull, each muscle of his shoulders perfectly articulated. Ren didn't like the bulk, but he couldn't help responding to the way the men were moving, their steps, their perfectly choreographed male lust.

"Not the sweet sensitive types, are they?" Sarah said into his ear. She was obviously getting turned on too.

"Was your ex sweet and sensitive?"

"He could be sweet," she paused, "and he was sensitive too. He knew just where to put the knife."

Ren could tell from the slight thrill in her voice that the cruelty excited her. "Nasty," he said.

"But when it was good . . ." she licked her lips and danced away from him. "These guys are colder than a snow-ball in hell," she said when she swung back. She was staring at a man in tight leathers cut out to show his butt."But they're sure gorgeous." Then before he knew what was happening, she'd thrown her arms around his neck and kissed him full on the mouth. He disentangled himself as gently as he could.

"Ren, can't you be with me, just for tonight. I'm so lonely."

"I know, sweetie," he said, "but I can't."

"Can't? Won't, you mean. Oh, forget it, it was a stupid thing to do."

"Don't let it ruin our night. Okay?"

She turned her head away and didn't answer. The strobe lights lashed their shoulders and the men around them, oblivious, whirled and thrust. Ren held her for a minute quietly and then they moved off the dance floor, not looking at each other, and took a taxi home.

CHAPTER ELEVEN

sleights of hand

"surely," said arthur, "with your foreknowledge
and magic you can avert your own destiny?"
"that is not so," merlin replied.

— Malory, *Le Morte D'Arthur*

They worked right up to the final dress rehearsal. Once
the changes to the end were firmly in place, Ellen blossomed. When Joe pushed her, instead of flaring, she waited, poised and cool as a cat. The two women seemed to catch
fire from each other and at each of the final rehearsals some
new gesture or detail was added. The concluding scenes were
both funny and unexpectedly tender. The tension built slowly
from the first scene, where the Wife, all charm, catches
Gawain in bed and pretends to make him prisoner, to the last,
where she comes in naked beneath a fur mantle.

Grace, with her showy good looks, was great as a
coquette. She flattered Gawain with practiced smoothness,
telling him archly that "if I had my choice of men, I'd take you
for a husband." Gawain, who could be seen observing her with
a touch of irony, responded that she was already married to a
better man. And besides, he could hardly be expected to concentrate on wooing when he is about to lose his head. Despite
his protests, Grace extorts a kiss.

At her visit the second day she is more blunt. "Are you
really Gawain?" Grace asks when he tries to engage her in
polite conversation. "Have you already forgotten what I tried
to teach you? Or is kissing me such a trial?" She cuddles up to
him and offers her mouth. He kisses her once and draws back.

"You needn't look at the door. It's well locked. No one will disturb us." She puts one arm around his neck, with the other strokes his arm. "You could take me by force if you wanted," she says, squeezing his biceps appreciatively, "unless, of course, I bore you."

Up to here Ren's play followed the original poem so that it would be clear to what lengths the Host's wife was willing to go to entrap Gawain. But now, before Grace's final visit, Ren let Gawain find the ax and realize who his Host really is.

When Grace arrives at Gawain's bed on the last day of the trial in a flowing mantle, her bosom and back almost bare, and offers herself, instead of withdrawing politely, Ren made Gawain lean his dark head close to Grace's blond one, caress the lustrous young skin of her shoulder, then suddenly take hold of her wrists and tell her straight out he knows it is a trap. Brushing aside Grace's terrified confession, he calms her and then gradually extracts her story, the tale of what it is like being a prisoner in your own home.

Ren could see Grace losing her coquettish tone and becoming more direct. When she says, "Believe me, I hated being a party to this," Gawain wonders what would happen if Grace stopped the game right now. "If you really don't want to see my head on the block, refuse to play. These aren't your rules. They do nothing for you. Think about it, don't be afraid," Gawain whispers, taking Grace in his arms. "It's up to you. You can follow orders or you can do something totally unexpected."

It seemed to be working. Ellen's acting had never been better. She was looser and freer and Joe's excess bluster had diminished. Still, Ren had never been under so much pressure and no matter how well a rehearsal had gone, he went to sleep with the dread that he'd wake up to hear the phone ringing and that it would be Marci, who was on night duty, or Henny, telling him there'd been a crisis.

Two days before opening night, coming back from the theater, he ran into Sarah a couple of blocks from his apartment. She gave him a friendly smile, so he guessed she'd forgiven him for not responding to her kiss. Most probably, high as she was, she'd forgotten it. They walked back slowly, fighting a bitter wind.

"I don't know how you cope with so much stress," she said, head down, chin tucked into her coat collar. "Jack, your show – if it was me, I'd be coming apart at the seams, or at least, stuffing myself with chocolates. By now I'd look like a Macy's balloon."

Ren told her he didn't know about the chocolates but he was going to have a little wine and cheese in the theater lobby on opening night. He hoped she would come.

"Wouldn't miss it," she answered. "But you need something sweet. Come to think of it, I have a friend at a great bakery who owes me a favor. I think it's worth a couple dozen chocolate chips, maybe a cake. I might even bake you one myself. Though it's been so long since I touched my oven, I'm not sure the damn thing still works." She smiled her crooked smile. "I used to do a wicked lemon custard." Ren was surprised and touched. He realized with a little chagrin that he'd thought Sarah's mental dramas didn't leave her much energy for other people's woes.

"You're a doll," he said, and gave her a big hug.

The final dress rehearsal was technically excellent but the actors seemed slightly constrained, as if they were holding themselves back, waiting for the audience. Ticket sales had been going well. Some of the NYU theater people were coming and several old acting friends from the Ridiculous Theatrical Company, as well as an Italian theater producer whose name Ren didn't recognize but who had a confident voice with an intriguing undertone of melancholy. Ren had invited them all to the party.

Tonight after the final run-through he'd gone back to check and recheck everything: costumes, props, projector, sound system. He was still worried about the backstage radio for the Green Knight's voice after the beheading. Ellen, who was there getting some minor repairs on her costume, had to tell Ren to go home and try to get Gawain out of his mind for awhile so he'd be fresh for the opening.

On opening night, Ren and Sarah went down in a cab a little early, taking the food. The taxi lurched to a stop at a light, throwing Ren against the warmth of Sarah's thigh, and for the fraction of a second he imagined it was Jack. That was how they sat, managing always to touch. Oh, bubbi, Ren intoned silently, be all right, you have to. He fingered the little red horn he was wearing around his neck, a talisman against bad fortune.

When they arrived at the theater Sarah handed the things over to an intern with instructions about how to set up and then joined Ren in the audience. He always liked to sit in the middle about three-quarters of the way back and she liked the first row, but she deferred to him and they settled in and sat, nervously watching the seats fill up.

"It looks as if you'll have a full house," she whispered, and he pressed her hand.

Full as it was, Ren kept looking towards the doors until he saw the blond hair and strong chin that reminded him so much of Jack. Then he jumped up and ran to welcome Henny and Franco. "I thought you'd never get here," he said, giving her a quick appraising look. The green eyes looked tired, but clear. Jack must be holding steady or she wouldn't have come. Now that she was here, Ren felt the ball of tension in the pit of his stomach relax. Luckily, there were a couple of free seats just in front of him. He hustled Henny and Franco over and introduced them to Sarah. Just before the lights dimmed, Ren saw his mother slip inside with her new beau. His mother, almost a head taller, was wearing an elegant black dress with a plum-colored boa and leaning on her friend's arm, talking excitedly. Ren was too nervous to get more than an impression of an attentive little man with a shiny bald pate before his mother blew him a kiss and the curtain went up on Camelot.

Ren was so used to the confusion of sexes in his play that he was taken aback when some of the audience giggled as the boy playing Guenevere saluted Ellen/Gawain in the opening dance. Sarah didn't laugh, but she gave Ren a quick complicit smile. A few minutes later, she seemed rapt, leaning forward in her seat as the Green Knight burst in. The mask's red eyes rolled as he looked down at the court from his great height. He coughed, stamped, cleared his throat.

"If anyone is so bold or so wild as to trade me stroke for stroke, I'll give him this," Joe stopped in front of Ellen for a moment and caressed his giant axe with a beautifully malevolent look. "No answer? All Arthur's famous crew silent? Are you so overwhelmed by one man's speech?" Then he roared with laughter, but before the laugh died down, Ellen had leapt to her feet and taken the ax.

"No one here fears your bluster," she said with a nice mix of pride and contempt. "I am as eager to begin as you are." Ren reflected that this was really a different Ellen. They were glaring at each other with an animal ferocity.

Ren relaxed and began to enjoy himself. The first act continued without a hitch and carried the audience with it. Since the play was relatively short, Ren had decided there was no need for an intermission. After the hunt dance, the action started its taut progress towards the climax. The concluding scenes had been changing so much right up to the dress rehearsal that Ren hadn't had time to let it settle and become part of him the way the rest had, so he watched them with increased attention.

The audience laughed delightedly as the Wife, all charm, caught Gawain in bed and pretended to make him prisoner. Grace's coquetry apparently worked as well in the present as it had in the fifteenth century. She was excited by

the audience's response and undulated ever more provocatively as she extorted kisses.

Ren hadn't been sure the audience would tolerate the
slow pace of Grace's visits, and when Grace turned up the heat
on her second attempt, Ren noted the men around him seemed
discomfited by Gawain's lack of response: what was the matter
with the guy? Was he impotent? Most of them probably didn't
get the original story's concern with mortal sin. Ren sensed the
audience beginning to get impatient – were they going to see
sex or blood? Whatever it was, they wanted it now.

On the third and final day, Grace arrived at Gawain's
bed in a flowing mantle, with her bare bosom and back, and
redoubled her accusations of coldness. Ren was struck by the
sensuousness of the caresses Ellen bestowed on Grace's shoulder. Around him, he heard appreciative murmurs and saw
people watching intently as Grace began to unbutton Gawain's
tunic, a button at a time.

Now, though he had seen it in the dress rehearsal, even
Ren felt a shock of surprise when Ellen suddenly took hold of
Grace's wrists and told her that she knew it was a trap. The
audience got very quiet. Ren felt his stomach contract with
anxiety. Were they going to accept what came next? As Grace
wept and told her story, Ren saw Sarah nodding in approval.
When Gawain whispered to Grace that what she did now was
up to her, that they could take history in a different direction,
Ellen sat bolt upright and opened her tunic, showing her
breasts. Ren was stunned by the confidence of Ellen's per-
formance. There was no denying what she offered. Grace
looked at her wondering for a moment and then slowly extend-
ed her hands. The audience gasped, then burst into applause
as Gawain and the Wife hugged.

Afterwards, when the Green Knight had been suitably
dispatched, doomed to live alone in his chapel while the two
women set off together, Henny leaned over her seat and
hugged Ren. "Cool end," she said. Sarah gave him a thumbs-
up and they inched their way along with the rest of the audi-

ence to the lobby. His mother, swimming against the crowd, Morris in tow, planted a big kiss on his cheek.

"Oh, sweetheart, it was beautiful," Thelma said, looking around her to make sure people noticed her intimate connection to the director. "Such costumes, and I loved that halo of gold light around Gawain's head. Morris liked it too."

"Pleased to meet you," Morris said, putting out a beefy hand. He had an unexpectedly strong grip. "I didn't know what to expect but it was very entertaining. Many people these days forget that theater is supposed to be entertaining. I sure don't go just to listen to people talk. I fell asleep in that show, what was it Thelma? Philosophy, math – I had enough of that in school."

"You're thinking of Tom Stoppard's *Arcadia*," Thelma said. "But that was an exception. Broadway shows usually have too much glitter and too little substance. You had both, darling. Oh look, Ren, isn't that Woody Allen?" She pointed her finger excitedly.

Ren glanced up and with a thrill of pleasure recognized the familiar figure – thinning ginger hair, glasses – coming down the aisle. "Please, Mom, yes, and that's great but . . ." He took her jabbing finger and gently pressed it down. "Give the guy a break. He might want a little privacy."

"If he wants privacy he should stay home," she said, piqued. "Or wear a mask." Seeing Ren frown she immediately relented. "Now don't let your mother monopolize you, dear," she said, brushing a fleck off his shoulder, "with all those people waiting to congratulate you."

Corks were popping in the lobby as two interns still in their court ladies' costumes poured champagne into plastic glasses. Ren took a look around and spotted the reviewer from the *Times* leaving the theatre and his heart started beating wildly. Back Alley had gotten some good notices for their production of Pirandello's *Naked*, but he really hadn't expected anyone from the *Times*. And he'd seen the reviewer from *The New Yorker* too. For a moment he was disappointed they weren't staying for the party. But of course, it wasn't done. No partying with the victim before slicing him to shreds. To calm himself he took a glass and went over to an old lover he saw standing against the wall, holding a metallic cane, clearly afraid of being knocked over. Mike had come to the party with a group of actor friends from the Ridiculous Theatrical Company. Ren knew he could count on him to be friendly.

"It's terrific. A real breakthrough," Mike said, embracing him. "Congratulations." He lifted the glass in a toast, then gave it back to Ren. "Being sick is such a frightful bore. But for two hours you had me rapt, totally." They hugged again and Ren went off to find him a stool.

Fighting his way across the lobby, Ren saw Ellen and Joe touching glasses with Grace.

"Hey, you were super," he told them. "I don't know where to begin. You were over the top." As Ren was enlarging on his praise, a man named Scott, a scene-stealing prima donna whom Ren had acted with and disliked intensely, interrupted him in mid-sentence. Ren hated actors who didn't understand teamwork. It wouldn't have been so bad if Scott had a big talent, but he didn't. Just a big prick.

"Oh darling," Scott raved as Joe and Ellen moved off. "It was so, so . . ." He was so eaten up by envy he couldn't bring himself to finish his compliment and fell back on a feathery kiss-kiss deposited on the air on either side of Ren's cheeks. "But a love story. I wouldn't have believed it," he cooed. "Where is the old cynical you?"

"I wouldn't call it a love story, more an anti-establishment fable," a bright voice pronounced, and Ren saw the wife of one of his friends smiling at him. She reached out and gave him a high five. Behind her, Genine, a queen he hadn't seen for ages, was struggling towards him with, of all people, his favorite female impersonator, Dame Edith, who was wearing street apparel and zany eyeglasses. Genine was dressed in a long gown and had a bouffant blond wig and long false eyelashes.

"I liked it a lot," she said, "but I didn't see why you used a woman for Gawain, when you could have had a real woman," she ran one long hand down her silk side, "like *moi* – one with really big boobies."

"There's more to a woman than her anatomy," Dame Edith said. "I thought it was lovely. You should take it to the West End."

Ren spied Edmund White at the other side of the room in conversation with a man he recognized by his bloodhound face, imposing girth and sorrowful eyes to be Harold Bloom. Ren finally managed to get to White, clasp his hand, and hear his congratulations. "Dynamite!" he said. "Really mind-blowing. You'll get raves – or they'll flay you alive for desecrating a classic. A Christian classic at that." White was a writer Ren revered for his honesty – he never confused fucking with love, never prettied things up in his work – combined with a sensuous, lyrical style. They'd met at a party when Ren's Hamlet was having some success and had a few conversations later about growing up queer. His praise really did it. Ren began to feel that he'd succeeded – that it wasn't just people who knew him and wanted him to do well who liked his show.

When the crowd had thinned out a little, a man came up to Ren and introduced himself as Brent Baldassare, a producer from Rome. He was a slender, handsome man whose blond looks seemed more New England than Italian, and who spoke with fluent assurance, clearly accustomed to getting what he wanted. He told Ren that he loved the play.

"The acting, the setting, the lighting – your interlude with those surreal images – everything, but I liked especially the ambiguity. You don't play it straight but it's not strident. It's playful and serious, *tutto insieme*. Very Roman." Here he laughed. "I'd love you to put it on in Rome this summer. We have a grant, so we'd pay airfare. The salary would be minimal but it would be exciting. We can do it in the Theatro de

Marcellus, you know, in the open air. We'd have to make some adaptations. But I think the setting would go beautifully with your epic vision. And you'd have more space for the dances."

He told Ren that he also had a penthouse apartment he could offer him. That in the spring, he always moved to Todi, a hill town just a couple of hours from Rome. The apartment would be empty.

It sounded fantastic. He told Brent he'd love to do it, but there were some things he had to check out.

"My partner's in the hospital," he said, when the man pressed him. "I have to see how things develop, I'll let you know as soon as I can."

The next morning at five a.m. the phone rang and Ren grabbed it, terrified that it was the hospital, that Jack had had a crisis. But it wasn't the hospital; it was Joe calling with a copy of the *Times* review.

"It's super," Joe was saying. "And long. He liked the acting, too, said it was strong ensemble playing." Ren grabbed a pencil after Joe hung up and jotted down what he remembered as the best points. "Allusive, rich, evocative, a mix of brutality and beauty, chivalry and humor with a surprise twist at the end. Joe Mowana was formidable as the Knight, vibrant playing by the young Ellen Jones as Gawain, strongly partnered by Grace McDonnell. Having McDonnell play a double role as mother and wife was a particularly clever stroke."

It was the sort of review he had dreamed about when he started directing. There simply wasn't anything negative. And this wasn't some small local paper, this was the *Times*. Ren was ecstatic. He could hardly wait until morning to go to the hospital and tell Jack.

CHAPTER TWELVE

Reprieve

he delighted all around him,
and all agreed that day,
they never before had found him
so gracious and so gay.

– *Sir Gawain and The Green Knight*

When Ren woke up again, it was nearly eleven. So late! Jack would have been miserably awake for hours. He jumped out of bed and got into his clothes without washing, then he took them off again and ran into the shower. He couldn't take a chance on bringing in bacteria. He shaved hurriedly, cutting himself on the chin, blotting it with a wisp of toilet paper that stuck there like a white flag, proclaiming his haplessness. He looked a fright, but Jack wasn't in any shape to notice.

On the subway, he sat down opposite an ad for Green Giant frozen peas – the Green Knight reduced to a doltish hawker of vegetables – and looked at his good reviews. Another had come in this morning from *Newsday*, the Long Island paper. It was incredible to him that he was getting such good press. In addition to praising the acting, the pacing and tight construction of the play, Blake Green had actually read the medieval romance and praised Ren's sensitive transformation of the ending, noting that the game playing seemed to serve as a paradigm not just of war, but of Western civilization at its most patriarchal. Ren glowed. He'd not only had a successful opening night, he'd succeeded in transforming a story that had haunted him since he was an adolescent. If only life were so simple.

Meanwhile Brent, the Roman producer, had given him what seemed like an unparalleled opportunity. But he certainly wouldn't leave with Jack still going through hell. Though he should know pretty soon if the transplant was taking. And then? He stared at the ad for Green Giant frozen peas. He had managed to tame the Green Knight. Maybe he should just treat all the tumultuous events going on in his life as plot elements and work with them as if he were doing a rewrite. As long as Jack was seriously ill, Ren assumed the role of chief actor by default – Jack was passive, nailed to his bed. And all Ren's efforts were directed to bringing Jack out alive.

He had literary prototypes for that, of course. Orpheus had gone down to Hades for Euridyce, and Persephone's mother had descended to the dark regions to bring her back. Even Jesus had gone down. Though of course none of them were traipsing after their boyfriends.

But bringing Jack out alive wasn't by any means the end of the story. Going to Rome with Ren would be tantamount to Jack's coming out to Malcolm, and it seemed likely that unless Jack had his father's approval, he wouldn't go. How would a playwright solve that one? The principal difficulty was that Ren couldn't rewrite Jack's part. Or Malcolm's, for that matter. This was where a *deus ex machina* might come in handy, an androgynous angel reaching down a delicate hand to stay the sword.

A crush of people got on at Forty-second Street and Ren distracted himself by thinking of plots in which a patriarchal blueprint is overturned by the sheer force of desire. No luck. Aeneas left Dido and went on to found the Roman empire. Orlando went mad with love but only for awhile, then manfully returned to war. Even Shakespeare couldn't imagine love's triumph – and Cleo wasn't even gay.

Ren shut his eyes and imagined an underworld of blue light getting colder and bluer as an armored figure strode down, trying to make out his love's shape in the misty shadows. He had a long sensitive face and Ren's big lips. His feet clanked. Sweat built up under armor that wasn't meant for a slow slog. But it was always the same – rocks and icy blue and the sense that though he was moving his feet, there was no progress.

When he got to the hospital, it seemed drearier than ever under an overcast sky. The thick black clouds seemed so low he could almost touch them. In the hallway of the transplant floor, he saw a young woman walking with her IV. Bald, pale as a ghost, she wove her way along the corridor.

Ren had the panicky thought that Jack had died while he was savoring his triumph. What if when he got to the room the bed was empty, or Marci was pulling off horribly bloodstained sheets? She'd lift her head and look at him and he'd see it in her eyes. What if Jack had died just at the moment when Ren was thinking of a quick pick-up? The way Jack's photo had fallen from the fridge door when Ren knocked a magnet loose.

He was flooded with relief when he looked through the porthole and saw him. Hairless as a slug, probably still feverish, but there in the bed. Luckily, he was heavily asleep and Ren tiptoed in and threw himself down in the yellow armchair.

When Marci came in around one, Ren was dozing. He heard the door shut and his eyes snapped open.

"Sorry to wake you," she said, giving him a quick appraising glance. "You look a bit peaked."

"You're too polite," he said, "I look like shit. But what's with Jack? He's never slept this late before."

"We gave him something to let him rest. He had a bad night," her lips tightened. "Constant emesis. But he never complains – he's such a sweet guy." Ren looked at her and she blushed. If she said it was bad, it really must have been. He wondered if she had a bit of a crush on Jack. Even in his damaged state, he was beautiful. Marci bent over Jack, picked up his limp wrist and felt for his pulse. It was hard to find. She pursed her lips, concentrating, looking at her watch. It was a

Mickey Mouse. Ren had never noticed it before. Maybe she had a son whose watch she'd borrowed – or a campy streak he hadn't suspected. Seeing her fingers pressing so hard against Jack's vein made him queasy. He had the ridiculous thought that the vein was a frightened animal trying to escape.

Jack strained to open his eyes. They were glued shut. Marci wiped off the gunk with a moistened wipe and he opened them half way. They shone dull green against his unnaturally white skin. "I've brought your stem cells," she said, as he blinked at her uncertainly. "Today's the big day. We're going to do the rescue. You don't have to do anything except relax."

This wasn't a question of cats or maidens. This was going to be the real thing. Ren didn't know what he'd expected. Drums, fanfare . . . a parade. A ceremony where they brought the magical stuff in on a velvet cushion in a crystal box with a gold lid. He imagined Dr. Stevens dressed in scarlet robes, the box in his hand. Nothing would have been too good, too precious for Jack's cells.

Adrenaline started coursing through Ren's body but he couldn't use it. No one to punch. No mountain to scale. Jack's doctor, Dr. Stevens, hadn't even bothered to show up. There was just Marci rummaging in what looked like a cooler. He went over to look. Sloshing around in icy water were some sacks, like giant bags of frozen peas, brought from some subterranean fridge.

"This, " he paused, staring at the ugly plastic sacks, "is all there is?" They were the color of raw salmon.

"Yup, just two of them. It's real easy, they go in just like regular blood," Marci said, misunderstanding him, "but we have to wait till they thaw to infuse them." She had turned on the TV, probably thought it would relax Jack, but the constant stream of mindless babble got on Ren's nerves. He turned it off and started to crack his knuckles. Somehow hope was harder to bear than the constant terror of the last few days.

"It's going to take awhile," she said, taking the sacks out of the water and laying them on the bedside table.

"Let me hold one, it'll thaw faster." He held out a gloved hand. Marci seemed to consider for a moment, then she passed one to him. He hefted it; it must have weighed about a kilo. He wished it weighed ten, was as big as a boulder. He lifted it over his head and paced towards the window and back again, trying to feel as though he were enacting some ancient rite. What he was doing reminded him of something and suddenly he remembered . . . he'd seen his aunt before her remarriage, carrying her bill of divorce around like that. Oh bad. Wrong symbol. He lowered his arms sheepishly.

"I was just getting into it," Marci said. "I was just going to start accompanying you." She started singing softly, "Got the whole world in his hands." She seemed to have understood a little of what he was feeling. Ren smiled at her gratefully.

"I should have brought my rain sticks – we could have done a healing dance."

"Anything that works," she said, "and believe me, I've seen a lot of things. I shouldn't be saying this, but it's a mystery who makes it and who doesn't. But Jack," – her tone was suddenly cheery – "is going to do just great, aren't you, fella?"

Ren turned towards the head of the bed. Jack was actually focusing on them.

"Sure," he croaked.

Ren moved up near Jack's head, holding the bag like a baby in the crook of his arm. "Hey, buddy, you're awake. How are you?"

"My feet itch," Jack whispered.

"His feet itch," Ren repeated to Marci. He was as proud of those three words as if they'd been Einstein's theory of relativity.

Marci lifted the bottom of Jack's blanket and looked at his feet. They were covered with reddish crusts. "It's the fungus flaring up. You can have a bath after the cells go in. That'll help."

"Thanks," Jack said.

"I'm warming up your cells so they'll really work for you." Ren squeezed the bag experimentally; it was softening. "The little devils will be so excited when they get in, they're going to be building blood cells on a round-the-clock basis."

"Pretty pink," Jack murmured.

When the bag went completely soft, Marci emptied it into Jack's catheter. The cells went in with a soft whoosh.

Then Ren and Marci walked Jack to the bathroom for his daily shower. Ren was grateful that she let him stay while she sat Jack on a wooden stool under the shower head and washed him all over. Ren watched while she soaped him carefully with antibacterial soap. She paid special attention to his itchy feet, washing between each toe. The steady plash of water mixed with Ren's exhaustion. Now she was stroking the soft under-belly of Jack's foot. "Feel better?"

"Feel better?" Ren heard his mother's voice as she rubbed soothing ointment on his foot. Once when he couldn't have been more than five, Ren and his father were in Central Park, on Sheep's Meadow, and Ren begged his father to let him take his shoes off, he wanted to run on the grass and feel it on his toes. But as he was running wild with pleasure over the thick grass, he stepped on a wasp, which had stung him right in the softest part of his foot. When he'd run to his father, crying, his father had scolded him and called him sissie. "Boys don't cry," he'd said. Somehow Ren had forgotten till now. It disturbed him.

He saw his father's disapproving face in the steam. It looked a lot like his own face, long and slightly sad. He couldn't pin the look down as the face appeared and disappeared in his mind. He tried to recall being punished, being spanked. Somehow that would have shown him his father cared . . . noticed him. But he couldn't remember his father's hand touching him at all.

"You'll need someone to help you with this when you go home," Marci was saying to Jack. "Your dad was talking about having a trained nurse. Probably a good idea for awhile. "

Ren felt a pain in his heart. So Jack's father was planning to take him home. He looked at Jack sitting there, naked and vulnerable as a baby, hardly able to get two words out. There was no way he could stand up to his father. No way Ren could even start talking to him about it. For a minute he pictured himself as Violetta sitting with her head resting on her arms after she'd renounced Armand. The father striding away in his Victorian suit and waistcoat. But tired as he was, he couldn't accept that for long. Better to confront Malcolm and tell him they loved each other and wanted to live together. That he was going to stay near Jack if he had to chain himself to his bedpost. Maybe it was good that Jack was too weak to protest. Plead for more time to break it to his father gradually. By the time Jack's mind was working again, it would be done. He guessed that Jack was afraid that his father would stop loving him.

There'd been a ghastly letter in the papers the other day from a man whose father had not only denounced him but was pushing a new bill against gay marriage. He was proud of me when I piloted a fighter plane in the war, the man had said, he was proud of my medals, now he's not talking to me. I'm the same man. I'm still his son. Ren shivered. Would he really have the courage to inflict something like that on Jack?

CHAPTER THIRTEEN

skirmishes, or, more games

> . . . the lord of the land is bent on his gaymes
> to hunt . . .
>
> — *Sir Gawain and The Green Knight*

The next day, checking on the ticket sales, Ren found that the show had sold out for the next two months and Patrick, their producer, thought they were looking at a two-year run. Joe and Ellen were in heaven.

When Ren came into Jack's room bursting with good news, he was horrified to find him still vomiting black bile. "His body hasn't responded yet," Marci told Ren, "but it will soon, trust me." She was right.

Five days later Jack's blood cells started to regenerate. His fever subsided and the vomiting stopped. The only thing they were giving him intravenously now was glucose. He was still dead white and hairless, but Ren could see that new nails were beginning to grow, their tiny edges just visible, pushing the yellow dead ones out. Jack couldn't taste anything yet – that might take weeks, Marci told him – but he could swallow water a sip at a time. He was terribly weak, exhausted after the smallest effort. But his beautiful eyes were clear of gunk and, though he spoke haltingly, he made sense.

He was supposed to be ready to leave the hospital in another two weeks and Ren was in an agony of indecision over what to do. He'd told Jack about Rome, of course, and he'd responded just as Ren had feared, by waffling. When Ren persisted, he told him that if the opportunity was too precious to miss, he should go by himself.

Ren ran through technicolor high-action scenarios of confrontation with Jack's father. They worked pretty well as long as he was alone in his bed at home. He could imagine himself knightly and heroic, and he could hear the strong, firm words he was going to say. But when he would meet the man leaving Jack's room the next morning, he'd shrivel up. Even saying, "Hello, Malcolm," made him sweat. Jack's father looked at him the way a blind man might, staring blankly. No, it was much worse than that because a blind man wanted to see what was there and would strain, whole face alert toward the sound. Malcolm simply looked through him at the wall. Ren had to glance down to assure himself his body was still there. He consoled himself that a confrontation was premature. He couldn't risk a blowup. Not yet.

Jack was getting better physically but emotionally he was very fragile – Marci explained it as a reaction to trauma. Like a shell-shocked vet, he cried at the slightest provocation, had night sweats and terrors, and spent much of the hospital day watching TV or just staring at the ceiling. Ren hated to think what would happen if his father made a scene in front of him. He might call a confrontation meeting with the rest of his family – that would be the sort of twelve-step thing he might do – and hire a brainwasher. Ren couldn't really guess what went on in Malcolm's mind; his polished exterior kept him off, like glass.

Though it was painful, Ren tried to think of what he had done in the early days of his relationship with Jack to make Malcolm dislike him so much. Once he started thinking more about it, a host of things came to mind. How he'd insisted that global warming was occurring despite Malcolm's assurance that it was all pseudo-science. Malcolm had been so irritated, his hand started shaking and Ren had wondered if he was going to have a stroke. Then Ren had disagreed with Malcolm's idea of separating black children from their parents and sending them to government-run camps. And worst of all, he'd said – rather heatedly – that tax breaks for the very rich were obscene. How could he have said that? Especially when he'd seen Jack shaking his head, begging him not to.

No wonder Jack's father hated him. He'd been acting like an adolescent. And he knew better. He knew when you were having dinner with a fundamentalist you didn't start talking about the beauty of evolution. He was sensitive enough in other situations. He was the first to be angry if someone made comments about bi's and gays. So why was he cutting his own throat?

If Ren were going to rewrite this, it would have to be pretty dramatic – on the level of Paul writhing in the dust on the road to Tarsus. He wondered if the old guy would believe him if he said he'd found Jesus and converted. Or even better, joined Jews for Jesus. Malcolm always found a way of uniting Christian values with his business practices. Or maybe a political shift would be enough. Congressmen shifted parties sometimes, didn't they? If it was expedient enough.

"Honey, I'm a changed man," Ren said in a husky Marlene Dietrich voice. "You've got to believe me."

He squared his shoulders and examined himself critically. His six feet made him look imposing, as much like an athlete or a movie star as a businessman. Standing straight was good, but not so straight that he looked threatening – stiff but humble. That was the ticket. He inclined his head slightly, practiced in front of the mirror.

"Yes, sir," he said, to the mirror. "Right sir" – clipped off syllables, jaw lifted, looking himself in the eye. Tomorrow, he'd buy himself a costume for the part, a pinstriped suit.

———

He revved himself up thinking of the moment the first review came in and he knew he had a success. It had been like a shot of vodka, hot in his throat and chest. He'd gotten a great review in the *Times*! He still couldn't believe it, had to keep opening it up and reading it again. If he just could bring Malcolm around and get away to Rome with Jack . . . but he needed to hurry. Brent wasn't going to wait forever.

Ren had always studiously avoided the hours when he knew Malcolm would be visiting. (That had been easy enough since he usually went late, after work.) Now, he purposely made their visits at the hospital coincide.

The first few times weren't so bad. He was quiet and respectful, called him sir, and even asked him about how his new book was doing. Jack's father made a few polite comments in return. When Ren overheard him telling Jack that he was thinking of running for some political office, Ren bit his tongue. The thought of all that business gelt pouring into politics was horrifying, but Ren smiled and wished him well. He even asked his advice about the stock market.

But when their visits had overlapped a second and third time, Malcolm began to ignore the fact that Ren was there. He directed himself entirely to Jack, who was propped up on pillows now, pale, eyebrowless, trying to manage tiny bites of cracker or canned – bacteria-free – fruit.

When Marci came in, Malcolm would address her with cheery managerial bluster, but he kept his face turned away from Ren. Apparently, he had seen a good review Ren had brought Jack, on the bedside stand, and it made him even more hostile. Jack told him Malcolm was furious when Jack said he was thrilled the play was being taken seriously. Malcolm had referred to it as "ridiculous campy trash." Ren would have felt like a ghost if Jack hadn't kept catching his eye. Sometimes, when he was out of Malcolm's line of vision, Ren would give Jack's leg a quick pat or squeeze his foot.

As the day of Jack's discharge grew nearer, his father seemed to get more and more nervous. He kept harping on how difficult all the pills and the cleaning routines would be to maintain. How Jack wasn't naturally organized, was in fact, sloppy, and how the trained nurse he'd had hired was going to have to keep after him. Ren sat by, boiling. It was true Jack was a bit sloppy, but he didn't need to be policed by Miss Ratched.

Then Malcolm started in about Jack's job at the Fisheries. The commute was long, the pay was terrible, he had to be out in all weather collecting samples. He knew it would be months before Jack felt up to working again, but when he did, why not switch to a comfy office job? Nothing would be easier than to work for his father. Ren had held his breath for a moment, praying that Jack could insert a casual remark about wanting to go abroad, relax in some beautiful place – at least start laying the groundwork for Rome. But all he said was, "Thanks, Dad. I'll think about it."

When he wasn't pressuring Jack in one way or another, Malcolm would complain about Henny. "This relationship of hers is ridiculous. I've tried all the reasonable arguments I know. When you're better, maybe you can talk some sense into her." One day Ren got there before Jack's father and found Henny talking animatedly to Jack. She and Franco were going to live together. They'd found an apartment in Brooklyn. "It's pretty reasonable price-wise, and there's a tree right in front of the bedroom window." She outlined a curvy shape with her hands. "I can't wait till spring when it gets green. There are lots of nice delis with all you can eat for as little as four dollars. And not too far from Manhattan."

Ren was just thinking how perky and self-confident she looked when Malcolm walked in.

"What's this . . . what's not too far?" he asked after he greeted them.

"Greenspoint, Daddy. I found a place."

"I thought you were going to stay somewhere in the Village – where you'd be near your grad school next year."

"Everything's so expensive," she said and rushed on before he could talk about money. "And besides, it's a great neighborhood."

"Polish immigrants," he said, "if I'm not mistaken."

Somehow she missed the edge in his voice and went on eagerly. "Polish newspapers, Polish store signs, families chattering in a foreign language. It's like being abroad without the hassle . . . I love it."

"How much can it cost to live in the Village? I'm more than glad to pay the difference. Pay the whole thing if it makes it easier for you. I don't like the idea of your taking the subway late at night . . . with all those perverts hanging around."

She laughed. "I'll be fine Dad, and it's so much safer once I get there."

"I don't want you to do this. It's dangerous."

"I'll try it for a semester. You'll see how nice it is and then . . ."

He looked at her and shook his head. "I suppose you're moving in with that Mexican fellow you picked up at the stables. Watch out – next he'll be wanting to marry you so he can get a green card."

Henny stared for a moment then slowly turned red. "He's Bolivian, Papa . . . oh, what difference does it make, you'll never understand. Anyway, you don't have to visit."

His voice changed. "Henny, Henny . . . I don't know why you're doing this to yourself, you're such a beautiful girl."

"And he's a wonderful man . . . he's kind and caring." Her voice caught in her throat. "All the good things."

"All the good things?"

She was trembling on the edge of saying "all the things you're not." Ren could see it in her face. But she couldn't. That little burst of energy was all she had. Now she was afraid.

"Things you don't notice," she said weakly, looking down at her hands. A few minutes later she left, saying she was late for class.

Malcolm sat looking glum. Shoulders stooped as though he'd been the one who was hurt. When Jack asked him what was the matter he said that he was getting old and would love to see him married. "Your sister is such a disappointment. I need some grandchildren I can be proud of."

"Even if I wanted to have children, I'm not sure I could," Jack said.

"Of course you could . . . that's why I insisted they freeze your sperm. You didn't want to think about it but I knew you'd be grateful later."

Ren stared dumbfounded. Jack hadn't breathed a word to him. He was beginning to understand Malcolm's power.

Ren was scared and angry. How much more of himself would Jack be willing to give up?

In the evening, Ren went to see his show again. Even in his depressed mood, it looked good and the audience was just as enthusiastic. Afterwards he went backstage to give them some notes. Joe had muffed a couple of his lines in the first act and there was a missed sound cue. "Just little things," he told them, "but I hope you'll all keep making adjustments. It's important if you want to keep the production fresh." Ren thought he'd come as often as he could.

That night, after waking up with insomnia at four a.m., Ren decided over a bowl of cornflakes with banana that manly aloofness wasn't getting him anywhere in his campaign against Malcolm – besides giving him no chance to talk about either Jesus or the Republicans, it felt so unnatural. It occurred to Ren in the first faint light of dawn that he might play this as a camp role and come on to Malcolm with grotesquely exaggerated submissiveness. Sometimes during really bad fights, he had accused Jack of groveling his way into his father's graces. Maybe in some fantastic miraculous way, it would relieve Jack of his disguises and make him a little freer. More important, it might give Ren access to Malcolm's decisions, his thinking. He'd become an enemy spy, a secret agent.

Later, looking in the bathroom mirror at the shadows under his eyes, he told himself the new idea was one percent invention, ninety-nine percent cowardice. "Forget the secret agent stuff. You never had any guts, girl, that's the truth of it. Furthermore, if you want to look appealing, you've got to get some more sleep. And get a chin strap. My God, the flab!"

He finished shaving fast so he wouldn't have to see himself any longer, and went back to the kitchen, where he made himself a cup of coffee to get his adrenaline pumping. He thought of the queens fighting the police during Stonewall while the clones stood by. But a girl knew that sometimes it was better to take a defensive position. That didn't mean it wasn't war. Ren would draw up plans and lay siege to Jack's father; there must be some way to erase the man's negative perceptions.

He bought some self-help books at the corner drugstore and then on an inspiration, he got Malcolm's book out of the Forty-second Street library. Wasn't the way to a man's heart his reflection in a girl's eyes? The book was thick, with a glossy black and white cover. At first he wondered why the publisher hadn't used color with gilt "bestseller" lettering, but then he realized how brilliant it was: the gloss managed to suggest success and the severe black and white meant getting the job done. Color would have been too shallow.

The book had nice big print and a section on efficient communication as a way of problem solving. Put your cards on the table, Malcolm said: trust that if you're forthright, your employee or your children will be too. Ren thought of himself as an adolescent, stealing women's clothes from the gym lockers so he could try them on at home. Hey, guess what, Mom. Yeah, sure. You could see this was bullshit, but maybe the guy believed it. Ren underlined the subheading "Don't be afraid to admit your faults. Be generous when an employee, following your example, admits his."

Admitting faults was something Ren could relate to. Things had obviously gotten much worse between him and Malcolm after that stupid fight Ren had had with Jack's male nurse during the cell harvest. Ren had to admit to himself that this had been a bad scene – he'd been hysterical with jealousy, might actually have done Jack some damage. And he couldn't really blame the guy for going ballistic when he saw his son's blood spurting from the tube.

He called Malcolm and told him he had something important to tell him. The man sounded cold, but to Ren's surprise agreed to meet him at a coffee shop on Broadway near the hospital. It had been much easier than he thought. Surprisingly easy. Though there was a strange hint of paranoia in Malcolm's voice, almost as though he'd been expecting something. Ren was too agitated to think what.

Ren dressed carefully in monochrome. He really looked sallow but squelched an impulse to put on a little rouge. Save your fire, girl, he told himself. It wouldn't be appreciated. He made a few faces at his image in the mirror. Pretty sincere, he thought, but maybe not manly enough. He bared his teeth a little like a monkey making a threat gesture. "Hey, there you are, Tarzan, ape boy." He scratched mockingly under his arm. "Go for it." Not bad.

He tucked his copy of Malcolm's book under his arm and went down his stairs two at a time. Should have bought it, he thought, then he could have autographed it for me. Crossing Broadway at 110th Street, Ren stepped in a puddle made by melting snow and it went down the inside of his shoe. He had worn his good ones in an effort to look regular. Now there was an unpleasant squishing sound at every step.

He walked into the coffee house, nodded at the man behind the counter and sat at a small black-topped table with chrome legs, looking out the window at the mushy snow and the people walking by. A Latina mother was coping with a tiny tantrumming girl, two beribboned pigtails sticking out from under her snow hat. While he waited, he could feel the damp spread inside his shoe. It had felt warm when he was walking but now it was icy cold. And it seemed to be taking his courage with it. He tried to remember an article he'd read about wet feet undermining morale, something about soles and souls. He reached down and slipped his foot out, blotted the inside of his shoe with his napkin. He wondered if he dared squeeze out his sock, maybe even lay it on the heat vent behind the table, but decided it was too risky. Malcolm was already ten minutes late. He slipped his foot back in the shoe and resumed his vigil.

An old woman with a thin, proud face walked by the window, slowly leaning on two canes. As she was almost past him, she slipped, but before she hit the ground someone had caught her arm and was lifting her up. It was Malcolm, and Ren noticed in amazement that his face had taken on a tenderly concerned look. She was obviously thanking him profusely and he just as graciously was denying anything special. His face changed so much, his expression was almost motherly: his eyes widened and rested on the woman's face, his mouth softened. But before Ren could grasp it, it was over.

The next minute, Malcolm walked in briskly, looking around him. Ren leapt up and stuck his hand out.

"That poor woman," he said. "Lucky you were there." Malcolm grimaced slightly as if he'd been caught filching from the till, then took his hand and gave it a perfunctory shake.

"More sensible to stay inside on a day like this, or have someone to walk with you – but old people often insist on being independent."

If Ren hadn't seen him helping the woman just a moment before, he wouldn't have believed that he'd done it. Would have thought he'd just scurry by with that blank stare. Could it be that his coldness was some sort of pose?

"I had an aunt like that," Ren said. "She was that way until she died . . . never would accept any help. Not even Meals on Wheels."

"It's admirable, really," Malcolm said, "but I suppose difficult if you're the one taking care." Ren nodded, venturing a half smile. Could it be that they were getting along?

The waitress came by with the coffee while Ren was still bemused by the hints of softness in Malcolm's face. He was so absorbed that when he lifted his cup to his lips, he missed and sloshed coffee on his tie. Without thinking he blotted it with his wet and dirty napkin and accidentally brushed against Malcolm's arm.

"Careful, there," Malcolm said, drawing in his chest defensively as he looked down at the brown pool in his saucer.

"Oh sorry, sorry, oh dear . . . Is there any on your clothes?" Ren hovered with his napkin at the ready.

"Please," Malcolm raised his arm, warding Ren off. "I'm afraid that will make matters worse. Waitress," he called, and the girl hurried over – the place was almost empty – "we need a fresh napkin and another saucer, if you don't mind." He gave Ren a look somewhere between scorn and pity.

"No problem," she said, snapping what looked like bubble gum. Pink and huge. "Anything else for you, sir?"

Red-faced and desperate for a sugar hit, Ren ordered a donut. Eating might give him a chance to collect his force and regroup. "They're expecting a big storm tomorrow," he said, hoping they could have a few minutes of truce, of small talk. But Malcolm wasn't helping him out. He just made a slight humming sound to show he'd heard, then took a sip of his coffee and sat stiff and silent, waiting.

"I was reading your book," Ren said finally. He could feel sugared crumbs sticking around his mouth, making him look ridiculous. "I liked what you said about putting your cards on the table," he said. "I'd like to try." There was no glint of recognition of his own words in Malcolm's eye. Perspiration beaded on Ren's forehead. He tried another line, the one he'd underlined. "I thought it might help if I admitted my faults." Still no response. Maybe the guy had his books ghostwritten or perhaps he'd written so many he couldn't remember individual lines. "Anyway, I'm really sorry for what happened with Jack's nurse."

Jack's father shook his cuff back and glanced at his Rolex. "I'm not sure I know what you're talking about," he said in a flat voice. "What nurse?"

"When I, you know, got excited and . . . I bumped his arm."

Jack's father looked at him as though he were mentally deficient.

"I gave up a meeting this morning because I thought you had something important to say to me. I'd appreciate it if you came to the point."

"Maybe you don't remember. When Jack was having the harvesting . . . I accidentally bumped his arm . . . the needle came out . . . and blood."

"Stop, stop right there. Yes, I remember, but it's not worth going over, it won't change anything." His voice seemed suddenly tired.

"But I want to apologize." Ren was leaning forward over the table. He knew he should stop . . . pack it up, retreat, but he couldn't. The man's coldness was driving him crazy.

"Don't you understand? I just told you, I'm not aware of anything needing an apology – and if you had any sense of yourself, you wouldn't be here."

"I was stressed out. I'm sure you were too."

"I was not stressed out, as you put it. I have my nerves under control, as you should know if you've read my book. We're clearly not organized the same way. When something unpleasant happens, I put it out of my mind."

"But it's affecting how we get along."

"We clearly don't get along. The best thing we could do would be to avoid each other. We have nothing in common."

"We have Jack."

"Look, Ren. You want me to put my cards on the table . . . tit for tat. Is that what you want?"

Ren nodded.

"No. What you really want is to work up a drama with me. But I just don't respond that way. You think if you say you're sorry, I'll forgive you. Isn't that the kind of thing you want? The sort of thing that happens in cheap movies? And we'll all live happily ever after. But it's not going to happen. Jack's been through a terrible ordeal and I'd be a lousy human being if I didn't acknowledge that you've helped keep him going." He rubbed his hand across his lips – almost, Ren thought, as if he were unzipping them. "But you're just not the sort of person I would have imagined as my son's" – he paused – "companion. Maybe you're not a bad person. The nurse told me how much you helped him. I can see you care for him. But I can't really see that he's going to be happy. And because I love my son, I can't just stand by and . . . Surely you can understand?" It all went by so fast Ren wasn't sure whether he'd filled the pauses correctly, whether Malcolm knew or at least guessed. Whether it was, in fact, exactly their love that he was so opposed to. Ren was just organizing his thoughts around this possibility when Malcolm leaned towards him.

"Believe me, I know it's a sacrifice and I'd like to make it easier for you."

Ren saw him reach into his pocket. Oh God, was he taking out his wallet? Did he think he could buy him off?

"No, please. How could you think . . . " he stopped, too upset to talk. Malcolm blushed slightly. It was a reputable business tactic from his point of view. He'd been so sure it would work. "Well . . . you win some . . ." he started, but then there was nothing else to say except, "Goodbye." Taking care to avoid each other's eyes, they pushed back from the table, Ren ostentatiously taking the bill. It wasn't until he got far enough away to make sure Malcolm wouldn't see him that he started to run, stumbling over his shoelaces, tears of rage streaming down his starched collar.

CHAPTER FOURTEEN

Temptations

and she called gawain to her bed and sweetly she spoke
each morning [when] the host went to hunt
he left his lady behinde that was so blythe

great peril between them stood
if mary had not remembered her knight.

— *Sir Gawain and The Green Knight*

Ren tore off his tie when he got home and threw it into a corner; he stepped out of his pants, then stomped on them, kicked them. He threw the jacket after the pants. The physical movement gave him some relief. "Nasty things," he said, "filthy, nasty things."

He paced the room. His toiletries were all set out on the dressing table, his silk kimono hanging neatly from its hook, the bed made. After awhile he couldn't stand to see the clothes abjectly crumpled on the floor. It wasn't their fault, after all, that their owner was such a nasty item. He thought of Malcolm's hand with its perfectly manicured nails, the square fingers a little like Jack's.

He'd have to think of some other plan; everyone had a weak spot somewhere. The Trojans, for instance, just couldn't resist that horse. He pictured himself for a minute hiding in the swelling wood body, fully armed. He could almost feel the jolting of the wheels as the horse was trundled inside the stone gates. He imagined Malcolm peacefully sleeping in a towered room, his scornful face relaxed in dreams, then open-mouthed as he woke to see Ren standing in the doorway. You know what I've come for, he'd say – Jack.

You irrational, stupid Mary, he told himself. First you let him insult you and then . . . then what? Tell yourself fairy stories. With you as the fairy queen. With your luck, the horse would lose an axle going in. He bent and picked up his trousers – the light wool was deliciously soft and had a faint tang of sweat. Then he folded them neatly and put them in a plastic bag along with the jacket. That was it with the suit disguise.

He spent the rest of the afternoon spelunking for ideas about how to spirit Jack off to Rome and came up with zilch. Everything required money – and though his show was doing well, the percentage he expected for a long run, $500 a week, just wasn't enough. Even if the apartment in Rome was free, he'd still have the cost of his apartment here; his landlady was adamant about not subletting. And he'd have the utilities to pay in Rome and food for them both and clothes, everything double . . . when he lived by himself he'd done everything as cheaply as possible, but he couldn't with Jack, and Jack would have other needs besides: medicines, frequent check-ups – all the extra things not covered by his insurance.

When he figured Malcolm would certainly have left the hospital, he called Jack. Jack sounded tired. Marci had made him get on the exercise bike that afternoon to try and get some tone back in his muscles. It had worn him out. Ren knew he shouldn't bring up Malcolm, especially not so soon, when Ren was still seething. But he couldn't stop himself.

"I saw your father for coffee this morning," he blurted out when there was a silent moment. "It didn't go well." It went like shit was more like it.

"What'd you say?" Jack asked, his voice tense.

Ren felt a flush of anger. Right away he's worried about his father's feelings, what about mine? Which one of us is it? "Nothing incriminating, if that's what you're worrying about," he said with an edge of irony. "I just apologized for my terminal lack of cool."

"Oh," Jack said. "Don't get huffy. I didn't think you'd mess up. You know we have to give him time to get used to things."

Ren bristled at the way Jack said "You know" – sort of the way you'd say to a child, "You know your spinach is good for you."

"Baby doll, I love you, but it's not working that way. I don't want to give you heartache. But I have to give Brent an answer about Rome pretty soon or he's going to look somewhere else. For God's sake, I tried, I really did, but it's no good. We're no further along than we were months ago or last year." Worse, much worse, if Jack knew how things had gone. The awful thought crossed his mind that Jack wouldn't be sorry for him, wouldn't kiss and console him, but would be horrified that the jig was up, that the old man would guess. "How can he get used to things, when you don't give him a clue?"

"I think he's beginning to get it," Jack said. "He's been talking about lifestyles a lot lately."

"Lifestyles! I bet . . . 'I just don't know why some people choose the self-destructive lifestyles they do,'" he said primly. "You mean like that?"

"Ren!"

"Sweetie, I'm not beating up on you . . . try not to hear it that way . . . try to listen. Think a little. You told me yourself how upset he was when a gay couple wanted to move into his apartment building."

"Yeah but . . . "

Ren could imagine the parts of the conversation Jack hadn't repeated to him: Just because some of them have business smarts, doesn't mean we want them ogling our prepubescent sons in the elevators. Once one of them gets in, all the rest will follow like a gaggle of geese and before you know it, it'll be a fag building. "Jack, face it, he hates gays."

"He's a good person, that's what you don't see, a decent person . . . he's got some prejudices . . . I admit that . . . It's the way he was raised. It's hard to overcome."

"That's how you were raised too. Are you prejudiced?"

"Believe it or not, I had to work on it. He will too. I know it. He'll come around."

"Work on it how? Work on it . . . after everything we've been through together, you're still ashamed . . . if you felt really good about yourself, you'd tell him." If he could afford it, Ren thought, he'd hire a hit man.

"No I wouldn't. He's not ready. He's been very good to me, Ren . . . He doesn't show what he feels the way you do, but it's there . . . he cares."

"If Hitler came along tomorrow and asked him to gas the queers along with the Jews, he'd do it."

"You're pushing it, Ren. I may not like everything he does, but loving and liking isn't always the same. I love him. You've got to get that through your head. Stop fighting it or you're going to . . . " he stopped. Ren could hear the tiredness thickening his voice.

"Going to break us up," Ren persisted. "Is that what you were going to say – blood is thicker than water?"

"I can't listen to anymore of this now, Ren, I've got to rest . . . "

"Wait, I just want to say one more thing," Ren said before he heard the faint click of the receiver being put down. Fuck it.

He threw on his coat and pulled on a knit cap and gloves. Then he bent, picked up the bagged suit and ran down the stairs. There was a little table in the entry hall where people put things they wanted to give away. He threw down the bag and walked out with his collar up. People usually left jars of pickles or books with tattered covers or broken umbrellas. He thought bitterly of some guy gasping with pleasure when he saw the Prada label. Well, let him enjoy it . . . the whole charade had been a mistake. Maybe if Ren had been truly sorry, the man would have responded differently. But he doubted it. He could no more have fooled Malcolm into thinking Ren was his obedient vassal – repenting his mistake – than Tiny Tim

could substitute for Babe Ruth. He should have known it
wouldn't work. He was on a different playing field, a field
where the costumes and the rules were fluid. He should have
tried to use what he had. But what was that exactly? It was easier to say what it wasn't. Tantrums, for instance, relieving as
they were, obviously didn't help much.

He started walking without thinking where he was going,
his hands clenched in his pocket. He passed the little boutique
where he usually liked to look at *tchatchkas* and scowled at
himself in the window. You look seedy, he thought, no wonder
Jack doesn't want to own you, no one would – then he stopped
himself. Arguments with Jack about Malcolm always
depressed him, no matter how good things were otherwise . . .
if he didn't watch it, pretty soon he'd be telling himself he did-
n't deserve his success. He thought briefly of going back and
making himself gorgeous, going out on the town: trendy director hits nightspots in Big Apple. But he was too upset and
angry to enjoy himself. Screw Malcolm. Think, he told himself, try to be rational, think. He stared at a lamp with a braided brass base. In comic books, characters were always having
light bulbs flash over their heads when they got a great idea,
but the only thing that came to Ren was that the neighborhood
was getting gentrified and someday his landlady was going to
raise the rent.

It wasn't too cold. The snow had been melting since
morning. He turned down West Street with its hum of traffic,
past the junky buildings until he got to the piers. It was well
after dark, the moon was up and almost full. For a moment,
he thought he saw a figure on the pier that reminded him of
Jack. His heart beat faster. The illusion was so compelling that
he was ready to call out. Then he saw it was some old boxes
covered with a tarp that flapped in the light wind like arms
beckoning. When he was in the mood for sex he misread signs
. . . quick freight would be "quick fuck," or rap center, "rape
center." He looked furtively at the pier. Nope, not even some
broken-down troll wanting a quickie. And if there had been?

He moved on, shoulders hunched like an old man. Even if someone was cruising, he thought, they wouldn't give him a second look.

He kept going through the park, where patches of dry grass were beginning to show like charred flesh through the melt. The Hudson stretched out next to the esplanade like a broad, dark avenue. He peered at it looking for signs of the pollution that Jack was always talking about – floating condoms, bottles. But it was all rippling black skin, lit here and there by moonlight. Poor Jack, trying to clean up everyone's act. Polluters of all stripes. Hidden dirt. He remembered Jack sitting in the kitchen before all this started, telling him about the latest disaster at work, an oil leak from a barge or something like that . . . his shirt had been open and he was looking so adorable that Ren had gone to him and kissed him, licked the jam off his cheek.

"Cut it out Ren, I'm trying to tell you something important."

But Jack still didn't understand that his father was one of the worst guys around. Even if the Green Knight's ax was directly in front of him, Jack would manage not to see it.

Ren walked along the esplanade, looking at the water and thinking angrily about Malcolm. There had to be some way to get at the bastard. He was beginning to feel the slightly drunken high you get from long walking. His legs seemed to move almost by themselves though his fingers were starting to feel slightly numb despite the gloves. He stuck them into his pockets and kept on going through Battery Park, then turned in towards the financial district. The huge skyscrapers stared down at him with their lighted, empty eyes.

He wondered if Malcolm's office was down here, in one of these fortress towers. In the daytime, the streets would be crawling with striding men and women clutching their briefcases containing their modern weapon: the laptop which could zap out into space and bring back riches – stock quotes, theater tickets, jewels – or could bombard a rival company with e-mails, spar with a rival CEO. There was something beautiful about it, which he glimpsed for a moment – the reach, the imagination that made it possible. But then his anger clicked back in and the buildings were again part of the evil empire. He ignored the striking silhouette of Trinity Church with its historic spire, and muttering about Caesar and God back to back, he continued in his slow loop towards home.

He had almost reached his neighborhood, when he began to drift imperceptibly west again. He was very tired but he couldn't stand the idea of going to his apartment. He had thought and thought, but was getting nowhere. His mind kept going round in a circle of vengeful fantasies that didn't do him any good . . . accidents, disease, anything to rid him of Malcolm. But always like a dark light behind the victorious scenarios was the knowledge that Ren wasn't going to get what he wanted. Jack wasn't going to tell Malcolm, and his physical weakness would make him a virtual prisoner in his father's house.

Ren had an image of Jack standing wistfully by his bedroom window after a brainwashing session with Papa. His cropped head was just beginning to show a faint golden fuzz, but as Ren watched, it grew into a long thick coil that Jack let down like Rapunzel for Ren to climb up and rescue him.

Deep in his fantasy, Ren hardly noticed the men who slowed down as they passed to give him a quick appraising look, flicking their eyes over him. When he saw a tall bearded man approaching him he flinched, expecting some sort of retribution for his secret thoughts – but the man slouched furtively by him, trying to hide his beard under his collar. At the same time, Ren noticed a tall long-haired trannie in a doorway, and he realized he was in the meat-packing district. The man was a Hasid. He watched as he approached the hustler and felt unexpected pity. Poor fellow, he probably had seven kids at home and a wife covered from prow to stern. If they caught him, his coreligionists would happily stone him to death.

He stopped in front of a dingy doorway. Without letting himself know where he was headed, he'd ended up in front of The Crown Jewels, one of the sleazier clubs. He'd been there once with a friend. He hesitated. They didn't cater to queens – and it wasn't the sort of place he would have gone to if he'd been dressed up – he wouldn't have wanted to dirty his costume. But he was in jeans and there was something appealing about the place tonight. It would be dark, no questions, no conversation, no faces that weren't Jack's.

He had no trouble getting in. He took off his clothes and put them in one of the tiny cubbies provided. No one else was there at the moment. The entryway was like a narrow tunnel leading to a swelling dimly lit space. Partitions had been set up dividing some of the space into irregular rooms using what was probably plywood covered with purple velvet curtains. At first he felt dubious. He could have done a better imitation of a Victorian brothel himself, could have made something classy, like the setting for the orgy scenes in *Eyes Wide Shut*. This was tawdry. But as soon as he went a little way in, the darkness and the odd spaces took him over. He seemed to shrink and then grew bigger. Soon he was lost, confused about his direction. He breathed in the dank musty smell mixed with the odors of sweat. Everywhere there were muffled sounds, as though some hidden animal were breathing. It excited him. While Jack seemed in acute danger of dying, Ren hadn't felt any sexual urges at all – his anxiety had kept them down. But as soon as Jack started to manufacture his own cells, as soon as his temperature stayed at 98 and he was lucid again, Ren's desire came back in a rush. He'd been doing the usual but it didn't seem to help.

He crept along, feeling the velvet walls, trying to accustom his eyes to the half-light. His fingers, feeling the velvet wall like a blind man, suddenly sank into the wall. He moved them further in and saw a pinprick of light. He bent to put his eye to the hole and saw there were candles on the floor and a naked figure splayed out on a table. A tall woman – probably a trannie – was wielding a birch. She was dressed in a heavy gown cut below her full breasts like the snake goddesses of Crete. The candle made her gorgeous.

What would it be like to give up your thing, he wondered, be spliced? He'd never been tempted, but she was sensational. He watched – bent over to the crinkled opening – as the rod came down with hypnotic regularity on the man's firm, tight buttocks and his white skin, silky and tender as a young boy's, reddened under the blows. The man writhed voluptuously against the leather restraint and for a moment Ren glimpsed hairy balls and a deliciously thick, straining penis between his open legs. The mix of strength and soft helplessness intoxicated him. There was no sound. It could all have been a dream.

When the man on the table started to moan softly, pressing himself against the table, Ren felt himself harden. As the trannie raised her arm, his own arm, which was up next to his face on the wall, tensed in response and he grunted as though he'd struck a blow himself. It felt good.

Suddenly he saw a collection of heavy paddles on the floor next to the trannie. Without thinking, he found himself groping for the door. When it opened easily he glided to the paddle and picked up the heaviest. The trannie took a graceful step back and nodded to him. He had never beat anyone but now he raised the paddle and brought it down with all his strength, with all the frustration of the day behind it, until the man cried out, "Enough!" and the snake woman motioned him to stop. Breathless with his exertion but with a giant erection, he stumbled out into the narrow corridor.

He could almost see now. Enough to make out a chamber pot attached to a wall. His fingers found the view hole and he peered through. Bathtubs with claw feet, figures lying in each of them while in each one a man stood holding his penis, like Mannikin Pis. Golden streams. Not what he wanted, but the sight of the soft penis of the man nearest him excited him. The man seemed very young and was wearing a white shift like an altar boy, which he was holding up above his waist with one hand. The boy had stopped and was shaking his penis, holding it delicately between first and middle fingers. He was almost near enough to touch. Ren had had fantasies about choir boys, about lifting those girlish robes and introducing them to sex. He thought for a moment of putting his arm through the hole, but it was too small. His erection was bucking like a horse wanting to get free of the rein. He gave himself a promissory squeeze. And kept on, stiff-legged with urgency, feeling his way down the narrow hall.

Finally, at the end of the warehouse, there were small bare rooms in which there was no pretense of artfulness. Several had lone men sitting on benches in the corner. Men obviously too old or unattractive to show themselves, skulked in the dark until someone came and offered. He hesitated, the man beckoned obscurely but Ren moved on, he didn't want that much contact with another person.

What he wanted was the room with holes at waist height around it and a matching room on the other side. And soon he found it. He wasn't thinking anymore. It was glorious in a way to be as intent as a hunting animal, every part of him focused on getting it off. The excitement built as an anonymous mouth closed on him from the other side of the wall, anonymous lips and tongue teased his prick, teeth encircling the head of his penis, adding the extra thrill of danger, then steadily moving until all the humiliations of the day were forgotten in a whoosh of juice.

Afterwards, he just wanted to leave fast. Hurrying out, he bumped into a naked figure coming equally swiftly from the room next door. Head down, he clutched at the man to steady himself, noted the slight paunch of a middle-aged body, grayish in the dim light, the long pale feet with a bunion. Vulnerable feet, he thought in that fleeting second. The man cursed under his breath – a strangely familiar sound, and then he looked up, scrunching his eyes into peering slits.

Even in the dim light, Ren could see that he knew the man – it was Malcolm. And his heart gave a great lurch. It was Malcolm standing there naked in front of him, then scowling and moving away quickly down the thin corridor. Ren's instinctive reaction was terror. Malcolm had seen him. He'd been trailing him. He was going to tell Jack. Or maybe – the thoughts took place in the fraction of a second under his mind's skin – the cops were doing a sweep and Malcolm had been put in charge. But cops didn't run around naked with dangling limp pricks.

As Ren fumbled into his clothes, the obvious fact hit him that Malcolm was there for the same thing Ren was. He might even have been the guy on the other side of the hole. His mind boggled at that. The shift in view was too sudden, like those figures of beauties who turn into hunchback witches when you tilt the page. Running out the front door of the club, it dawned on Ren with full force that God or some demon had delivered his enemy into his hands.

CHAPTER FIFTEEN

SECRETS

gawain knelt on his knees, neck bared for the blow.
the knight dreadful in green, made two feints with his axe
then sayde he low "your secret i wiss,"
and lifting his great axe knicked the skin of his neck
so the bright blood flowed his shoulders bye.

– Sir Gawain and The Green Knight

Once outside, Ren took in great gulps of the night air. He was exhausted but exhilarated, drunk with adrenaline and the sense that unexpectedly he'd gotten the advantage. The sky was just beginning to freshen, gearing up for dawn display. Even the hookers had gone from their doorways, except for one who was grimly waiting with hand on hip for morning trade.

It was so cliché, Ren thought, as he turned the corner and headed home. Like what was that movie? American something, where the fag-hating marine turns out to be gay? He could see the headlines: Basher Businessman Has Pink Undies. Industry's Prime Knight Caught with His Pants Down. Green Giant's Escutcheon Smirched. Right-Winger Shows Wrong Stuff.

A garbage truck rumbled by, jolting over the cobblestones. Maybe he should have run after Malcolm. Should have caught his arm and said something like, "Well, darling, here we both are . . . shall we go out for a drink and have a laugh? Is it all going to be one big happy family now? Is that what it's going to be?"

As he got nearer his place, he walked in the middle of the street, liking the look of the cobblestones in the fresh light. When he got to the outer door of his house and tried the lock he saw his hands were trembling. Nerves overloaded. He let himself in and went up the creaky stairs, thinking about how he'd seen Malcolm's pale feet in the hallway of the club . . . and the mind-blowing second when he'd recognized his features.

His mind was racing too hard to let him sleep, so he just lay on his bed, fully dressed, listening to the gurgle of water in the pipes. Above it, he heard the yowl of a cat, probably Horace. Poor Sarah, stuck with that crazed cat and her fucked up love life. Someday he was sure he was going to wake up and see the ambulance men carrying her out on a stretcher. God, how astonishingly lucky he was to have found Jack. A moment later, something clicked into place like the tumblers of a lock. Ren jumped out of bed and gave a shout.

Then he went over to the table, tore a sheet from his production notebook, sat down, and began a letter:

Dear Malcolm,
    You and I both know how things stand. The question is, what are we going to do about it?
    You thought your family was keeping you safe. Okay, you're not the first to do that and I'm not into outing people.

He stopped and made a thick line through "and I'm not into outing people."

    But I hate . . . I really can't stand . . . the way you've treated me. Was it really necessary to make me feel like shit? More to the point, to make your own son terrified to tell you the truth about himself? What do you think it did to him seeing you publicly support antigay legislation? What kind of a message . . . (here his letter broke down into fragments peppered with ellipses and dashes) . . . you hypocritical bastard . . . you don't deserve him . . . don't deserve a son like Jack.

He ground to a halt. It was all true but somehow wrong. Too personal. He looked around his dimly lit room. His glance traveled around the walls, taking in his blue wig on its hook, the animal masks on the wall, an elaborately framed photo of him and Jack on a Hudson pier, and came to rest on the mock-up of the Green Knight's head that he was using as a paperweight. He took up another sheet and wrote all in a rush.

Dear Malcolm,
How would you like seeing your name all over the front page? Well that's what's going to happen if you don't deliver $100,000 in unmarked bills . . .

Oh, shit no, that sounded like a grade B movie. But it gave him an idea. What if he were directing a play whose climax hinged on a letter? Yes, maybe thinking of it that way would rouse his instinct for the right gestures. He started the way he often did, with mood. The lights would be dim the way they were now in his room, but there wouldn't just be him, there'd be Sarah asleep on the bed like some character from Tennessee Williams – and there'd be a yellow spotlight on Ren and a blue gel on Sarah . . . to stress the contrast between them . . . one going up toward freedom and the other, stuck and sinking. You should be able to see from the lights alone that in no way did Ren want to end up like her.

Ren gave a strangled laugh. It was bizarre, but the mental experiment was helping. His stomach stopped contracting and he was able to take a few deep breaths. The next second it became obvious that he shouldn't give Malcolm the satisfaction of seeing how much he'd hurt him. It was gratuitous and certainly wouldn't get results. Malcolm had already shown he enjoyed hurting him. Pretending to be a street tough wouldn't work either. Ren crumpled his last attempt into a ball and sat squeezing it slowly, waiting for it to tell him the shape of his letter. When he picked up his pen, he didn't feel vindictive, certainly not criminal – feelings that had inhibited him before. By some inner alchemy what he was doing seemed almost virtuous:

he was engaged in telling a simple truth, being painfully hon-
est. The letter almost wrote itself.

> Dear Malcolm,
>   I want to take Jack to Rome with me as soon as he
> is well enough to travel. He'll need an allowance. He'll
> also need your tacit approval. The same goes for when
> we return and set up house together. I don't like to
> threaten, but I'm sure you wouldn't want our surprise
> meeting talked about.
>
>   Yours,
>   Ren

He wanted Malcolm to get it first thing in the morning, so
he opened his laptop, typed it in and sent it off. Luckily, he'd
noted the address when Jack's phone was down and Jack had
sent his father an e-mail. Then Ren got into bed quietly and
fell into a deep sleep.

At ten, when he woke up, he made himself a strong cup of
coffee and went into his e-mail. He sipped the hot liquid, feeling his heart begin to pick up pace, and brought up Malcolm's
answer.

> Dear Ren,
>   I can't imagine what you are talking about. I was
> playing cards with some friends last night (who would be
> glad to vouch for me) and didn't go out at all. If you
> thought you saw me somewhere (and that this gave you
> some kind of leverage with me), I am forced to conclude
> you were drunk or high. In any case, it would be my
> word against yours. Someone less benign than I am
> would probably bring charges for attempted blackmail.
> I'll settle for an apology. I think by the way that it
> would be a good idea for you to go abroad for awhile. It
> would give Jack a chance to recover and get on with his
> life.
>   Yours,

The letter wasn't signed. Ren sat still for a minute in shock. The awful arrogance of the man. He'd baldly denied it. And not only that, he'd threatened him. That suggestion that he go abroad was surely a veiled threat. Was it also an offer to pay him off? To pay him to leave town? And if he didn't? Would Malcolm really bring charges for attempted blackmail? Ren didn't think he'd do it because of Jack, but if he did, it would be a nightmare. As Malcolm said, it was his word against Ren's. What could Ren do?

One thing was clear: he had to get something or someone to validate his story. Find an old lover or an enemy who was willing to talk. But he knew so little about Malcolm's life or the people he saw. It wasn't as though they frequented the same circles. And Malcolm had never even had him over to the house with anyone else. If he tried to pry information out of Malcolm's maid, whom Ren knew by sight, she'd probably go right back and report it to her employer. Malcolm probably didn't bring pick-ups back to his apartment anyway. Maybe Ren could hire a detective? The way people used to do before no-fault divorce. Ren rejected that immediately. It would cost way too much, but it gave him an idea. Why couldn't Ren do the footwork? He could find out where Malcolm worked, observe his comings and goings – from a safe distance of course . . . and pray that something useful would turn up.

Last summer he'd seen a spine-tingling detective thriller where the hero had tailed a suspect through the streets of Paris, trying to catch him red-handed. The detective's patience had paid off, but even if it hadn't, Ren might have tried his approach. It appealed to his need for action and used his skill at transformation.

First, Ren found Malcolm's work address – he already knew where he lived – and when he usually visited Jack at the hospital. Then, since he decided it was too risky to trail Malcolm without changing his appearance, he carefully selected several different disguises.

Ren's play was up and running well; he figured the actors could do without him for awhile. For the next few days, wearing different costumes, starting with shades, a hat pulled down low and a lined raincoat similar to the one in the movie, he shadowed Malcolm. He was nervous about being spotted and kept a cautious distance, but he needn't have worried. A seasoned actor had to be adept at vanishing into the background when it was necessary. No one looked twice at him, strolling along with a newspaper tucked under his arm.

And keeping track of Malcolm wasn't as difficult as he'd feared. Every day Malcolm went jogging around seven o'clock and was off to work by eight-thirty. He didn't go out for lunch. Once Ren had determined that Malcolm was more or less chained to his desk during work hours, he felt free to visit Jack again during the day. Malcolm stayed at his office until six o'clock. Then, during the hospital dinner hour, he visited Jack. By the third day, Ren, wearing a knit cap and a fake beard, began to worry. Was Malcolm just going to shuffle innocently back and forth between office, hospital and home? That night when Malcolm left the hospital, Ren noticed a handsome man approach Malcolm, swaying his hips provocatively. Ren tensed expectantly, but Malcolm walked right by.

Could Ren have imagined the whole thing? Or if he hadn't imagined it, maybe The Crown Jewels was an anomaly. A one-shot occurrence. Unprovable. Still, Malcolm seemed restless. When he took an express down to the Village, Ren followed him, swaying on a strap, watching from the next car. After an hour of seemingly aimless wandering past shops and bistros, it started to spit, half snow, half rain.

It was eleven o'clock and Ren was about ready to call it quits when Malcolm stopped in front of a bar, looked around – Ren ducked quickly into a nearby doorway – then went in. Ren stared at the painted sign: The Trojan Horse. He felt adrenaline surge through him. A gay bar. Malcolm had just gone into a gay bar. And it wasn't just to ask for a drink of water. Ren could have done a victory dance right there in the street – he hadn't been hallucinating and Malcolm had given him a second chance.

Ren stationed himself in a doorway where he could see the entrance. In a few minutes Malcolm came out again with a pick-up. The man was wearing a pea coat and a knit cap like Ren's – definitely rough and very drunk.

This was Saturday night and Malcolm went to the bar Sunday, too – Ren thought these were probably his regular days – and each time he picked up someone different. But both of them were big, husky men with slightly foolish drunken smiles. One was wearing leather and resembled Joe. That gave Ren another idea.

"So that's it." Joe looked up from studying Malcolm's e-mail, which Ren had printed out, and which was now spread out on greasy oilcloth at the all-night diner near the theater.

"Definitely not a nice guy," Joe said, disentangling a gold earring ensnared by his black turtleneck, "and not about to give in easily . . . you obviously need someone to catch him in the act."

"Will you help me?"

"I don't see myself as your fellow detective, Ren. Tina Turner, yes, detective no . . . " He rolled his eyes. "But, seriously, sure I'll help. You know what a romantic I am. If Romeo and Juliet were to run in here right now, I'd help them too. What do you want me to do?"

"Malcolm's giving one of his inspirational readings at Barnes and Noble on Astor Place tomorrow night. You have no show that night. I want you to go, get a good look at him."

"Oh goody, a pick-up." Joe batted his eyelashes, which were exceedingly long and lush. "The compliments will be so thick, he'll need a shovel to deal with them. Oh, *che grand uomo* . . . what a great speaker you are . . . such power, such big success . . . I love ze big success, it turns me on." He shivered suggestively and despite his worry, Ren couldn't help smiling at the speed with which Joe could drop into a character.

"Actually, I just want you to be able to recognize him when you see him again. I think it would be better if you came on to him in the bar he frequents. He probably likes to keep things separate. At the reading there'd be a chance that someone he knew would see him. This way, you'll simply show up on the next bar stool." Luckily, there'd been no photos of Joe without his make-up as The Green Knight, so there was no chance Malcolm would recognize him.

"What makes you think he'd like me?" Joe eyed himself in the dusky mirror lining their booth.

"He likes big men with easy grins . . . and you're not bad looking."

"Not bad looking! I'm gorgeous . . . I wonder what I should wear. I've a perfectly fantastic cocktail dress – no pun intended – black, low-cut . . . but it's probably not the thing." Joe grinned. He was clearly enjoying this, but Ren was sure it wasn't all fun and games. He remembered a conversation where Joe had described the nastiest of his new boyfriend's commanding officers as "a vicious closet case."

"Sorry. He doesn't like pretty, he likes hunks," Ren said, "naive hunks, I think – there was a sort of country bumpkin look about his pick-ups."

"Thanks a lot." Joe said.

"It was just a suggestion."

"I've turned enough tricks in my time to know how to do this. I even have a hole in my bedroom wall that will be perfect for taking pictures . . . Don't ask me how I know . . . " Joe cupped his chin demurely. "No, seriously, I have an old lover who I'm sure will take them for us, he likes 'interesting' situations . . . and he's an undiscovered Mapplethorpe."

"We don't need art – we just have to see Malcolm's face while you two are doing it. It has to be clear."

"It'll be clear. Don't stress. Do something relaxing for a few days. Read. Meditate. Masturbate. Personally, I like crocheting." Joe grinned and reached for Ren's hand – Ren noticed his perfectly manicured nails – and gave it a bone-crushing squeeze.

When Ren went to see Jack the next day he was afraid that Jack would read on his face that he'd been up to something. But Jack was oblivious and, to Ren's great relief, feeling a little stronger. His sense of taste was returning. He'd been able to taste the sweetness in a chocolate milkshake. And his ability to concentrate was improving. He'd actually been making some sketches of nesting behavior in pumpkin-seed sunfish for some brochure his fishery was going to put out. He had gotten tired after about fifteen minutes but he was still excited by it. It was a beginning.

He showed Jack his sketches – the male fish circling around on the river bottom using its body and tail to scoop out a round hollow where the female could lay her eggs. Then, like Horton the elephant, he would stand guard. For quite awhile now, Fisheries had been thinking about doing something larger than brochures, like a book of Hudson River fish and aquatic plants. They knew Jack's work – he had done a lot of watercolors for his own pleasure. If they wanted him to help with this bigger project, he wouldn't have to go into the office for months. It would be the perfect convalescent activity. He could work at home from photos.

Or Rome, Ren was thinking. He could picture Jack sitting at a little desk, the window open to a sun-drenched terrace, his blond hair beginning to grow back. He called Brent. "Jack seems to be through the worst," he told him. "It looks like we're going to be able to come." That afternoon Ren went to a small travel bureau near his house and asked about tickets to Rome. Then he got some brochures with glossy photos of Piazza di Spagna and the Coliseum.

Joe called him late on the night before Jack was to leave the hospital. "Honey, you'll be proud of me," he said. "We've got some beautiful pictures. Malcolm's face from the side, unmistakable, mouth open, just going down on me. Of course, my prick is what supplies the beauty."

Ren asked him to come right over. They sat at his little table. "I don't want to see the pictures," Ren said, turning his head away. "I just need to know we have them."

"And an audiotape too, don't forget the tape."

"I'm not forgetting anything."

"The weird part is that the guy really loves his kid. Afterwards, he couldn't stop talking about him . . . told me all about the transplant, what he'd been through. How terrible it was to see him suffering. How he would have taken it himself if he'd been able. Then he started telling me stories about him when he was a little boy . . . things he'd done . . . how he'd had a bad bronchitis once and it had scared him, but nothing could have prepared him for this."

"He may love Jack, but he certainly isn't good for him. Jesus, Joe, what are you trying to do? Am I going to have to feel sorry for him? Feeling sorry for people has always left me up shit creek."

"That's the trouble with being sensitive," Joe said.

"No really . . . this shakes me up . . . should I?"

"Should you give up Jack?"

"I just wish you hadn't told me this."

"Black and white is easier than gray," Joe said, " but you don't need to fall apart. If you haven't learned to deal with guilt by now. I mean really. Now sit down and write him a nice little note." He patted the chair seat invitingly. "Look, here's an envelope right on the table, let's get it over with." He flipped through the photos, took one and put it in the envelope. "Hurry up, don't think, just write something, anything. Do what you have to do; you can feel sorry later."

Ren sat down heavily and wrote. "There are more where this came from, and a tape of your voice. I'll use them if I have to. You must understand by now, I can't do without him. I understand how painful this is for you, but you have to let him go."

CHAPTER SIXTEEN

grief and grace

the lady bends down
sweetly kisses his face
with speech they expound
on love's grief and grace

– Sir Gawain and The Green Knight

It was a **Wednesday** in spring. All the traffic in the old parts of Rome had been stopped and Ren had the sensation as their cab entered the heart of the historic center that he had been reborn in another century. Gods and goddesses were all around them. Jack's pale face lit up as they passed the Trevi fountain with its sea horses plunging as the water poured down in sparkling sheets. Ren wondered if Jack had any notion why his father had suddenly relented and let Ren take him off this way. Had even given him the money to spend some time on a restorative holiday. No, of course he didn't.

In the weeks before they left, Jack had been so bemused and grateful that his father seemed to tolerate Ren. Ren would come over to Malcolm's Park Avenue apartment where Jack was installed in his old bedroom with a practical nurse, and mix himself a martini from the fixings on the blond wood sideboard. Then he'd sprawl on the orange silk sofa; sometimes he even took off his shoes and put his feet up, daring Malcolm to object. Malcolm had been pointedly, exaggeratedly polite.

"Do make yourself at home," he'd say in a bitter parody of lordly politesse.

He had been stiff with Jack as well, but he was always that way, more or less. Only Ren was aware that it meant something different now, that Malcolm was withdrawing. He had the preoccupied eyes and the grimly set jaw of an aging man losing a young lover – Ren saw him dart yearning looks at his son when he didn't think anyone was watching. It was painful to watch him struggling to keep up his magnanimous Host act when the truth was, he was a scared old queen.

Gradually, Jack had become aware of some subtle shifting of the dynamic between them. "There's something going on, but I don't get it," he said to Ren after a particularly glacial dinner. "Why is Dad referring to himself in the third person? As if he's dead. Your father this, your father that? What's with him? I know it's not you. He's being great with you but he seems so . . ."

"Uncomfortable?" Ren finished. It was a weak word for what Malcolm must be feeling. Jack nodded unhappily. "Well, why not ask him? It's probably just something at work."

Ren knew that father and son had always had a formal relationship and Jack couldn't bring himself to ask Malcolm why he was acting so distracted. "I'm afraid it's having me at home in such close quarters. It cramps his style," Jack said. The thought clearly made him miserable.

Never mind, Ren told himself, Jack's a big boy now, he'll get over it. Besides, he planned to make it up to him, to be the perfect father as well as the perfect mate, not to leave him any room to want anyone else. Ren imagined Gawain doing something similar with the Green Knight's wife after he stole her away.

Ren quietly supported Jack's hunch that taking care of him constituted a burden for his father. That way, the contrast with what Ren was going to do for him would be even greater. He could feel his chest filling with the sort of manic exhilaration he had felt that night at The Crown Jewels. Like Gawain, against all odds, he was winning. But defeating a brutal, controlling man wasn't enough. Ren wanted something better, a different model based on love, not power.

The color of their *palazzo* on the Corso Vittorio Emmanuele was a light lemony yellow. It stood on a busy corner near the Tiber bridge with its Bernini angels that led to the ominous Castel Sant' Angelo, a dark circular fortress that had once served as a papal refuge, afterwards, a prison. On the other side of the river, broad avenues led to the Vatican. The narrow street facing the Castel Sant' Angelo held a little cafe with chairs and tables outside on the sidewalk. Ren eagerly pointed it out to Jack as the cab drew up alongside the massive door set in stone blocks. It would be a perfect place for breakfasts. Just across from them was a news kiosk hung with papers and glossy magazines.

"We could buy the *International Herald Tribune* and take it with us while we drink our lattés," he said.

The car stopped and the cabby took the bags out of the trunk. While Ren was standing dreamily on the curb fantasizing about chocolate croissants, Jack grabbed the handle of his brown leather bag and lifted it out of the black and white checkered trunk.

"This'll strengthen the old muscles," he said, cheerfully as he headed towards the door, then he groaned. "My legs feel like spaghetti."

Ren saw him stagger and almost fall. He took three big steps and was alongside him. "No way, sweetie," he said, reaching for the bag's handle and tugging. Jack tugged back.

"I'm not a cripple," he said, glaring at Ren with a mixture of exhaustion and bravado. "I've got arms, I even have legs, look," he nodded down at his khakis, "see!"

"Yeah, but this was a long tiring flight. You have a compromised immune system."

"Fuck you."

"Sure, fine, cool." Ren backed off with what he hoped was amusingly exaggerated haste and watched Jack wrestle the bag over to the door. Sweat was breaking out on Jack's forehead. Jack's irritated insistence on independence was new and Ren didn't know what to make of it. But he knew enough not to take out his hanky and wipe off the perspiration. He pushed the buzzer and a tenor voice responded, "*Pronto?*"

"We're here."

"I'll buzz you in," the voice said, "the elevator's straight ahead. Take it up to the last floor and then up the stairs. I'll meet you there."

Luckily the elevator – a tiny box crammed into the marble stairwell – was only a few feet from the door and the floor was level. Jack managed to get his bag in without too much trouble. Ren piled the other bags on top of each other and they squeezed in beside them.

"Sorry for yelling," Jack said as the contraption lurched up past wrought iron railings and shiny brass door knockers. "But you're such a nervous Nelly. You make me nervous." They continued up in silence.

Ren had thought that once he got Jack away from his father, it would be smooth sailing, but somehow it wasn't. Jack had let his father micromanage everything for him without a peep of protest, but when Ren simply made a prudent suggestion, Jack would blow up.

The elevator stopped on the third floor and an old man with a small boy in his arms opened the outer door, peered in, said, "*scusi*" and banged the door shut again. They jolted on. Ren wondered if Jack's touchiness had gotten worse after his father had said he wouldn't visit them in Rome – he hated the place, he said, a lot of decadent slackers who took three-hour lunch breaks and never got anything done. Ironically, Jack had thought of asking him because he and Ren had seemed to be getting along so much better. Poor kid had thought that they were putting aside their differences because of him.

When they got to the fourth floor, they still had to walk up a flight to get to their apartment. Ren tried not to look worried as Jack started up the marble stairs slowly, holding on to the curved iron railing. Strengthening his muscles? Who was he kidding? When they got to the atrium outside the door, Brent rushed out to greet them. Since their meeting on opening night, Ren had had several talks with him about various matters of production. He learned that Brent was half American; his father was an Italian count of some sort. Jack had never seen him before and was looking him over curiously. Brent was wearing tan slacks and a soft green shirt that complemented his blond good looks.

"I'm so glad you're actually here. There have been so many strikes, air, land, sea, I was worried you wouldn't make it. I am impatient to start work. I've already started getting some actors lined up. But we can talk later on the phone. Now you want to get comfortable."

Before he took them inside, Brent showed them how to turn the alarm off by pressing a little black device into the wall socket, waiting for the inset red light to glow and stop.

"You have to hold your hand over the bulb to see it in the daylight," he said, looking sideways at Jack. Ren could see the wheels clicking as he noted Jack's thinness and pallor, wondering if it was really AIDS, not cancer. Afterwards, he showed them how to work the heavy locks and cautioned them to be very, very careful to engage them all.

"Have you had many break-ins?" Jack asked nervously.

"Only one," Brent said. "They came down over the roof and broke the sliding door, but that was before I put in the alarm. *Niente problema*. Not to worry."

He closed the heavy black door behind them and they stood in the entry – a small oblong room with a sofa and bookshelves crammed with books – looking through the picture glass window on the opposite wall. "You are looking at one of the famous hills of Rome," Brent said, pointing to the gently curving landscape, "our Gianniculum." The buildings showed as faint smudges of ocher topped with green. "Now come."

Jack seemed to hesitate, so Ren took his elbow and steered him ahead. The entry room narrowed to a sort of hallway with beautiful dark brown ceiling beams and a double bed tucked snugly under the slanted eaves. A mirror was hung so it reflected the hills behind and you could see it from the pillow.

"It's incredibly romantic," Ren said, sneaking an arm around Jack's waist. Jack didn't draw away and Ren gave him a proprietary pat.

"My cleaning lady, Erminia, thinks the mirror's there for some obscure sexual purpose," Brent said, "but my partner loved to read in bed, and I hung it so if he looked in the mirror he'd see the view." He sighed and Ren could see he was still hurting. He guessed there'd been a painful break-up.

"Kitchen's over here, living room ahead," Brent said in a flat voice as he ushered them into a large room with big view windows and shuttered glass doors. Ren recognized the sound of depression. Poor guy, such an amazing paradisiacal place and his Adam had flown the coop. But he was in good shape, Ren thought; he shouldn't have much trouble finding a replacement. Having some funds and an undoubtedly large theater network wouldn't hurt.

Brent slowly slid open the shutter, then the glass sliding door and Ren saw a terrace bathed in light.

"*Bello, no?*" Brent asked.

"Fantastic," Ren said, standing on the sill looking out. There were low brick walls on two sides, a white couch, an umbrella for sunny days, a red terra cotta floor. He turned and beckoned Jack – thank God he had him. He inhaled deeply, puffing out his chest like Pavorotti before a big aria.

"*Vieni,*" he sang, softly, "*vieni,*" imitating Don Giovanni's seductive call to Zerlina.

"For me, this suggests something else," Brent said unexpectedly.

"Well go for it." Ren was annoyed at the interruption of his mood but he didn't want to offend him.

"I can't sing," he said. "But if I could, I'd sing that bit in *Tosca* where she is begging Mario to get up after his execution." He walked quickly to a compact disc player in the corner under the eaves and a minute later, Maria Callas was sending her desperate cries into the spring air. "*Su, su,* Mario, *su.*"

"Can't compete with that, Ren." Jack said wryly.

Ren felt a chill – that scene where Tosca realized her lover was dead always left him in tears – but he made himself laugh. "Well, we can't all be divas. But why Tosca?"

"Because you can see the Castel Sant' Angelo from the terrace – the walls she jumped from are right out there. Almost in front of you." He swept his arm out in a large gesture. "And there are other reasons besides. Basically I'm a pessimist. Life is full of tragic ironies, no?"

"Tragicomic," I'd say," Ren answered. "Right now I'm stressing the comic."

"Good for you if you can do it," Brent said, gliding back with an ambiguous expression on his face as all three of them moved from the dim cool inside to the brightness of the terrace.

It was like bursting into the center of a flower shop. The space in front of each wall was packed tight with flowers and blooming trees. Large, low pots of pink geraniums and roses, flowering rosemary, small palms with interesting twisted trunks, huge lacy ferns so thickly planted, Ren wondered how you could get a hose in between their stems to water.

"Wow," Jack said, inhaling. He seemed galvanized by the brightness. He bent his head back and looked at the trellis overhead covered with large passion flowers. "Anyone who could do this can't be a pessimist," he said to Brent. "I love your color scheme – pinks and purples now, reds and yellows in autumn." When he saw Ren looking blank, he explained. "See this date palm, it'll have yellow fruit come September, the mock tomato will have red fruit, the passion flower, red leaves, my God, there's even a mini-pomegranate. It's terrific. A plant lover's paradise. And a budding olive. Do you make your own oil, Brent?"

"I haven't yet," Brent said, not meeting his eye. "The plant's too young . . . maybe next year."

Jack fingered the gray-green leaves gently and then bent to examine a small bronze plaque. "In memory: John."

"It's his garden, really," Brent said. "He was the tactile one. I'm more cerebral."

"Oh."

Ren could hear the exhale of breath. He felt he had to say something. Especially since he'd misjudged the depth of the man's grief. He felt ashamed. There they were flaunting their happiness in his face, more or less on their honeymoon – asking Brent about his lover was the least he could do.

"I'm so sorry," he stammered. "Was it recent?"

"Last year," Brent said.

"Did you expect it, or?"

"No, it was horribly sudden, actually." Brent ushered them back inside. When Jack stumbled and Ren grabbed his arm, he could see Brent studying them.

"We were jogging. He bent to lace his sneaker and he smiled at me. I smiled back and then suddenly he dropped like a stone, flat down on his face – broke his poor nose." Brent paused and Ren could feel him trying to collect himself.

"How awful," Ren said. They looked at each other. "Sometimes you don't know what to wish. If you have time to say good-bye, then you have to see someone you love suffer. I know that doesn't help."

"I did say good-bye, though. I sat with him in the morgue. It was a dreadful place, all white and chrome, just the kind of place he would have hated. I held his hand and talked to him so he wouldn't be afraid, and he was there, you know. I could sense him there somewhere around the window. I could almost see him . . . you know how you look into a fog, and gradually you see a shape?"

"I think I know what you mean," Ren blurted out. "When Jack was very sick, sometimes I'd feel him hovering just outside his body."

"What did it feel like?" Brent turned towards Jack, "that's what torments me, that I can't know. The doctors said he didn't feel any pain but . . . "

"I can't remember really," Jack grimaced. "Don't want to either. It's gotten to the point where if I saw the nurse who took care of me there I wouldn't recognize her."

"I understand that," Brent said. "For months I couldn't talk about what happened to John – and now I can't stop talking about it. It's droll."

Droll or not, Ren wished he would stop. Jack didn't need to hear this now.

Jack had been leaning against the wall; now he plumped down in a heavy armchair with an embroidered cushion, his head almost touching the slanted ceiling. Light came from the little dormer windows behind his head and back-lit his hair.

"You're tired," Brent said.

"A little," Jack admitted. Good boy.

Brent apologized profusely for tiring him, they played a little back and forth game of apology and denial, then he showed Ren where the fuse box was. As soon as Ren had rested up a little, Brent wanted to meet and go over the production schedule. They had seven weeks till production, but he wanted to start thinking about casting. He had the wild idea of using some Neapolitan transvestites, *femminielli*, for the court ladies.

"They're gorgeous," he said. "They'd give the play a slightly different tone, but I think you'd like it. I was even thinking of proposing one for Gawain. They are more female than real women, you know."

"Sounds intriguing," Ren said, "I'd like to see how they do it." He wondered if the *femminielli* took hormones. Breasts seemed essential to the discovery scene at the end.

"Homosexuals here are friendlier to the female principle than they are in America," Brent said mysteriously, as Ren opened the front door and let him out.

Afterwards, Ren made Jack some tea in the pocket kitchen and brought it to the chair. When he came back Jack was looking out the big glass window at the terrace. On either side of the window were two marble busts – one that looked like Queen Victoria and the other one equally imposing.

"Oh my God," Ren said, making his voice determinedly cheerful. "Did you see these? Two queens. What a riot. They make me feel right at home."

"I doubt if it was meant that way," Jack said sharply.

"Really? It seems pretty obvious." Ren had the feeling Brent's story had gotten to Jack and was producing its own cycle of black thoughts. Or maybe it was just exhaustion.

"They're fun to look at, however they're meant," he said carefully. This didn't seem the time to mention how great it was to be in a gay-friendly house – the coffee table art books filled with gorgeous boys, the bits of Greek statues. He could relax.

"I don't see why you had to blab out everything to him that way," Jack said. "Do you have to say everything that comes to your mind?"

"Well, he was telling us, being so open . . . "

"That doesn't mean you have to be." Ren didn't like the way Jack's jaw was set. He was staring at a photo of a man with his wife and son, displayed on a low shelf – the man was about Ren's age, had dark curly hair, an infectious grin. Brent had mentioned to Ren that his partner had been married before they started living together and that he had children. That they saw each other frequently.

"They look like a happy family," Jack said in a faintly accusatory tone, "or they were before Brent came along. The wife has a sweet look."

"Celluloid smile," Ren said, but Jack didn't look at him. "What's the matter, bubbi? It's sad about Brent, but he's no one close to us. I don't quite see why you're so upset."

"I'm not upset, I was just wondering about the happiness-cost ratio."

"Oh." Ren stared. It didn't sound like Jack. "Maybe the guy's wife liked Brent too."

Jack didn't smile. "Don't be flip, Ren. I mean, maybe she put up with him for her husband's or the children's sake." Jack's chin wobbled and Ren wondered for an awful minute if he were going to cry. "There's another photo of her in the front room," Jack continued. "Maybe she thought she had to *like him* if she wanted to keep any connection."

"Well? What's so wrong about that?" Ren was getting irritated. "What's all this sympathy for an unknown family? She was a shrill bitch for all you know. Anyone can look good in a photo." Jack didn't answer. A few minutes later, he undressed and crawled under the covers of their romantic mirrored bed.

He slept through the afternoon while Ren unpacked their suitcases, hanging up their things in the matching *armadios* on either side of the bed. As he folded Jack's T-shirts and put his socks and briefs neatly into the drawers, he wondered if Jack was missing his father. Worse, what if he were blaming Ren for his father's strange withdrawal in the weeks before they left? No, he couldn't, couldn't guess.

Around eight Ren woke him up and got him to eat some canned soup he'd found in the kitchen. It wasn't at all what he'd planned for their first supper, but the poor kid was obviously exhausted. He didn't even get out of bed and when he finished the bowl, he lay back down again. Washing the dishes in the tiny kitchen, with Jack sleeping peacefully right in view under the eaves, Ren felt his fears calming. He told himself it was natural for people to get cranky when they're exhausted, especially after they've heard a story like that. When Jack woke up, he'd forget about it and let himself be happy.

Around midnight Jack woke up screaming. "I was back in the hospital," he gasped, "covered with bugs."

"Here, come here, baby," Ren reached out and took Jack into his arms. His body was wonderfully warm, it sent a shock of longing rippling through him. For a minute he thought of seducing Jack into making love. He kissed him tentatively but Jack didn't respond, and he could tell by the slight tensing of his muscles that he wasn't comfortable. It'll come back, he told himself. Be patient.

"Hey, I'm the one who has nightmares," he said, "not you. You're a sound sleeper, remember? No?"

Jack sat up and hit his head on the slanting roof. "Ouch!" Ren switched on one of the reading lights next to the bed. There was a small stack of books next to it.

"Let's see what his taste is . . . Oh, Andrew Sullivan." One of the most provocative gay writers. "Too heavy for middle-of-the night fare." Ren heard himself babbling but couldn't seem to stop. "Hey, Woolf's *Orlando*, that's a thought. Why don't you let Mama read to you? It'll make me feel better, that's for sure." He put it that way because Jack had gotten hyper-sensitive about needing so much care. Jack grunted an assent and Ren started leafing through the book, looking at the illustrations of Orlando's metamorphosis from man to woman.

"Quite a character, this lady. I wish I'd known her. She probably wouldn't have been overjoyed to meet me though. What do you think? She was a bit of an anti-Semite, hated the hoi polloi . . . still, she could really write. It's depressing, isn't it, when people write like angels and have the nastiest prejudices." Jack tried to smile but he was still obviously under the spell of his nightmare.

"I just remembered how you sang to me in the hospital," Jack said with surprising tenderness. "You have a beautiful voice. Read whatever you like, it doesn't matter. I know I'm being difficult. Try to bear with me, will you? I'm still trying to adjust to being alive."

Ren put his arm lightly around his shoulder. "*Niente problema*," he said. No pressure. Just a light touch. Jack shivered even though it was a warm night. There was a woolly throw on the end of the bed and Ren drew it up and tucked it around Jack. Poor kid. His temperature regulators had all gone haywire. Jack laid his head on Ren's shoulder and Ren could feel his body soften as the tension went down.

He opened the book and began to read the first page of *Orlando*: "He – for there could be no doubt of his sex – was in the act of slicing at the head of a Moor which swung from the rafters. Orlando's father, or perhaps his grandfather, had struck it from the shoulders of a vast pagan." He hadn't remembered how Woolf had started with the young prince doing the proverbial male thing. Slashing off heads. Somehow the coincidence thrilled him and he read on, engrossed.

Then the prince cuts his enemy down and strings him up again, "so that his enemy grinned at him . . . through shrunk, black lips, triumphantly."

When Ren looked up again, Jack was fast asleep. Ren shut the book and switched off the light, but now he felt wide-awake. Images of Malcolm came obsessively to his mind: the stiff way he unfolded his napkin at the table, like a Victorian patriarch, the patronizing way he talked to his Chinese chef, in a sort of pidgin.

Get out of it, he told himself. We're gone now. Isn't it pointless to keep on running the tape? But why, he wondered finally, was Malcolm so afraid Jack wouldn't accept him? Why couldn't he risk telling him? He couldn't think Jack would be horrified by the sex part, could he? But maybe it was the hypocrisy. All that mouthing about the family and telling it like it is, but then he'd kept half his life a secret. His "prejudices" wouldn't seem so excusable now; they'd seem like the worst self-hatred. It seemed hopelessly tangled. Ren couldn't figure it out.

He put on a sweater and went out onto the terrace and smoked a joint – against Jack's advice, he'd brought it through customs in his carry-on bag – hoping that it would soothe his mind. It did. The rooftops seemed a pleasant jumble under the full moon. Tosca's castello was rounded and softened, and a little way over even the Palace of Justice seemed less severe. He slipped into an easy, dreamy state. The smell of jasmine mixed with the sweet odor of the joint. He was tired. The last weeks had been exhausting. He really hadn't had time to think things over. He'd just been on a roll, acting and reacting with only one thought in his mind: to get Jack away from his father, to be with Jack, not to be harassed. Then why did he have this faint sour taste in his mouth?

The Palace of Justice just in front of him glimmered white yellow as the moon rose. Ren noticed that the angel on top was drawing her sword – or was she sheathing it? He told himself that what he'd gotten was only justice. He couldn't be punished for that, could he? Would that be fair? He looked up at the angel for clarification but her face was in shadow, and he couldn't make out her expression.

CHAPTER SEVENTEEN

Interlude

now peaceful be his pasture, and love play him fair!
— Sir Gawain and The Green Knight

he angel looked better in the daytime, and by the end of a week Ren was convinced she was sheathing, not drawing, her sword. Jack seemed to feel better too. He drank the hot milk possets and other restorative drinks Ren made him without complaint. His appetite was definitely improving. Ren fixed lunches of healthy steamed vegetables with thick creamy cheeses and freshly baked bread from the small grocery on their corner. He sometimes caught a glimpse of himself in a storefront, scuttling along with his net bag like one of the neighborhood grandmas. But he didn't mind, as long as the haunted hospital look was leaving Jack's face.

They ate on their *terrazo* under a white umbrella. Even the saying of the word, *ombrellone*, made Ren's mouth and tongue happy. He looked forward with voluptuous pleasure to the simplest things – to setting the outdoor table with Brent's woven mats, or pouring Jack wine from the blue glass decanter. The first time Ren had given wine to him straight, Jack put the glass down with a start.

"It burns my throat," he explained, coughing. "It's still pretty raw."

Ren ran into the kitchen and brought back a pitcher of water.

"Are you crying?" Jack asked, when Ren bent down to

pour, turning Ren's face with his hand so he could see his eyes. "It doesn't hurt me that much."

"I'm just happy," Ren sniffed, tears trickling down his cheeks. "I'm a sentimental fool, I know, but it's the beginning of our life together."

"We've had meals together before," Jack said gently, "slept in the same bed."

"I know, but it's different."

Ren stopped himself from adding, "I have you all to myself now."

Ren redoubled his efforts to make Jack love Rome, to make him happier here than he'd ever been anywhere else. Only that could justify what Ren had done to get them there. He tried to be sensitive to Jack's wishes before he expressed them. When Ren noticed that Jack was curious about the Roman water system, he got a book about it and they spent days looking at the ruins of ancient aquifers. When Jack spoke nostalgically of his fish and wondered how they were doing – he had sublet his place – Ren persuaded him to get out his sketch-pad and start working on his Fisheries drawings a little every day. To inspire him, he bought a couple of tropical fish and a small aquarium. There were things here that needed care too, he told him, pointing out the withered brown geranium flowers and the small bugs on one of the roses. Ren bought him some new plants at the outdoor market at Campo Dei Fiori, then encouraged Jack to pluck and prune and water until he began referring to the hardy Roman blooms in the same affectionate terms he had the scrawny specimens at home.

"I have to get some spray for the aphids," he'd say, and thumb through the dictionary to find the word. Then together they'd try to figure out the best place to get it. Most of the flower sellers in their neighborhood knew Jack by name.

"Oh, signor Jack," they'd say delightedly when he came by, "*Buon giorno*, I have something special for you."

Brent arranged for the two transvestite actresses to come up to the apartment on a Sunday afternoon the next week. Apparently Saturday was the big night for business in Rome.

"Naples has the most beautiful queens in the world," Brent explained to Ren, "but it's hard to earn a living there. Here the pay's better, so the *femminielli* come up every weekend to work. If we can get these two, we'll be lucky. I've seen both of them in little theaters here. They're a little rough but they're born actresses."

Brent arrived with Lauretta and Toma punctually at four and Ren ushered them to the living room. Brent had warned him but it was still astonishing to see how sexily feminine they looked in their short skirts and black wrap-around tops – Toma's cut rather chastely, Lauretta's plunging and ruffled.

Toma was dark with typically Mediterranean looks, an aquiline nose and big eyes, and Ren could immediately imagine her as Gawain. Lauretta was more glamorous, an Ava Gardner type with abundant long hair and voluptuous breasts, covered by soft folds of black silk.

Jack brought in Camparis and some olives, then went out discreetly to the terrace while the actresses perched on the edge of the soft seats like exotic birds. They weren't at all shy. On the streets they'd dealt with all sorts of men, including American tourists and servicemen.

Lauretta had been raised as a girl by her mother. She had a thing about the false macho of American men, how if they recognized who she was, they would jeer and laugh and then would sneak back for a quickie.

"Your Americans," she said, pressing a white fist against her belly, "are afraid of their feelings. They have lost touch with what is in here."

Ren sympathized. He liked Lauretta.

"Because they're scared, Americans put everything in separate boxes; prick here," she said in her husky, seductive voice, sketching a square shape in the air in front of her bosom, "pussy there," she shaped a second one to the side.

"Oh, fa," she made a typically Italian gesture of disgust. "We *femminielli* are not like that. We've learned to live with our complications, like Pulcinella. You know Pulcinella?" she asked Ren. He shook his head. "In Naples you see them all over in the stores, maybe not so much in Rome. He's a man who is a woman too, he carries his babies in his hump and gives birth through his *cullo*."

Ren laughed. Lauretta would be a more temperamental Wife than Grace had been. But it could be interesting. There was something poignant about her view of herself as a hermaphrodite like Pulcinella.

When Ren asked Toma about herself, she told him she was from a poor family, that her father had died when she was a child, and she had saved herself from hunger by going on the streets in Naples's Spanish quarter. She had supported her young brother for years, helping him with his education. Now he was finally old enough to get a decent job and she wanted to leave the street and work full-time as an actress.

"I prayed to the Patron Saint of Naples, San Gennaro, to help me," she said.

"He was beheaded just like the Green Knight," Brent explained. "At the same season, too. Every year his blood liquefies in the spring. It's a holdover from pagan times." Brent raised a sophisticated eyebrow. "They refer to it as the menstruation. It might be fun to work in allusions to it in your show."

"Why not? The original has plenty of mythic references. They'd probably mean more to an Italian audience."

"The Saint bled three times this year!" Toma went on enthusiastically. "So I'm sure I'm getting very good luck." She hastily made the sign of the cross.

"She's superstitious," Lauretta said, "but she's a good actress."

"Gawain was a believer too," Ren said, smiling. Toma would probably love having the Virgin on her shield.

"Brent has told me about your play," Toma said to Ren after they'd chatted for awhile longer. "I would like to play Gawain. I know at the end Gawain reveals herself as a woman. I have nice breasts, you know. I just finished paying for my hormone treatment – small, but nice. I could show them to anyone . . . would you like a preview?"

"It's not necessary," Ren said quickly. "But I do want you to come to tryouts next Saturday. I'd like to hear you both read along with the actor Brent has in mind for the Green Knight . . . to see how you would work together."

"You will see. It will be good, *molto buono*, very good. *Grazia*," they said in chorus. Then he took them out on the terrace to join Jack and see the view and they talked a little longer. The girls wanted to know about transvestites in America, how the police treated them. Ren told them about some of the drag stars like Joey, who was called Mr. New York, or Ru Paul, who could be seen in full-page ads for running shoes in the *New Yorker*. Ren also told them what he knew about the cop-ridden hustlers in the meat-packing district. "It's not great, but I guess you could say it's not a nightmare either."

Finally Toma said they had to go. One of their friends was getting married to a furniture refinisher in Trastevere. Ren couldn't make out if the guy was gay or straight, but it prom- ised to be a great occasion. Before they left, Toma confided wistfully that she hoped to get married one day herself. She wanted a church wedding.

———

For the next few days, when Ren wasn't talking to Brent about their production plans or getting additional people lined up for casting, he and Jack spent leisurely hours in further exploration of the narrow streets that fanned out from their palazzo, on one side to Piazza Navona, on the other to Campo Dei Fiori.

Ren had never seen streets so unbelievably rich in their texture and variety. Of all the things he liked about Rome, the best was the human dimension. Even the biggest palazzo had the right scale for a human being. Ren hadn't realized how much he disliked New York's looming skyscrapers and harsh, grid-imposed streets. Here, churches, palaces and fountains not only had the right proportions but there was a playful spontaneous air to the interactions of soft and hard, of straight lines and curves – like the corkscrew spires of Saint Ivo.

Ren liked the sense that ten different routes would lead to the same place. You could get deliciously lost. The small alleys and streets propelled them in bewildering directions and opened out on surprises like the Pantheon under a full moon, or, when they'd walked unsuspecting around a corner, the Trevi fountain with its astonishing gallons of cascading water. It was like a succession of stage sets but much more immediate. Everything seemed physical and close, like sex or dreams.

Ren made each excursion short so as not to tire Jack, and they always included a stop for coffee or juice or gelato. They tried all the squares in their neighborhood. They sat under umbrellas in the piazza of the Pantheon watching tourists clicking cameras at each other in front of the brick round that brooded like a tawny lion in the golden light. Jack figured out the Latin inscription, *M. AGRIPPA, L.F. COS. TERTIUM FECIT* (Marcus Agrippa, son of Lucius, consul for the third time had this building made), and Ren oohhed over the tomb of Raphael. One evening a boys' chorus sang surrounded by candles and, at the end of the concert, roses rained down on the spellbound audience from the round opening in the dome.

But their favorite spot was the great oval of Piazza Navona, where they sipped brightly colored liquids on the loggia of an old palazzo turned into a cafe. The high stone loggia afforded some protection from the milling crowd and faced Bernini's fountain. Ren never tired of looking at it. Of its four immense marble forms, Ren loved the huge Moor best – tilted vertiginously backward with his cape over his head. Ren felt the swirl of foam on his cappuccino against his lips and imagined he was an escaped slave, looking out for the first time at his freedom.

Rome's chaos of forms lent itself to daydreaming. When Ren wasn't looking at the fountain, watching lovers, or reading small items from the newspaper aloud to Jack, he fantasized being a chariot driver in the old days when the piazza had been a hippodrome. Now kids on tricycles pedaled in circles. Still, as he watched an occasional horse-drawn carriage rumble by over the uneven cobbles, Ren could perfectly imagine his chariot bouncing as it turned the curve and raced down the stretch in front of the ochre and pink houses.

One day an unpleasant incident interrupted his reveries. They were lazing at their cafe when a heavily rouged older woman with a newspaper in her hand approached their table. She was monumentally overweight and her fat forearms were covered with bracelets that jingled when she walked. She leaned over confidentially and started saying something in Italian. She spoke quickly, rolling her eyes as though talking to herself. The man at the next table started laughing.

"She makes up the headlines," he explained to them in halting English, "now she say the prime minister lost his *coglione*, what do you say, his balls, to a mafia *capo*. You have to know Italian politics to understand." The woman shook the newspaper in front of their noses. "Priests ordered to marry by tomorrow, she says now," the man grinned. "She's a *characteraccio*, a real character. But you're lucky she likes you. She tells you that she has always looked for love but never found it and that if she'd only learned to behave herself, she'd be a happy woman now." The man had stopped laughing and looked moved. "*Povera creatura.*"

The woman suddenly advanced a fat finger under Ren's nose. "*Sia buono!*" Even he could understand that – "Be good" – in the tone you use with children. And in fact the woman drew back her hand and made two swift spanking motions, one palm against the other – whop, whop – her bracelets giving off a tinny clang. He knew she was only guessing, the way fortune tellers often did – most people felt guilty about something – but it unnerved him. It felt as if Malcolm were peering out of the women's shrewd laughing eyes – as though they couldn't escape him merely by crossing an ocean. Somehow he was still there between him and Jack. Ren flinched, inadvertently blushing, and she burst into raucous laughter.

"Are you entertained?" Ren asked Jack cautiously after the woman went away. "Or is it too much like a Fellini movie?"

"It's a zoo, but it's fun," Jack said, scraping the last bit of sugared slush from the bottom of his cup. "Or it would be if you'd stop giving me those worried looks. I feel as if you're taking my emotional temperature." He shook an imaginary thermometer. "Don't need to, sweetie. Really. I'm on the mend. I'm going to be fine."

Jack did look a little more like himself, Ren thought. The fishbelly pallor that had been so disturbing in the hospital was gone and he was getting a slight tan. "I'm glad you didn't mind her."

"Why should I? She's a critic of morals and manners. Like that local satirist – what's his name? – the one they have a statue of on the Corso." Jack studied Ren. "You have a sheepish look. What's the matter? Did she hit a nerve?" He dipped his finger in Ren's coffee and, extending his arm, deftly sketched a mustache under his nose. "Ohhhh, I'm in love with a mafioso."

Ren laughed and licked it off but he felt vaguely threatened. He pressed his leg against Jack's to reassure himself that this – the air, the spring sun, the stone, the gushing water – wasn't going to suddenly vanish. Damn that old woman. She had almost succeeded in undermining his mood.

Strolling along later, they noticed placards for an exhibit of Roman festivals at the Palazzo Venezia. Ren had read about it in the *Herald Tribune* that morning – a "brilliant re-creation of city festivals from the sixteenth century to the Republic." It featured a special section on the so-called ephemera – elaborate stage sets for important events which exploded at the end in bursts of fireworks. The placard tempted them with a magnificent float crammed full of maskers in brilliantly colored costumes. Ren was immediately curious to see what the Renaissance Romans thought important as well as the nuts and bolts of their illusion-making.

"Oh goody, dress-up time," he said, imitating what he called the Roman rooster walk, somewhere between a swagger and a roll. "I've always wanted to be somewhere fun during Carnivale – New Orleans or the Bahamas." He adjusted an imaginary necklace. He'd seen the necks of male Romani – not just the queer ones – adorned with gold chains and virile coral horns to keep off the evil eye.

"I'm afraid I haven't been much fun for you," Jack said, shielding his eyes from the sun. "It's taking longer than I thought to feel like a normal person."

"Normal, schnormal, we're beyond normal, we're supranormal. We're inventing a new category, didn't you know?" Ren skipped a few steps ahead of him pretending to play a pipe. He knew he was being silly but he didn't care. He needed to get back his feeling that they were suspended in a kind of translucent medium filled with infinitely varied shades of pleasure.

They were threading their way through a narrow, curving street that didn't let the sun in. The sidewalk was so narrow that to walk alongside each other, one of them, usually Ren, had to step into the street, maneuvering around the cars that lined the edge. Still, except for the motorcycles, which macho tradition required the rider to roar at pedestrians, it was relatively quiet. And every few feet they found something to admire. In one curving block they passed a painted façade – rare in Rome – of two medieval buildings, recognized by their narrowness, and a small piazza with pink and green facades and a central fountain surrounded by tables overflowing with tomatoes, eggplant and zucchini. That was one of

Rome's special beauties. Away from the main streets, the lovers were transported to an earlier time – the little piazza could have been the central square of a village.

Suddenly they came to the end of an alley and emerged into a wide open space drenched with sunlight that reflected off the gleaming white surfaces of the Victor Emmanual monument – the monument to the first king of a united Italy. Cars careened around them, and a group of Japanese tourists following a leader with a raised red umbrella dashed to get across the street.

"Back to the future," Ren said, cocking his head as he studied the monument's dazzling white structure. "It's Las Vegas without the slot machines."

"It's not so bad," Jack said. "It's so excessive, it's almost good."

"It's a perfect emblem for centralized power," Ren said, "brutal, heavy and ugly. It's a Fascist building." He felt himself getting hot with indignation. If someone had given him a sledgehammer, he would have attacked it right then and there.

"Looks like a wedding cake to me."

"It's relentless, it's . . . " Ren glared at the oversize gilt statue of the king on his horse. "The thing must be forty feet high. It's all groom and no bride."

Jack giggled. "Let's not argue about a building," he said soothingly. "It doesn't seem worth it on such a beautiful day. Anyway, here we are," Jack looked up at the poster over the entrance to Palazzo Venezia, the severe stone rectangle which housed the show, while Ren made an effort to collect himself.

"Sorry," he murmured, "I don't know what got into me. That building hit me like a slap in the face."

"It's okay, bubbi, I love your sense of drama. You should write a guidebook: The Emotional Language of Monuments."

They paid for their tickets in the entry and went into the first room of the exhibit – a large stone room filled with huge oil paintings of carnivals at different periods.

"Now *this* is my city," Ren said, as they walked past

depictions of masked men and women dancing in the streets while others looked from flag-draped windows.

"I don't think I'd like the crowds," Jack said, good-humoredly. Ren gave him a grateful smile. They were so different but Ren never felt that Jack was trying to make him over, and their Roman holiday was obviously doing him good. The hollows in his cheeks were filling in. If only they had their sex life back, things would be perfect.

"Don't worry," Ren said. " We'd go in a carriage like the aristocrats. And if we got out, I'd put my cape around you to protect you." He squeezed Jack's arm and Jack didn't move away. Ren wondered if he was less careful here than in New York because men in Rome touched each other much more. They walked with arms linked, stood breathing in each other's faces when they talked, kissed on both cheeks.

They moved slowly through the rooms.

"Can you imagine, Jack? These people didn't just party once a year, or once a week, they had a festival every day. Every single day was choreographed as carefully as a dance. It's fantastic, unbelievable."

"They didn't have television," Jack said wryly. He lowered himself onto one of the shiny wooden benches in the middle of the room.

Ren stood next to him and stared at a wall of paintings celebrating princely marriages or victories. In the grandest, a tournament was set up in the courtyard of an imposing palace, the windows all hung with gilded drapes printed with coats of arms. He caught himself looking for a knight dressed in green. Brent had astonished him by telling him there was an Italian folktale about Gawain – lifted from Mallory, of course – in which Gawain's task was to find out what a woman wants. He meets a hideous crone with tusks like a wild boar, one curving up and the other down, who says she'll tell him if he promises to give her anything she asks.

"And what was it?" Ren had asked.

"Women want dominance over their men," Brent told

him, laughing, "and Gawain has to repay this unpleasant revelation by marrying her. She gives him the choice of having her beautiful by day and loathsome at night or vice versa and when he leaves it up to her, she commends him for his wisdom and says she'll be beautiful all the time."

Ren supposed Brent's version fit the Italian obsession with La Mama. But he didn't much like the way it resolved the issue of power by shifting it onto the other sex. He studied the painting in front of him. It was loaded with mythic allusions. But the knights were dressed in red and yellow and white with matching plumes on their helmets and their horses' trappings. Anyone who wanted to see the Green Knight would have to come to Ren's play.

Jack had swiveled around on his bench and was looking at the opposite wall. Along with other canvases depicting religious processions, there was a painting of Pope Pius VII returning to Rome with his cortege. The path of his procession to the Vatican had been decorated with ephemera made of papier-mâché and stucco. The painting depicted the pope's arrival through the triumphal arch at Piazza del Popolo, accompanied by gorgeously attired horsemen. Spectators lined the square, framing the spectacle.

"Wouldn't that be fun?" Ren asked as Jack craned his head to see, "to be following the route of the Caesars' loaded down with jewels on every finger, a peacock plume fan waved over your head? Those ancient Romans really knew how to do things." Ren loved the way the real city was reinterpreted through the symbolic processions with their fragile ephemera.

"I'd rather sit in the grandstand and throw roses," Jack said as he slowly got up and stretched. "Hey, isn't that Brent?"

Brent emerged from the crowd and greeted them with courtly courtesy. He had on a white summer suit and looked quite elegant, with only a hint of melancholy.

After asking them if the plumber had fixed their leaking pipe yet, and finding that all was well, he confessed to sharing Ren's fascination with the ephemera. "Everything nowadays is real, in the dullest sense of the word, even the TV shows, and not just in America – *Survivor, How to Marry A Millionaire* – how banal can you get? That's why I like your play so much. It creates an imaginary world with very real people in it. Speaking of theater, have you seen any of the little dramas in Piazza del Popolo?" Brent nodded his head towards the painting where the pope's procession was wending its way towards the piazza's central obelisk with its four surrounding lions. "It's particularly known for displays of adulterous behavior. Moravia used to quarrel with his mistress there every morning. There's also a reigning gypsy, Rosita. She's superb if you like florid theatrics – she has a way of sashaying after the men," here Brent gyrated slightly, "shaming them into buying her roses."

"Sorry I missed her," Ren said, "but I saw Lauretta and Toma there with a group of their friends. They really want the parts, and some of their friends seemed eager to try out for the court ladies."

"Handsome bunch, aren't they?" Brent asked. "I thought you'd be pleased." He followed them into the next room which featured a mock-up of the Castel Sant' Angelo with a cascade of fireworks behind it. "Recognize your castle?" he asked them.

"Of course," Ren said. He wished he'd mentioned it first – he would have pointed out the full moon to Jack and reminded him it had been like that their first night. But he wasn't going to do that with Brent listening. "What's that in the background with the lit facade?"

"Saint Peter's." Brent leaned to read from a placard on the wall next to a painting. "The Vatican celebrates."

"I prefer my fireworks without benefit of clergy," Ren said rather pompously, "fireworks of the human spirit." He had just noticed the intent way Brent was appraising Jack's body and he didn't like it.

"Ren," Jack warned him with a glance, and Ren remembered the shelf of religious books in the library of their apartment. Who knows? Brent might be a devout Catholic. He didn't want to alienate his producer.

"Oh, sorry," he said. The tracts had been next to a small but fine collection of pornography.

"No problem." Brent's cell phone suddenly rang and he took it out of its holster, listened, then spoke rapidly in Italian. After a minute he hung up looking pleased.

"Good news?" Ren asked, curious despite himself.

"Very. The props should be completed next week. And by then we should have finished casting and be ready to start reading rehearsals. In the meantime, I want to go over the video you took of your production in New York. We'll need you to help our designer decide how to adapt the sets to our outdoor space."

"It shouldn't be hard. Basically, we pare down."

"*Benissimo.* I'll take you to see the Teatro di Marcellus whenever you're ready. Let me know." He turned to Jack, and inclined his head. "I hope you'll come too – it's an evocative space, ancient stones, very suggestive." Ren noted that his nose was aggressively Roman in profile.

"He seems awfully taken with you," Ren said as soon as Brent was out of sight. "Is it mutual?"

"Don't be a silly ass," Jack said. "For godsake, he was just being polite to ask me along."

"Are you sure? I saw the way he looked at you."

"Sure, I'm sure. Whatever my interest in him, it's only because he's working on your project."

"As long as we don't have to have him over for supper."

"I won't go with you to see the theater, okay? – though I'd think you'd be pleased if I want to. I won't see him at all until we give him back his keys, if you like. Oh, please, Ren, you're giving me a headache."

Even to Ren's gimlet gaze, Jack seemed totally sincere.

"Sorry, baby," Ren said. "I guess it's hard to believe I'm enough for you. I make every third person into a threat."

"You said it, not me," Jack said.

Ren took his arm, "Come close to me again. I promise to act normal. Maybe it will get to be a habit. Can you take one more room? It looks even more fantastical than the rest. I feel as if it's going to give me ideas."

"For what?" Jack asked leaning against him.

"Not sure yet. Something new." A grinning devil leered out at them from the top of a fire machine painted with the word *trasgressione* (transgression).

"Maybe I should take that as my motto," Ren said, reveling in the outrageousness of the artists' imagination. They built all this amazing stuff, he thought, and then at the end of the day, they exploded it. The floats themselves were complicated. Giant griffins belched fire next to gilded figures on embellished thrones stories high. Everything pulsated with life. The elaborate baroque structure of one float groaned under a load of gilt fauns and satyrs; then, like buttercream icing on an already overrich wedding cake, the float's creator had it drawn by horses caparisoned in gold and riders whose red and white plumed headdresses made them seem like giant birds. Animal and human, man and woman, white and black were mixed in suggestive ways as satyrs; Moors and half-naked women wove their way through the crowd with goblin fruit.

So much work, so much effort. Ren could hardly believe the enormous labor that went into these ephemera, only to be burst apart at the end by water or fire.

"I'm getting tired," Jack said.

"Oh," Ren was startled out of his dream. "Sorry. I felt you hanging on my arm but I thought you were just snuggling. First I have an attack of the green-eyed monster, then I don't see you're ready to drop. I'm not seeing things too clearly today, am I?" He cocked his head towards a chubby, blindfolded cupid in papier-mâché who was leaning towards them from the doorway. "At least I'm not the only lover who's blind."

Jack gave him a rueful smile. "Enough already. No guilt."

"Fine." Ren ran an imaginary zipper along his mouth. "Let's go." One of these days, Ren thought, he'd have to work hard on his jealousy. What he had with Jack was too good to risk blowing up.

CHAPTER EIGHTEEN

SORROW and grief

now i am faulty and false, though afraid i've been ever
of treachery and untruth, both bring sorrow and care

— Sir Gawain and The Green Knight

en began to realize that the play was going to flourish in
its new surroundings. The theater of Marcellus turned out
to be truly evocative, a semicircle of ruined stone below
the Capitoline Hill, near the Temple of Vesta. They would be
playing behind the ruined amphitheater on a raised platform
set against two ancient stone pillars. You could almost feel the
ghosts of the ancient Romans. In fact, Ren was thinking of
having some ghostly presences just out of the range of the
lights, as an historical chorus.

The tryouts went as planned. Gianni, the actor Brent
wanted for the Green Knight, was a Nordic type as different
from Joe as possible. He seemed very good, though Ren would
have to become accustomed to seeing someone so sophisticated
and aristocratic in the part – the Green Knight as a
Renaissance prince. Both Lauretta and Toma read well with
him. Ren would miss Grace and Ellen, but he was excited at
having yet another way of playing with gender. Unlike Ellen,
who'd been antagonistic to Joe from the beginning, Toma
seemed quite smitten with Gianni.

When they started the readings, two days later, Ren
noticed that Toma's face and voice revealed admiration just
below the surface even when she was directly confronting the

Green Knight. In the scenes with the Host, there was a sense that she understood the type of man he was – power games and all – if it hadn't been for the need to liberate his wife, she might even have arranged some sort of a deal. Her interpretation of the lines struck Ren oddly as a tilt back toward his original conception of the play, in which Gawain and the Green Knight bond.

As Ren worked out the blocking for the first act later in the week, he thought more about it. He couldn't let Gawain submit and obey – he'd gone beyond that, though he still felt the tug of his original fantasies, his wish to be reconciled. But maybe Gawain could be more magnanimous at the end. What if Gawain offered to have all three of them, himself, the Green Knight, and his wife, live together in a *ménage à trois*? The thought made Ren laugh out loud.

It was what Noel Coward had done in *Living Dangerously*, the play that had given Ren his first starring part. He could do it so that no one of the trio had mastery over the other, and they could combine in any way they pleased. Toma's barely submerged yen for the Green Knight could play itself out (Ren had heard her the other day referring to Gianni as "*un animale magnifico*," roughly, a gorgeous brute). Toma's wry acceptance of her dual nature would add new richness to the play, which Ren began to see as a delicate balancing of hate and love.

Since they'd arrived in Rome, Jack hadn't heard from his father. Ren could see that it bewildered and hurt him, but he felt sure it would pass. Ren had succeeded in making Jack happy, there was no doubt about that; from the time they woke up in the morning to the sound of the gulls outside their window, until Ren closed the shutters at night. Still, he felt their happiness had a tenuous quality – as if they were floating in a shimmering element that might not continue to support them.

Ren remembered a commitment ceremony he had witnessed in a tent on a big estate in the Santa Monica Mountains at the home of a famous old set designer. It had been his sort of thing: a golden chapel on a bluff overlooking the mountains, a wildly chaotic mix of French antiques, Asian temple ornaments and dancing until early morning.

Ren tentatively mentioned his idea to Jack, but Jack didn't think they needed any ceremonies.

"We're happy as we are," he said. "I thought you'd be the last person on earth to want something as corny as a 'commitment rite.' Weren't you the one who pointed out to me the drawbacks of bourgeois marriages, the loss of fun? As a matter of fact, at that very ceremony you made a tasteless joke about last rites."

"'Lost rights.' It was a pun," Ren mumbled, "and perspectives change." The truth was, he wanted Jack engaged in making their happiness, not just being dragged along. "I've never wanted it before," he said, "never had anyone I could envision getting old with."

But of course, Jack was so much younger. Ren had a way of thinking they were the same age. Even when he saw photos of them together, he thought of them as age mates. In his clothes, Ren was still very youthful looking, tall and straight-backed, his face showing only faint wrinkles around the eyes.

One morning shortly after this conversation with Jack, Ren had just finished shaving and was putting on his under-eye wrinkle cream – thinking that it was way too expensive and wasn't doing enough good – when the entry phone rang.

Usually it was just the garbage man or the mail for the building, but this time it was an express letter. Jack buzzed the mailman in, unlocked their triple lock and stood with the heavy door open, waiting for the *postino* to come up on the elevator. When the man sprinted up the last flight of marble steps and handed the letter to him, Jack stood for a moment looking at the envelope.

Ren emerged from the bathroom, still in his pajamas, and for a second he was afraid that the letter was from Malcolm. What if he'd decided to tell Jack about Ren's request for funds? (That's how Ren put it to himself. He never used the nasty word blackmail.)

"It's from Henny," Jack said, and Ren breathed a sigh of relief. Jack took the envelope over to the sofa under the aggressively red painting in the entry hall and patted the seat next to him. "Come on, it's addressed to both of us."

Hand over his heart, trying to calm his breathing, Ren settled into the plump cushions while Jack tore open the envelope with his fingers – Ren had given him a crystal letter opener but he couldn't get him to use it. The tufts of golden hair on Jack's knuckles made Ren want to kiss them but instead he sat quietly and read along. Maybe later, they'd go back to bed.

The dull tan paper seemed sexlessly plain against Jack's brilliant green pajamas. There was a little sketch of a horse above the large childish script. "Dear Jack and Ren . . . " Ren surmised that she'd included him because she was grateful for his kindness at the horse show. It couldn't really be called support. What had he done, for christsake? Just exchanged a few friendly words and not judged her.

"I'm sick and tired of being patient and trying to win Dad over. Sick of trying to convince him that Franco is a human being. You met him, Ren," she wrote, "you know what a decent person he is."

Ren didn't know much after one short conversation, but he had smiled at the irony of their parallel efforts to win over Malcolm. Now Henny wanted to have a June wedding. Malcolm, of course, didn't want to have anything to do with it. Wouldn't even set foot in the church. The long and short of it was that she wanted to come to Rome and have it there. "You're the only family I have, Jack. Let me have it there with you."

Ren was amazed at how exhilarated he felt at the thought. And it wasn't just relief at not being called to account for anything. "Of course she can come, poor kid."

"His side of it is a bit different." Jack toyed with the letter, looking down so as not to meet Ren's eyes.

"Oh?" Ren felt his heart beat again. "I didn't know you'd heard from him." Outside on the window ledge, two gulls set up a clamor, fighting over some scrap.

"Yeah, I got a letter a few days ago. You were out buying milk." The words were casual but Ren felt Jack's body tense against his and registered the fact that Jack hadn't told him about it. "He said she insulted him. That he invited her over for dinner and she started screaming at him."

Ren could hear the special pleading in Jack's voice and it was as grating as chalk on a blackboard. The warm glow he'd felt a moment before subsided. "Just like that?" he asked, in a sarcastic tone. "Henny didn't want to come and she just started screaming at him over the phone?"

"No, well, she came," Jack muttered, embarrassed.

"And?" The morning sunlight was pouring in through the picture window. Ren could feel the pleasant heat through his pajamas. If they hadn't been quarreling they could be lying naked on the rug.

"He invited a young business associate – it seems perfectly natural – and the guy asked her if she'd go out for coffee or dinner, I don't remember which, the next night . . . and she said no."

"Doesn't seem like a criminal offense," Ren said. "It . . . "

"Hold on, will you? I haven't finished." Jack was obviously getting flustered, but the faint pink in his checks just made him more attractive. "I don't need you to be sarcastic right when I'm in the middle of telling you something."

"Cool. Fine, go ahead. Tell me." If Jack would just admit that Malcolm acted badly, Ren would have comforted him. He sighed, feeling heartburn start in his chest.

"Dad said Henny was just plain rude," Jack continued doggedly, "and he told her to mind her manners. Ren, why are you making that face? Can't you even try to see his point of view? I thought you two were getting along better."

"We are . . . but can't you see he insulted her? He would-
n't invite her boyfriend and he invited some Suit instead."
Malcolm had probably fancied the guy himself. The discom-
fort in Ren's chest moved towards his throat and he got up
abruptly and started towards the terrace.

"Where are you going?"

"To take in the wash." He picked up the laundry basket
and went out, unlocking the little gate that led to the service
terrace where the maid had hung the wash. He ducked under
a large blue sheet and started unpinning a row of red and purple briefs. "Seem a bit garish in full sun, don't they?"

Jack followed him, the sheets slapping against him. The
air smelled of laundry soap and rosemary. "Ren, you know
you're paranoid. If someone closes his eye because he has a
cinder you'd see an insult."

"I'm sensitive."

"Look, *even if, even if* he made an error of judgment . . . "

"Ah ha. You admit it!" Ren held up a pair of red silk
Armani bikinis like a flag for a bull.

"I don't."

"You do, you do," Ren danced around him.

"She didn't need to scream at him in front of his guest. It
was childish and it embarrassed him." Ren took the under-
wear and put it on his head like a hat. "Oh Ren, stop it, you're
being ridiculous. Let's stop. It's pointless. You're not funny.
You're hostile."

"Hostile? Oh lordy, shrink talk." Ren took down a sheet
and swirled it around him like a robe.

Jack was so upset that his ears were turning crimson.
"Angry then, closed-minded."

"Sweetie, you're dead wrong," Ren said, unwinding the
sheet, folding it, and putting it in the basket. "But let's forget
Malcolm for a minute. Let's talk about Henny. You love her, I
know you do. When you were sick and thought you were going
to die, you told her that if you got better, any time she needed
to come to you, you'd be there for her. I heard you. Now she's

asking." He reached out to break off a dangling thread from the sleeve of Jack's pajamas. "And I guess since neither of us was in the room with them, we can't really know what went on."

"Right." Jack said. Ren noticed his Adam's apple moving under the skin of his throat. Swallowing down his anger.

The next day when the subject of Henny came up again, Ren had a better idea of how to handle it to get the results he wanted. "But surely it's not your fault if Henny takes it into her head to visit," he suggested mildly. "No one could *reasonably* blame you for that."

"Yeah," Jack looked at him dubiously. "But if Henny really wants to get married here, and he's still . . . no, I can't do it, it's going to piss him off. She should have worked it out with him, not put me in the middle."

"You don't have to decide anything today. Remember we're on Roman time – it's always *domani*, always tomorrow." Here, Ren noticed Jack gave a faint smile. The electrician had just told them for the fourth time, "Tomorrow for sure."

"Who knows?" Ren said. "Maybe Malcolm would be glad to have the whole thing out of his hands. When it's over and done with, he might even come around."

That was bullshit, of course. He was sure Malcolm never forgave an injury anymore than Ren did, but it seemed to calm Jack. Ren decided to push a little further. He wouldn't have been able to articulate it just then, but Henny's coming here and marrying would provide some sort of closure. In some obscure way it might even vindicate him.

"As a matter of fact, he doesn't even need to know you went to the wedding."

"Oh no, I'm not into keeping secrets, Ren, I'd have to tell him."

"It's not a secret, really. You are just not telling him something that you think might upset him. After all," he paused, wondering if he could risk it, "you didn't tell him about us."

"Ouch. I hate to be inconsistent," Jack said, in a softer voice. Ren saw that, unexpectedly, he'd scored a point. Even for Jack, there were secrets and *secrets*. By the next morning, Jack had agreed to let Henny visit. What she did after that was her affair.

Ren lay wide awake in bed, listening to the muffled sounds of traffic from the Corso. He had met with the designer to talk about how his set might be adapted to the outdoor space. Though they were still in the reading stage and would start the blocking next week, Ren began to visualize his play in its new incarnation. Surrounded by the decay of ancient Rome, he thought it would be more sophisticated and more poignant at the same time.

He drifted easily from thinking about his show to daydreams of a splendidly choreographed wedding. Henny and Franco were coming in a few days, and though he hadn't discussed the wedding again with Jack – who still lay deeply asleep beside him – it was obviously going to happen. Ren thought Jack would come around. Even if he didn't, Ren determined to make it something unforgettable. A class act. It would be natural for them to ask his advice since he had been here for awhile and knew the city.

To prepare himself, he checked over likely sites. The small baroque churches attracted him for their sense of presence. He could imagine them as characters in a drama, his drama: *The Triumph of Love*. The churches floated in front of him – trying out for their parts – while he luxuriated against his pillows, reviewing their strong points. The Quattro Fontane had a perfect jewel-like inner space that seemed almost to dance, Saint Ivo had a sense of whimsy and strength combined. After awhile, images of a procession rose in his mind and setting the scene for its progress became as important as the church itself. Saint Agnes wasn't terribly exciting, for instance, but it had that magnificent fountain just outside. The fluorescent electric clock ticked loudly and he noticed that it was three a.m . . . the traffic sounds from outside had almost stopped.

An ambulance went by squealing and Ren instinctively turned towards Jack and tried to make out his face in the dark. He could just see the vague shape of fist curled against mouth. He felt such love for him. So then why was he so set on making his life difficult? Jack clearly hoped that whatever Henny did would make as few waves as possible with their father, whereas Ren wanted her wedding – directed by him – to make a statement. He *wanted* Malcolm to know about it. He thought he might even send him an engraved invitation.

But why did Ren have to send it in anger? He'd done a pretty nasty thing with the blackmail. Wouldn't it make him even more the winner if he could cancel that out? It occurred to him that he'd been blaming Malcolm for a lot of things that weren't really his fault. Malcolm wasn't there when Ren's father had walked out on him, when his mother alternately whined and petted him. Was it Malcolm's fault that Ren's adolescence was hell? Did Malcolm make him choose to work in a marginal profession? He could have gone to business school or become a computer programmer. But who wanted it? He didn't. Didn't want it any more than Malcolm wanted to struggle with a script and high-strung actors.

Malcolm was an arrogant, controlling hypocrite but that didn't make blackmailing him right. And more to the point, Ren was beginning to see that even if he was the best mate in the world, and a better father than Malcolm could ever be to Henny, he couldn't replace the old man. Jack not only still loved his father, but was suffering from Ren's entrenched dislike of him – suffering every time they fought about him.

What if he confessed to Jack, got the whole thing off his chest, then told Malcolm he'd pay back the money little by little – work another job if need be? But could he stand it if Jack was disgusted by what he'd done? What if Jack put Ren on probation? If he narrowed his eyes and talked to Ren the way he talked to the oil people about their spills. What if Jack couldn't forgive him?

No, it was too risky. He'd wait until after the wedding – Ren couldn't help wanting to make sure of his triumph first, but also to make himself more safe and secure. Jack didn't know it, but Ren planned to offer him a token of their commitment. If he accepted it, Ren's confession would be met by their strengthened bond. Then, who knows, maybe after the money had been paid back and Malcolm realized that Ren was actually making his son happy, Malcolm might forgive him for Jack's sake. Ren imagined Jack's beaming face. Who knows, maybe Malcolm might even come out of the closet. Ren smiled to himself and fell into a peaceful sleep.

He was awakened by the raucous screams of the gulls perched outside on the window ledge. Traffic had begun down on the Corso and the gray, predawn light flickered at the edges of closed shutters. He lay back on the pillow, willing his night-time scruples out of his mind. He would give Henny something to make her know how precious and special she was, Henny, who had Jack's chin and eyes and her own exquisite blond hair. He could envision the wedding, but when he tried to get beyond it, to see them as some sort of family, the images dissolved as fast as he formed them. He couldn't get much beyond the idea that came to him just before he fell asleep, of a wedding dress with heavy sleeves inset with embroidered panels in the medieval fashion.

Ren went to the airport to pick up Henny and Franco. He got there just in time to see them emerge from Customs, looking rumpled but cheerful, and rushed up to envelop them in a hug. They were both wearing worn jeans and light cotton shirts under jean jackets.

"*Benvenuti!* Welcome to Rome! The most beautiful city in the world! How was the flight? Did you manage to sleep? You look great!"

Henny laughed as they hugged him back. "We're fine. Hardly fashionable, but so glad to see you. Where's Jack?"

"I wouldn't let him come," Ren said, leading the way to the taxi stand. "He overdid it at the gym yesterday and I wanted him to get a little more sleep."

"Oh dear, I knew we were coming too early – seven-thirty in the morning is such a ghastly time."

"Don't worry about it. I'm up every morning at dawn," Ren told her. "There's a mother gull on the roof outside our terrace who makes an enormous racket at sun-up – I suppose she's telling her chicks to be good while she tracks down breakfast." Ren picked up Henny's roll-on and put it into the trunk of a waiting taxi next to Franco's and they settled gratefully into the back seat. "Somehow, Jack sleeps through it. He needs more rest lately because he's just started a new exercise program. But he promised to have coffee ready when we get there."

"I'm so glad he's getting his strength back," Henny said.

"You'll be amazed to see how well he looks. Rome has been good for him."

"You've been good for him," she said, pressing his hand.

Jack kissed Henny before she was over the threshold. Ren noticed him hesitate for a second before embracing Franco. Ren was sure Franco noticed too.

"I am afraid it is too much for you to have us stay with you. We should stay at a hotel," Franco said quickly. "I suggested this to Henny. I . . . "

"Nonsense," Jack interrupted with real warmth. "I wouldn't hear of it. You're family."

The boy smiled. "Then you must tell us if you are tired," he said earnestly, "if you need a rest or don't feel like talking.

We could shop, help cook. If we stay here you must use us." Franco looked over at Henny for confirmation. "Isn't this right?"

"Definitely," Henny said, and Ren saw Jack begin to relax.

"So that's settled, come, let me show you around." Jack took Henny by one arm, Franco by the other and walked them down the hall.

"I know you're better when you start taking charge again," Henny laughed and leaned happily into Jack's shoulder. "What a terrific place you have here. I love all the wood and the antique stones."

"Are you really sure you have room for us?" Franco asked with a slightly worried look when they'd finished the tour. Ren thought he'd probably noticed the absence of a second bed and the scanty shortage.

"The sofa bed in the living room is already made up for you," Ren said, walking over to it and pulling off the pillows. "It's easy." He grasped the bottom and illustrated with a sharp pull. "You just need to fold it out. And I've freed up a closet in the hall. I hope there's enough space."

"Henny can have the closet," Franco offered, smiling with obvious relief. "I'm used to living out of suitcases."

"But first, let's have breakfast." Jack slid open the door to the terrace. "*Ecco!*" He'd made coffee and picked up some still warm *cornetti* from their local cafe. After breakfast Ren helped them set themselves up in the living room and hung a curtain from the big overhead beam to give them a little privacy.

Though they were excited and grateful and very much in love, having them at such close quarters was quite different from Ren's fantasies. Because there were no divisions in their apartment, Ren was jolted awake every time Henny or Franco trooped by their alcove bed on the way to the bathroom. He and Jack were never really alone anymore. And all of them suffered from the enforced chastity.

On the positive side, not only were Henny and Franco delightful guests, expressing appreciation of everything from their local trattoria to the Borghese Gardens, but Franco turned out to be extremely knowledgeable about both Roman and Renaissance history. He brought the Forum to life for them. They strolled through it in the late afternoon when most of the tourists had gone home, and the marble seemed lit from within.

Franco gave a brief history of the Roman arch, and regaled them with colorful tales about the Borgia princes. And this was the man Malcolm had assumed was uneducated, Ren mused, because he came from a South American town with an unpronounceable name! Malcolm probably didn't know half the things Franco knew. And he was relaxed and gracious besides.

Jack had been tense with them at first, but one night after Franco had exhibited yet another skill by making them all a perfect *pasta con vongole*, he admitted, mopping up the sauce with his bread, that Henny had made a good choice. And love had galvanized her. Her green eyes sparked with energy, her chin held the confident tilt that it used to have only in the arena. Her intern work in the school system had not only made her see how sheltered and privileged she was, but had given her the courage to fight for those with real handicaps. She had taken part-time work tutoring children in a public school in Harlem. "I was feeling too sorry for myself, but I just had Dad to deal with. These kids get put-downs from everyone and everything." Luckily, they had spring break now or she couldn't have brought herself to leave.

She was working with the worst cases, the ones who fell behind year after year. It was exhausting but gratifying and she felt if she could make a difference with only one child, it was worth it. Dipping a *cornetto* into her cappuccino, she'd told them with breathless excitement about a little girl who was finally learning to read. The breakthrough came after the child asked Henny what her favorite color was.

"I said orange or maybe, gold – Marisa put her hand next to mine and asked me, do I like brown? Well, it was pretty obvious what she was thinking, so I said yes, that I wore brown a lot. Then she got a little bolder and asked me if I liked my skin. 'Yeah,' I said, 'it's okay. Do you like yours?' And she said 'No!' just like that. I asked her if that was because she was so dark – she was this deep beautiful blue-black – and she said yes, that the kids teased her about that. So I told her that everybody gets teased who is different but that her skin was beautiful, it was just like ebony."

"You've gotten to be almost as much of a do-gooder as your big brother," Ren said, moved almost to tears. He knew Jack couldn't help being impressed – these were all his values. And besides, Henny was so pleased and grateful for the hospitality that in a few days brother and sister were laughing and playing together the way Ren imagined they must have done as children.

Jack even got enough into the spirit to come with them to look at churches. Most of the nicest ones were booked for all the weekends in June, but since they didn't mind taking a weekday afternoon, they managed to get a beautiful church on the Aventine, with Greek plaques built into the wall, surrounded by orange trees that bore fruit and blossomed at the same time and made the air fragrant with a honey sweetness.

Ren insisted on designing and paying for the wedding dress himself – the lovers barely had enough saved to take themselves on a camping trip through the Cinque Terre. Ren shuddered to think of a honeymoon in a sleeping-bag with insects crawling over them, but they were young and it seemed to make them happy. Meanwhile, Brent recommended an excellent costuming seamstress. Ren brought the sketches of his concept and she produced an elegant pattern. Ren chose the fabric, a gorgeous ivory satin. He persuaded Henny to have inlaid embroidered slits in her sleeves, a form-hugging bodice, and to dye her satin pumps green.

"Do you want to invite your father?" Ren asked her suddenly one day. They were at the Villa Borghese – Jack had just gone off to the head – in front of one of Caravaggio's sexually ambiguous but infinitely suggestive paintings, *A Boy Bitten By a Lizard*. The boy has been arranging fruits and flowers. He draws back his finger in pained surprise – mouth open, his shoulder voluptuously bared, one white rose shining amid a mass of black curls.

"He's too much of a hypocrite to come. Not to speak of his being furious at you."

"For taking away his baby?" Ren asked lightly.

"The whole shabang," she said with an odd expression.

"Well, it won't be a traditional wedding if that's what you mean."

She started to say something more but just then Jack came back from the bathroom and she turned back to the painting.

"Caravaggio was gay, wasn't he?" she asked.

"Well, he certainly liked boys, but it wasn't as much of an identity issue," Ren said.

"It's more tolerated in Latin cultures," Franco explained. "It's just part of a sexual spectrum."

Henny was still looking at the painting. "It must hurt to feel you have to hide," she sighed, and Franco put his arm around her shoulder protectively.

The next afternoon they picked up Jack at the gym – Ren had gone in to get him among all those sexy oiled bodies – and they walked home together. On the way through a narrow street they were stopped by a black Cadillac trying to maneuver. The driver wanted to turn around by backing into another little street. Everyone was out on their stoops or in the doorways of their shops watching and giving advice. "*Americani*," someone said laughing, "too big," and made an obscene gesture.

"The driver looks a bit like Dad's chauffeur," Henny said and Ren's stomach lurched. Of course he wasn't, but the car was right. It was the same car that Malcolm used to send for Jack to take him to the hospital, and it would be like Malcolm to bring such an oversized machine into the medieval street.

A man in an apron was banging on the side of the car as it inched past a parked truck. Finally, it came free on the other side and everyone applauded.

The black Cadillac belched a cloud of carbon dioxide into their faces and Ren kicked it again in impotent rage as it finally heaved past them so close they had to cower back against a building.

"*Capitalisti*," a woman next to them murmured, "*criminali*."

Suddenly it seemed vital to Ren that Henny ride to her wedding in something other than a car. If they'd been in Venice she could have arrived on a barge like Cleopatra, or an exquisitely decorated gondola. He could see himself gorgeously gowned, leaning down to help her from the boat.

When Ren wasn't making suggestions about the new sets and going over the script with the actors – they were still in the reading stage, though Ren planned to get them off book in two weeks – he worked on his wedding surprise. For the first time, since he was a child, Ren felt that his dream life and his real life were coming together.

It had taken Ren some time to find a cabby who was willing to submit his horse and carriage to the elaborate makeover Ren wanted. His additions to the carriage would frighten the horse or be too heavy or constitute a public nuisance, he was told. But finally he found one who was actually enthusiastic. It helped that he was flamboyantly gay.

"Drive it too, if you like, I'm-a tired of driving. I wear-a my toga," he told him. "I wore it in the parade, the *primo* for

omosessuali. Why not?" he'd asked. "You should'a seen it" –
giving an affectionate pat to his own trim butt – "*che bei
ragazzi*, what pretty boys! *Mai pensato.*" Ren had never
thought he'd see that in the city of the pope.

Getting together a wedding party was less difficult. First
of all he'd invited two of the neighbors from their building. On
the floor beneath them there was the fruit and vegetable man
Antonio, who owned the small shop on the corner. Antonio was
a big coarse man with a wart on his nose, but kindly enough.
Ren had gotten friendly with him on his daily shopping trips.

One day Ren introduced Franco to Antonio as his cousin
and told him he was here to get married in the most beautiful
city in the world. Antonio took an instant liking to Franco
when the young man, speaking a mix of Spanish and Italian,
spontaneously offered to help him carry in some vegetable
crates. Though he seemed a little surprised to be asked, he
said he'd come to the wedding – "*con piacere.*"

Antonio's daughter and her husband and their two-year-
old child lived in an adjoining apartment on the same floor
and Ren invited them too. The signora, a squat woman with a
powerful voice, could usually be heard shouting rapid-fire
reproaches at her husband, all seeming to end in "*basta!*" If
this occurred on the landing or in the elevator, their daughter,
who had aspirations to gentility, would shake her blond mane
and look away in disdain. Once she had left her front door
open and Ren had peeked inside on his way downstairs and
seen lots of blue velvet and a large chandelier. He was surprised at the amount of money they had to spend.

Ren imagined they'd dress in their Sunday best, but
except for the blond, that was likely to be pretty sedate. "I
don't know how you'd feel about it," he asked Franco and
Henny, "but I'd like to have the cast and some of their
friends."

"As long as they don't upstage my bride."

"Nothing could, she's positively radiant. Some of them
sing . . . and I thought they could wear their costumes."

"Why not?" Franco grinned. "Maybe Guenevere could knight me after the ceremony. Sir Franco of the golden girdle."

"Will the neighbors get along with them, do you think?" Henny asked a little nervously.

"With enough to eat and drink, everyone will get along fine," Ren said. He told them he thought it would be nice to invite Brent's mother too. She lived in their palazzo on the second floor and they sometimes saw her in the elevator – a modestly dressed Italian lady with white hair. Ren was fascinated by the fact that Brent talked to her every day, and that when his lover was alive she had even cooked for them – brought stuff up steaming hot from the oven! She could be the stand-in for Big Mama, the mama everyone wants.

Of the theater people who were coming, Henny and Franco had already met the Green Knight briefly – Gianni, the blond Milanese – but they hadn't seen Toma, the young queen who was playing Gawain, or Lauretta or any of the other *femminielli*. Since they were indistinguishable from women, except for their genitals, which were taped down in elaborate ways under their tight provocative skirts, Ren had thought of introducing them to Henny as potential bridesmaids. They could carry her train or stand alongside her, flanking the altar. Toma had told Ren they loved weddings. It would be such a treat for her.

Jack thought Ren couldn't do that without telling Henny who they were. So he did, and to his surprise, Henny and Franco laughed and agreed. "Not quite ordinary, but then nothing about our romance is ordinary," Franco said.

"Great!" Ren loved the way the mix was shaping up. "It seems like the city itself, big-hearted enough to hold everyone."

What struck Jack, he told Ren one night when they were cuddled together in bed, was how Italian mothers seemed to accept their children. He went on to say that he'd been thinking, partly as a result of seeing how protective Henny was of

Franco, how identified with him, that he hadn't been protective enough of Ren in New York.

"I never admitted it, but I let you take the flack from Malcolm. I was too concerned about looking like the perfect Ivy League boy to see that you were taking the social heat for both of us. I kept toning you down, shushing you up because I was scared. I wouldn't even let you hug me in public, except in a safe house."

Ren hugged him. "I don't need your apologies for anything."

"It's just that I'm finally seeing this is how you're meant to be, florid."

"And a bit crazy."

"No. You know what you're doing. You're purposely outrageous. I let you love me, take care of me, but I wasn't giving back."

"You were sick."

"I was hiding. I should have supported you more. Even if I didn't want to tell Malcolm about myself – and maybe that was wrong – I should have stood up for you. I could have told him we were going to live together. I mean he has been fine about it, why couldn't I have told him long ago?"

"It's okay, bubbi, you weren't ready," Ren said, but he was thrilled. It was all coming together. Beauty and sex, male and female, love and respect for who he was. He felt so exuberant that he went out and bought red coral fertility horns for him and Jack and Franco and Henny to wear around their necks on the big day.

The church was an old Roman basilica from the fourth century – long and somewhat severe – but the assembled guests filled it with color.

Franco and Henny had written their own script for the ceremony. Fortunately, the local priest was young and open to things that brought people into the church – which tended to be filled mostly with old women in black. "I know how it is," he said gravely, "in America they play the guitar at Mass, and afterwards they kiss."

"We're not going to do anything so drastic," Henny said. Their vows followed the traditional ones except for the "obey" clause. "Obey is banished," Franco had said, "obey is defunct," and she had given him her glowing smile. On the morning of the wedding, Ren got a telegram from Joe with congratulations and best wishes from Grace and Ellen. The ceremony itself went without a hitch, from Jack's walking Henny down the aisle – she'd insisted Ren walk on her other side – followed by her "bridesmaids" dressed in violet gowns with spaghetti straps and slits up the side to the thigh, to the priest's brief remarks – he'd insisted on making them in English – then the burst of music from some theater musicians at the conclusion.

Brent had gotten together a quartet as a wedding present: two violins, a viola and a cellist whose hair was tied back in a pony tail, and the music – Ren thought it was Brahms – was sonorous and rich.

Afterwards the party moved to the orange tree grove overlooking the city, where they were served white wine (contributed by Antonio) and *hors d'oeuvres*. The musicians continued playing a mix of pieces. Then the cellist took out a double bass, shook out his long black hair, hunkered down over his instrument and started playing jazz. Plucking and strumming. He had a lithe, young body and great hands.

The rhythms were contagious. The guests, who had been eying each other warily for the first few minutes, began to loosen up and mingle. Lauretta and Toma started shaking their bodies to the music, their beautiful legs flashing through the slits in their violet gowns. Henny and Franco circulated, gesturing and smiling the way people do when they don't have a common language. Jack followed them with his new camera, snapping candid shots.

Leaning over the low wall, Ren thought it was a great success. He even thought he could make out their palazzo windows glinting far off in the distance, but he always got his directions confused. Certainly it was a beautiful sight with the Tiber winding just below them overhung by trees in full leaf, and the domes and spires and palaces of Rome beyond.

When the party was starting to wind down Ren slipped back into the church and got into his costume. It was a version of what some of the ancient emperors wore in their triumphs: part dress and part armor. He'd known the Mediterranean's reputation for olive-skinned boys and homosexual love, but what he hadn't known was that the ancient Romans had an androgenous ideal centuries before he had. What made those guys so smart?

There was quite a commotion when Ren clattered up to the garden gates driving the horse-drawn carriage, with the cabby standing on the running board next to him, giving him directions and reinforcing them with verbal commands to the well-trained animal. The horse, excited by the unfamiliar driver, pranced; his light-tasseled covering shimmered in the sunlight and the carriage, enclosed by a papier-mâché shell, glinted like pure gold. Embossed Cupids played hide and seek across its gilt surface and tiny bells laboriously attached by Ren along the hood rim with colored ribbons made a silvery sound at every step.

"It's divine," Lauretta said, running up – she'd taken off her high heels – "like a golden Easter egg."

"Or a shell," Toma added, "with wings. Oh, I would love to ride in such a thing when I get married."

"Maybe you will," Henny told her, pressing her bouquet into Toma's hands. "It'll be the start of a tradition." The horse turned his plumed head and tried to eat one of the flowers. Toma shrieked and drew back. The horse stamped and pawed and Henny laughed and patted his neck.

"Don't worry," she said to Toma, "he won't hurt you. He's just impatient to get going. Me too." She stepped to the side of the carriage and looked up at Ren, her eyes shining. "I knew you were up to something . . . but this is fantastic. It's

not a cab, it's a chariot . . . those gilded sides. . . . It's magical. It seems ready to fly. How did you ever do it?" She gathered her ivory satin skirts and looked around for Jack to help
her into the carriage.

Ren smiled down at her, then tried to catch Jack's eyes,
but Jack looked resolutely down. He seemed annoyed. For a
moment it seemed as if he wouldn't follow Henny in, especially when he saw people gathering to point and stare. Some were
even coming up to have their pictures taken next to it, pointing out the golden cupids with their arrows drawn and the
phallic fish.

But then Jack seemed to catch himself – Ren could almost
see him remembering his resolve. He reached out and touched
Ren's mantle, a flowing swirl of multicolored silk.

"If you could bear to part with it, I think I'd like to wear
it," he said. "I feel underdressed." Ren couldn't quite believe
what he was hearing but Jack was grinning, so he undid the
cord and shook out the brilliantly colored silk over Jack's
shoulders.

"How does it feel?"

"Festive," Jack said. "Do I look ridiculous?"

"You look like a prince."

It was no longer a cab but a golden chariot that felt
almost winged in its lightness and the soar of its gilded sides.
Ren felt like an emperor beginning his triumphal ride through
the city after a hard battle. Henny looked like a princess in her
ivory gown with inset sleeves of the palest peach, and an
antique veil Ren had found in a boutique and trimmed with
peach-colored rose buds and fragrant narcissus. Franco sat
next to her in a white suit, his knee pressed tight against hers
– he couldn't seem to stop smiling. Jack sat across from
them, in back of the driver's seat. Ren reached back and ran
his hand lightly over Jack's head. The hair had grown back
just enough to cover it with a golden fuzz that caught the sun.
The brilliantly colored cape brought out the green in Jack's
eyes.

"Stop the carriage a minute," Jack said, "there's something I need to do," and when Ren did, he climbed up to sit beside him on the driver's seat. The gilded shell rose around them, holding them in its comforting arms.

As they set off down the Aventine they could see across to the Palatine hill on the other side and the palaces of the Roman emperors. Continuing down, the smell of the roses coming from the public gardens on both sides of the street was almost overpowering – their massed colors, red, pink, coral, yellow, were like flares lighting their way. Their bursts of bright color reminded Ren that he had wanted to blow up the carriage at the end, have it dissolve in a rain of fireworks after they dismounted. But the cabby had squelched that idea pretty fast.

Ren pulled the horse to a halt, gave the reins to the cabby to hold, and darted over to pick a huge pink rose for Henny. Fold after fold of luxurious petals deepening to a vibrant crimson in the center. She bent her face and kissed the flower. He took his time getting started again. He loved this ride and wanted it to last as long as possible.

All too quickly, they approached the Lungo Tevere. They could already see the Circo Massimo, the huge oval of the ancient racecourse. Ren could imagine the chariot races they must have had there. With a roaring crowd sitting on the hillside seats and a laurel crown for the winner.

As they turned, Henny caught sight of a small Romanesque church. "Isn't that where the Bocca Della Verita is?" she asked Ren. "Let's stop for a minute. I want to see it." They drew up in front of the church and Henny and Franco and Jack got down. Ren said he'd stay with the carriage.

The Bocca was a grinning stone mouth – the Mouth of Truth set into an outer wall of the church. The story was that if you lied, it would bite off your finger. He heard Henny laughing and guessed she was trying it. Ren knew it was ridiculous but he felt queasy about sticking his finger between the stone lips.

"I don't know, Ren," Henny said when she came back, "are you sure you're not hiding some deep dark secret?" They all laughed and Ren turned up the Tiber towards home.

By a stroke of good luck, they'd picked one of the car-free days that were being tried out in the city. The long avenue beside the river, usually so noisy and filled with the stench of exhaust fumes, was quiet except for bikes, scooters and pedestrians . . . so quiet they could even hear the sound of the water.

When they got closer they cut into the side streets. The cabby stood hanging on the outside and told Ren which streets were one-way. As they jigged and jogged through the narrow streets, alternately gaped at and cursed by cyclists for their width, the chariot's gilt became abraded in places by rubbing against the walls. But though somehow it wasn't quite the mind-blowing thing he'd planned, still it was good. And at the end, just before he drew the horse to a halt in front of their palazzo, he reached into his pocket and took out the signet ring he'd had made out of a Roman coin. As Jack got down from the carriage, Ren took his hand and slipped it on Jack's finger. Ren half expected Jack to take it off, but he didn't; he pressed Ren's hand.

What happened later was a confused blur. They had gone back to their terrazzo and had a light supper – oysters, caviar and champagne – under the full moon. Henny, giddy with the fact that she was actually married, sat clutching Franco's hand and drinking champagne. She lifted her glass and toasted.

"To Ren and Jack!"

Then Ren toasted her and Franco, Henny drank to the moon, Ren toasted the angel. They had gotten to the end of the last bottle and Franco offered to go out and get some more at the wine store on the corner – he thought it was open late. "All

right Francuccio," she said, "but don't take too long," and
then somehow – it probably wouldn't have happened if she
hadn't been unused to alcohol and had realized how intoxicated she was – Henny looked up at the moon and toasted
Malcolm.

"To you, Dad. You should have been here. You would
have liked it, you old fake."

"Henny, "Jack said, "that seems unnecessary."

"Well, isn't he a fake?" She turned to Ren. "He would
have liked the costumes, wouldn't he, Ren? Or is he only into
Victorian?"

She winked at Ren and he choked on his champagne.
What was she doing? What did she know?

"No really, brother mine. How did it hit you? I mean
after all his family patter. Not that anything's wrong with
being . . ." she ground down, confused, and started on another tack. "Seriously, no, seriously, if you hadn't done what
you did, I wouldn't have had the courage to stand up to him.
Sure I was shocked, I admit. I was surprised, but it made him
more human somehow. He had feelings under all that bluster.
Maybe he even loved someone in secret. Do you think he
did?"

"What you talking about? Was he having an affair or
what? That's no big deal. He's not married anymore."

"You don't have to pretend to me, Jack. I'm not a baby
anymore."

"Pretend?"

"It's the wine," Ren put in quickly, "she's not used to it."
He kicked her under the table.

"Ouch. What are you kicking me for?" she asked, but she
didn't answer Jack. Instead she turned and looked straight at
Ren.

"You know," she said, her voice low, "I used to fantasize
that he was old and senile and completely dependent on me.
I'd have complete control over him. I'd imagine tying him to
the bed and making him take castor oil. I'd gag him and make

him listen to all the things he'd done to me all the times he'd
made me feel like shit."

"Henny, that's grotesque," Jack said.

"Are you sure you never had thoughts like that? Never
felt how controlling he was?"

"He was trying to do the best he could for us."

"I bought into that too . . . but really it was always him,
his image, the way he looked to people, his big book, his effi-
ciency theory, him as the big expert about other people's lives.
It was hard to resist. But you know what? I don't see him as a
power anymore. I just see him as a defeated old man. He cried
when I went to say goodbye, told me he knew he hadn't been a
good father. I'm almost sorry for him, aren't you Ren? Didn't
you almost want to invite him to the party?"

"Sure," Ren said. It was surreal, the soft night breeze,
the muted traffic sounds, the smell of jasmine, and yet it was
clearly all going to blow up. Still, despite his horror, for a split
second Ren saw Malcolm as a human being, not a storybook
monster. And Henny was just a kid reacting as a kid, to hurt.
And though he couldn't see himself as clearly, he wasn't so different. It was ironic that he had to see it now when everything
was going to hell in a handbasket.

Henny was getting more agitated. "You could have made
it a condition that he appear in drag," she made a sound
between a laugh and a cry.

Jack took her by her satin-covered arm and shook her.
"What's going on? What are you two talking about?"

"You know as well as I do. About Dad being gay or bi or
whatever he is. About Ren bumping into him at a sex club. I'm
trying to tell you, you don't have to shield me. It did me good
to know."

"You've gone off your head."

She looked at him genuinely puzzled. "Are you trying to
tell me you didn't know? Didn't you write your letter together? You were the one who knew Dad's e-mail address. I saw it
on his computer. He was late – we were going to have dinner –

and I needed to send an e-mail. I was looking through his inbox afterwards. You know I'm always curious about what makes him tick and . . . "

The look on Jack's face told her that she had made a terrible mistake. "Oh God! I thought . . . " and she clapped her hand over her mouth.

"Ren," Jack said, "you better talk fast."

Oh God, this couldn't be happening. Not now when everything was so perfect. Ren had an impulse to throw himself at Jack's feet, confess, beg for forgiveness. Why hadn't he done it before? When Jack would have believed it was sincere. Now he was afraid it was too late . . .

"There was no reason why he shouldn't give you a little something for your trip," he said, his voice quavering.

Ren thought Jack was going to hit him. His hands balled into fists and he was breathing hard. "Something! Something! Money. You can't even say it, 'Money.' That's blackmail, Ren. How could you?" he hissed. "You always wanted things to be different, better."

"It wasn't planned," Ren stammered, "it just happened. I ran into him at . . . "

"Don't tell me. I've heard more than enough to last me a lifetime. I don't want to know anything more about it." Jack put his hands over his ears. "Whatever he did doesn't excuse you. Damn, damn everything, Ren. I don't know if I can forgive you."

It all happened so quickly. Just a few minutes before they had been sitting with warm faces, warm hearts, touching, laughing like any family group, and the next minute Jack pushed his chair back and jumped up, upsetting the umbrella and the table, which fell heavily on its side against the tiles.

Dishes slid off and broke. Caviar specked the white cloth like bits of bloody entrails. The candles still burning in their bronze holders fell onto the crumpled tablecloth, igniting it. It was a big cloth and heavy, and in a moment it blazed up, making an orange question mark against the sky.

Jack, who had been heading for the terrace door, turned back while Ren stamped on the burning cloth, which was no longer white but rapidly changing to dirty black.

"Get help!" Ren shouted to Henny. "Antonio said he was going to stay out. Bang on his daughter's door tell her to call the fire department." Henny rushed off through the terrace doors.

Just then the breeze freshened and the toppled umbrella burst into flames. Jack leapt away from it, the bottom of his light jacket on fire. Ren ripped off his own jacket and tried to wrap it around Jack in an attempt to suffocate the flames, but Jack wrenched himself away. "Don't touch me," he screamed, throwing himself on the tile and rolling back and forth.

Ren felt as if he'd been slapped. He staggered back against the ancient outdoor water heater. Its rusted legs crumpled and the tank toppled over, pinning Jack's legs under its weight. It took only seconds for the broken gas line to catch fire and begin spewing flames with a hideous roaring sound. The curtains on the glass terrace doors flared and the fire moved inside.

For a moment Ren was too terrified to move; then he crouched next to Jack and shoved the heavy water tank off of him. It immediately began to leak a stream of steaming water.

"Damn, shit," Jack swore, twisting away from the hot pool. "I think my leg is broken."

From the corner of his eye, Ren could see the fire had caught the oriental rug just inside the door, and flames were licking at the sides of an old armoire.

"Go on," Jack said, "get out."

But there was no place to go. A bottle of *aqua minerale* had rolled over next to Jack. Ren opened it and soaked his wedding handkerchief. Then he lay down next to Jack and handed it to him. "Put this on your face. The smoke's more dangerous than the fire."

"Go fuck yourself," Jack said, but he didn't sound as angry as he was before. Lying there with the still cool tile against one cheek and smoke billowing out over their heads like the smoke from an exploded stage set, Ren moved tentatively closer to Jack, not quite touching. "Jack?"

Jack turned his face away.

The flaming umbrella canvas was sending off burning fragments that kept landing on them. So far he'd brushed them away, but it occurred to Ren that maybe the firemen wouldn't get to them in time. Everything in Rome happened so slowly. Including rescue. The ambulances often wailed beneath them for precious minutes caught in traffic. And fire was so swift. There was an explosion somewhere and Ren gasped as a fragment of roof shot by like a flaming meteor. Maybe the whole lemon-yellow palazzo would go up. Maybe the whole block on the Corso Vittorio Emmanuele. Maybe they'd suffocate or burn together.

Ren pictured them fusing together so close that not even Henny could tell them apart, their flesh dripping like wax. Even that would be better than losing Jack. Ren started to cry silently – tears dripping down his nose onto the tile. He sniffed. Then he heard the big engines screech to a stop below the palazzo and the sound of ladders being placed against the walls.

Just before the first red helmet pierced the smoky cloud above the wall of the terrace, he felt Jack's hand move across his back. It wasn't quite a hug, but it was certainly something. He held his breath. . . .

Acknowledgments

I am extremely grateful to Patrick Dooley and the Shotgun Players for arranging for me to sit in on rehearsals and for instructing me on the intricacies of stagecraft, and to designer Michael Frasinelli for describing the construction of the giant's head that I used for the Green Knight.

I am also grateful to the staff at the Hudson River Fisheries, who spent many hours answering my questions, informing about their work on the river and sending me packets of information about the fauna and flora. *The Riverkeepers*, by John Cronin and Robert F. Kennedy, gave me additional information on pollution and the struggle to reclaim a compromised environment.

For an account of the *femminielli* and *Pulcinella*, I am indebted to Frank Browning's descriptions in *A Queer Geography: Journeys Toward a Sexual Self*.

Particular thanks to Jayne Walker and Alan Rinzler, who gave me detailed criticism as the manuscript progressed.

I owe a debt of gratitude to my agent, Juliette Popkin, for her efforts and her friendship, and to my publisher, Bryce Milligan, for his dedication to making the book beautiful as well as factually accurate.

And finally, I must acknowledge my husband, Ira Lapidus, not only for reading and commenting insightfully on every draft, always insisting it was his pleasure, but for his generous belief and unfailing support.

About the Author

Brenda Webster was born in New York City, educated at Swarthmore, Barnard, Columbia, and Berkeley, where she earned her Ph.D. She is a freelance writer, critic and translator who splits her time between Berkeley and Rome, and she is the current president of PEN West. Webster has written two controversial and oft-anthologized critical studies, *Yeats: A Psychoanalytic Study* (Stanford) and *Blake's Prophetic Psychology* (Macmillan), and translated poetry from the Italian for *The Other Voice* (Norton) and *The Penguin Book of Women Poets*. She is co-editor of the journals of the abstract expressionist painter (and Webster's mother) Ethel Schwabacher, *Hungry for Light: The Journal of Ethel Schwabacher* (Indiana 1993). She is the author of two previous novels, *Sins of the Mothers* (Baskerville 1993) and *Paradise Farm* (SUNY, 1999), and a memoir, *The Last Good Freudian* (Holmes and Meier, 2000). The Modern Language Association recently accepted for publication Webster's translation of Edith Bruck's Holocaust novel *Lettera alla Madre*. She is currently working on a novel about the tragic death of Freud's most brilliant disciple.

Wings Press was founded in 1975 by Joanie Whitebird and Joseph F. Lomax as "an informal association of artists and cultural mythologists dedicated to the preservation of the literature of the nation of Texas." The publisher/editor since 1995, Bryce Milligan is honored to carry on and expand that mission to include the finest in American writing. To that end, we at Wings Press publish multicultural books, chapbooks, CDs and broadsides that enlighten the human spirit and enliven the mind. We know well that writing is a transformational art form capable of changing the world by allowing us to glimpse something of each other's souls.

Wings Press uses as much recycled material as possible, from the paper on which the books are printed to the boxes in which they are shipped.

Colophon

This first edition of *The Beheading Game*, by Brenda
Webster, has been printed on 70 pound paper containing fifty percent recycled fiber. The text has been set in
a contemporary version of Classic Bodoni. The font
was originally designed by 18th century Italian punch-
cutter and typographer Giambattista Bodoni, press
director for the Duke of Parma. Titles and initial cap-
itals have been set in Kells, a contemporary typeface
derived from the *Book of Kells*. All Wings Press books
are designed and produced by Bryce Milligan.

Our complete catalogue is available at
www.wingspress.com